A Meeting Under A Banyan Tree

Grahame Kerr

Contents

Dedication

To my sister, CarolLynn, for her comments on the content and for assisting with proofreading and editing.

Acknowledgment

My thanks to staff at the Imperial War Museum, London and the Ford Museum, Singapore for helpful tips and further information on sources.

About the Author

The author lived in Singapore during the late 1940's and his family lived there for 25 years. He enjoyed a successful career in university management before taking up a career in the law serving many years as a magistrate. He has lectured extensively on the colonial life in Singapore and the Malay States in the period before and after WW2.

Preface

The Japanese surrender in August 1945 happened so fast that the colonial powers had little opportunity to prepare governments for the Malay States, the Dutch East Indies and Singapore. It happened so fast that there was only half a dozen Allied soldiers in Singapore to agree a temporary truce until a formal surrender of the Japanese forces in South Asia could be organised. For the British and Dutch Governments, the surrender created a new problem because they wanted their colonial outposts to return to the status quo whereas the Indonesian, Chinese and Malay peoples had other ideas and wanted independence.

The Japanese 25th Army based in the Malay States was still a very capable force to confront. In addition, remnants of the Japanese armies that had been based in Indo-China, Thailand and Burma were also making their way south into the Malay States unbeknown to the Allied military command. Fortunately, most Japanese accepted the decision of their Emperor to cease fighting although there remained many who found the sudden decision to surrender too difficult to contemplate.

The Allies landed 40,000 troops on the west coast of the Malay States expecting to deal with a Japanese force of around ten to twenty thousand men only to find that the Japanese Army confronting them was more than double their size. In the end by late

1946 nearly a quarter a million Japanese soldiers were processed through the prisoner of war camp set up on Rempang Island, south of Singapore. The majority surrendered without any resistance but there was a great deal of tension with Allied Command anxious to keep matters low key as they had their own troops demanding to be returned home after six years of war. An amazing fact is that the Japanese prisoners looked after themselves, building their own camps with only a few Allied soldiers overseeing the discipline and welfare of the camp. The British Government, at home in London, penniless after six years of war, was anxious to get rid of the problem with the Japanese soldiers shipped off to Japan as soon as possible. Yet as late as 1947 significant numbers of Japanese soldiers were still emerging from the jungles of Southeast Asia.

In Singapore gone was the calm, orderly colonial life of the 1930's. War damage was still very evident, in some places extensive. The population was starving, with little work available and outbreaks of disease. Singapore had always depended on its staple diet, rice, being supplied by Thailand and communication with its northern neighbour was practically non-existent. Much of the open spaces within the city of Singapore, an urban crescent around the south of the Island, had returned to jungle with snakes and wild dogs quite a common feature. Rabies was a regular problem. The single line railway that linked Singapore to Bangkok was severely damaged and in parts, the jungle had taken over.

Malaria and other tropical diseases were prevalent, and it was not unusual to see lepers walking the streets begging for help.

Before the war the Island had had a population of around 450,000 Asian people with the majority being Chinese, with a sizeable Indian community and a small population of Malays. The British and European community had been perhaps around 40, 000 but this in 1941 had greatly changed in shape with many of the younger men going off to fight in Europe. The result was that the number of middle aged and older men was disproportionate. Many of the women and children of British and European men who worked in the colonial outposts of Southeast Asia and had gone off to fight in Europe, had ended up in Singapore and only latterly did they try to escape the Japanese advance, leaving it far too late; perhaps only half of those trying to escape, survived the ordeal.

The geography of Singapore in the late 1930's was nothing like the layout of the modern state of Singapore. A crescent of urban European style dwellings existed around the south of the Island interspersed with airfields and army camps that were mainly built during the 1930's. A state-of-the-art Naval dockyard had been built on the north-east of the Island ostensibly to be away from any attack from the sea with the planners never imagining that an invasion would come from the direction of the Malay States to the north. Apart from a few temporary army camps built, just before the Japanese invasion, in the north of the Island, the Island was still essentially jungle and swamps with a few kampongs of Chinese and Malay farmers interspersed with small rubber and coconut estates.

Pre -war Singapore had been the commercial hub for Southeast Asia. It collected the rubber and tin so essential to the needs of Britain and to a lesser extent the USA. After the Nazis had seized control of the Netherlands the Dutch East Indies increasingly relied on Singapore for the continuation of its commercial interests in particular oil and timber. Singapore as a financial centre therefore became very important.

In September 1945, when the Allies took back control of the Island and Malay States, the British Government was suddenly in charge of Singapore with nearly a million inhabitants including thousands of refugees. It found very quickly that they had no means of managing a population of starving people; a population that had doubled since the surrender to the Japanese in early 1942.

The Japanese through its programme of "Sook Ching" had removed a great number of the middle class and intellectual Chinese population who could have created problems for them during the occupation and would have been of great use in managing the population from September 1945. The Japanese Government later only admitted to a few thousand deaths, but other estimates say it could have been as many as a quarter of a million Chinese were forcibly pushed out into the sea to drown. Significant numbers of the remaining "coolie" working class were later shipped off to build railways in Thailand and Burma. The majority of these coolies did not survive this terrible ordeal.

The Indian population largely compliant at the time of the Allied surrender in February 1942 suffered later in the war when the Japanese forcibly used them to build defences in preparation for an Allied invasion. The Indian population that remained in Singapore in the aftermath of the war took the opportunity to support the independence riots in India, at a time when the bulk of British and Australian troops were returning home. Indian troops, based in Singapore, were not thought reliable enough to police their own kin in these circumstances and there was then the bizarre situation of the Army Council, who governed the Island, having to employ platoons of Japanese soldiers to control looting and crime on the Island.

In the Malay States, in particular, the Allies had worked with the Nationalist Chinese Party (Kuomintang) and the Malay Communist Party (MCP) in fighting the Japanese 25th Army throughout the years until the Japanese surrender. The Allies had armed the MCP to fight a jungle war accepting that the MCP guerrilla fighters would be paid as soldiers with a similar arrangement existing for members of the Kuomintang although much of their contribution was interrupted by the Japanese removal of whole sections of the middle-class Chinese in Singapore, Kuala Lumpur and Butterworth.

The local currency, Straits dollars, continued to be used during the occupation although the Japanese also imposed their own currency. Gold became a much more useful currency to pay for a guerrilla war and was preferred throughout the peninsula, as well as in Singapore and the Dutch East Indies and indeed the practice of gold coinage continued until well into the late 1940's when local currencies became stabilised.

Just before the Allied surrender in 1942 the British Government managed to get some of the large gold stocks it held in its banks, and the Government's Treasury, away to Australia although it soon became evident that arrangements had been made to keep a quantity back to pay insurgents to continue the fight against the Japanese.

The Japanese knew that there was gold on the island probably through Lai Tek, the MCP leader who was acting as a double agent although to this day there is a belief that the Japanese also had agents in the British civil service. Throughout their occupation the Japanese made strenuous efforts to find the gold and many British and Chinese, died under interrogation, without it seems the Japanese finding the hidden gold.

In this cauldron of chaos sits Robert Draper, a young banker, captured by the Japanese in 1942, and later tortured in the quest to find the gold. He survives although many of his bank colleagues did not. In the two previous books about him I show how he has grown into his role as a banker and leader of a local community defence unit. He has decided to stay in Singapore after the War whereas most civilians on being released from the internment camps quickly make their way back to their homeland. In my earlier books I concentrated on how the British, European and Eurasian communities developed their own cultures and class structure and how forms of apartheid existed. In this novel, interwoven with true events, I have tried to show how he now seeks to establish a permanent life in his adopted homeland and how he takes part in changing the colonial strictures of the time.

I must thank personnel at the Ford Museum, Singapore and at the Imperial Museum, London who assisted me in checking facts about the Japanese invasion in 1941-1942 and their subsequent surrender in 1945. Hours of reading the BBC War Records was also a must in understanding the parts that individuals played in surviving the terrible war years and the immediate aftermath.

Writing this book, indeed all three about Robert Draper, has been a pleasure bringing back so many memories of my childhood, living in Singapore immediately after the War, of the stories my parents later told me of events and people they met during their time in Singapore and in my own case reliving conversations I have had over many years with people who had lived in Singapore during the momentous 1940's.

I make the offer as I have done with the previous two books that should a reader want to contact me on Facebook or by email, pellwall@hotmail.com, to find out more then please do so. As to the missing gold take it from me there is no good information to say that it was ever found or exactly how much there was.

Grahame Kerr

Chapter 1

Airmail

Salisbury Crags

Tanglin Road

Singapore

8 September 1945

Dear Sir John,

I hope you have received my telegram advising you that I was released from Sime Road Internment Camp on 31 August. The situation here is somewhat chaotic with large numbers of Japanese soldiers still on the Island although there are many being marched off to Johor until they can decide what to do with them. It maybe sometime before the Allied troops can get a grip of the situation. In fact, the Japanese have not actually surrendered; there is to be a ceremony in a few days and in the meantime the Japanese have agreed to remain in their barracks. Many Allied troops have landed here in the last few days much to our relief as up to now there has been a mere handful of British and Australian troops on the Island although there is a large flotilla of ships just off the Island. They have at last started shipping off some of the very sick to hospital ships.

I have been down to Fullerton Square and I must advise you that the bank premises are in a sorry state. Fortunately, the records would seem to be largely intact although the humidity and the termites have caused some damage and I fear that some records may be irretrievably lost.

My understanding is that my appointment as Assistant Manager ended with the cessation of fighting, and I am therefore unsure of my authority, but I feel I must do my best to ensure the safety of records and the security of the bank in Fullerton Square. I am endeavouring to find some of our Chinese clerks to see if they can help with getting the mess sorted. I should appreciate an early reply to this letter advising me as to any authority I hold.

I am also trying to find a locksmith to repair the doors both to the Square and the side entrance to make the building secure. Most of the windowpanes are also missing and currently I have not been able to find a local glazier able to undertake the repairs.

I am sorry to have to tell you that Cedric Meadows, Head of Security at KL, died in Adam Road camp in 1942 from wounds sustained in the fighting. Stuart Meldrum, one of our clerks at Fullerton Square was with him in the Volunteers and told me the news when we met briefly yesterday. Stuart is now on his way home to Australia on one of the hospital ships. I did say that he should contact the Bank's Sydney office once he has recovered which may be many months away.

Although the Japanese troops have agreed to stay in their barracks and voluntarily disarm there are a number of them wandering the streets causing trouble, mostly looking for food. The Indian population has also been very uncooperative and refusing to obey civil orders set down by the Army Council that has being set up to manage the Island. As so few Allied troops are around the decision has been taken to use Japanese troops for temporary police work over the next few months: a good many of the Allied troops are already being shipped off to Europe, Australia and the United States.

We are also desperately short of food and heavily dependent on supplies being shipped in daily, mainly by the Americans.

I will be staying in Singapore as it is now my home so I shall be very happy to follow any instructions regarding the Bank premises in Fullerton Square.

A Meeting Under A Banyan Tree

Airmail

Salisbury Crags

Tanglin Road

Singapore

8 September 1945

Dear Peter,

Free at last. We were told this morning that the Japanese have agreed to stay in their barracks until they are sent off to a temporary camp in Johor although there is a plan to house them in a POW camp possibly on one of the Dutch Islands just south of here. We are told that Mountbatten is on his way to take a formal surrender. Let us hope there is no change of mind by the Japanese as it would be the thousands of civilians that would suffer most in any fighting. In fact, the Japanese on the Island only voluntarily surrendered on the 4th September despite some Allied troops having arrived on 31 August and the internment camps being opened up that day. The Japanese have insisted that we do not antagonise the situation by being too prominent, not that this is likely as most of the camp internees just want to get on the ships that are lying off the Island. I have moved up to Tanglin so I am fairly close to the remaining Japanese troops now based in Tanglin Barracks but I haven't thankfully seen any. My understanding is that the Allied troops that

11

landed this morning are prepared for fighting both here and on the Malay Peninsula as all the Japanese have not agreed to their Emperor's instruction to surrender.

I spoke to Eric Cassidy, a Captain in the Paratroopers (he worked in the Loans Section in Piccadilly up to December 1939) and he says that the surrender on the peninsula has been piecemeal and some Japanese want to continue fighting. When Eric turned up at the camp with half a dozen para's you can imagine my surprise and joy, but it took his senior officer some very delicate discussions to get the Japanese commanders to see that the game was up. We were literally starving, and the Yanks dropped food and drugs to us the next day and finally Allied ships arrived on the 31 August. I understand there is to be a formal surrender ceremony in a few days' time including hopefully of those Japanese forces in the Malay States although as I said the situation is very tense.

Where do I start? Singapore is a mess. We are short of everything and by the looks of it we will depend on the Americans for years to come. The bank is in an awful state, and I have written to Sir John and briefly told him of the situation and await his instructions as I am not quite sure what my position is at this time.

I went down Margaret Road this morning and I am sorry, but your house is a ruin. It looks as though the fighting was very close to it and it was hit by shells. I will go back in the next few days and see if there are any personal items that can be rescued.

Henry, I know will be writing to you with his news. He has managed to get a berth on one of the hospital ships and will be dropped off in Bombay where he will go on to Shimla to collect Mona but he intends to return immediately as he is to be Acting Station Master – the railway is not active currently. I understand that Brian and Martin are still in the Army. I think both are in Burma, at least that is where they were last stationed. We are trying to find some trace of Arthur and his family but there is no news at all. I will be doing some voluntary work at the Civilian Internees Registration Centre so I have hopes that I might get some information from internees that are being brought over from Sumatra. Nothing on Harry either. Still, it is very early days, so I am not giving up hope.

Michael Davison and his family leave tomorrow for Blighty, and I have taken the liberty of providing them with your address in Wimbledon as they will be staying not far from you in Clapham, with his sister. Michael will, I know, want to see you. He became our hut leader from just before Xmas 1944, something he seemed desperately keen to do at the beginning, but I suspect he was glad to get rid of at the end.

I hope you and Ethel are both well and that the news of Geoffrey is good. I am presuming that he was released from POW camp in April or May. Please write and give me all the news.

Best Wishes

Grahame Kerr

Airmail

Salisbury Crags

Tanglin Road

Singapore

8 September 1945

Dear Dr Connor and Mrs Connor,

I suspect you don't know that Joyce roomed at my house in the last few weeks of the fighting with the Japanese, in 1942. She and her friends Sally and Morag were bombed out of their accommodation and ended up using the ground floor of my house. I am told that the Colonial Office will be in touch with you to advise that Joyce is on her way home although I was told that she will probably need to have a period of recuperation in Ceylon before travelling the final part of the journey.

I'm afraid that she is quite ill, and she has been put on one of the first hospital ships leaving Singapore. I wasn't allowed to see her other than on a few occasions towards the end of our internment in Sime Road Camp and on those occasions, she wasn't lucid for a good deal of the time because she had a high fever. However, I know from the many times we played tennis together that she is a fighter, and I am confident she will be much stronger by the time she gets home.

14

All I know about her being a prisoner of the Japanese is that the ship she left Singapore on the 13th of February 1942 was sunk somewhere near Banda Island and she spent the greater part of the next few years in a women's camp on that Island and later somewhere in Sumatra. Sally Cheeseman, who was a colleague at the High Commissioner's Office, and a fellow internee, is also on her way home and she has promised to be in contact with you as soon as possible. Should there be any mix up in these arrangements Sally's home address is Kenton Hall, Great Chipping, Wiltshire.

Kay Skipton, a friend, is also on her way home. She nursed Joyce during the last three months in camp and has also said that she will be in contact with you. I'm afraid I didn't get her address before she left as things, as you can imagine, are a bit chaotic here. However, I understand she will be going to live with her parents in Heaton Mersey in Stockport and that this is only a few miles from you. So, I hope she will be in contact with you in a few weeks' time, as she sailed on 5th September.

Please be strong for Joyce when you see her as she suffered badly in the camp on Banda Island and give her my fondest wishes. I look forward to hearing that she is making a good recovery. Please write when you have a chance and for my part, I will do my best to give you more information about Joyce's last three years as I am learning more every day.

Chapter 2

As Robert limped up the steps and into the Municipal Building, he saw Neil Forsyth coming towards him looking very thin but resplendent in his police uniform.

"I thought you said you were going back to Blighty," Robert said as they shook hands. Before Neil could answer Robert added, "You look strange back in uniform."

Neil grinned back. In his broad Scots accent he said, "It does feel a bit strange, especially socks and shoes. I've decided to stay at least for the next few months until things are back to normal."

Robert just raised his eyebrows at what Neil said before saying, "It seems to me you have taken on a can of worms." He spoke as he looked at the pips on Neil's shoulders. "Is that promotion I can see?"

"Acting Superintendent, to be confirmed by the powers that be in a few weeks."

"Well at least you speak Japanese."

Neil was grinning back at Robert knowing what he meant. "A bit of a turnaround, Bob. The Police Commissioner thought it was a great idea and the Army Council agreed. We can't trust the Indians because they are sympathetic to the rioters, and the Army doesn't want to be involved, so what do we do – we use Japanese prisoners of war as policemen." Neil was shaking his head as he spoke. "The world is mad." With that Neil clapped Robert on the shoulder and set off from the building shouting as he went, "I have given Mary a list of evacuees that left on the ships last night. Pound to a penny their names were not passed on to you."

Robert waved his arm in the air as acknowledgement and continued limping towards the rooms that had been set up for the registration of internees and evacuees. Inside the room the electricity was working at a greatly reduced capacity and the overhead fans barely moved round shifting only a little of the stifling air. Mary Dyson was sat at one end of the room he had entered, with three other volunteers, sifting through boxes of cards. One of the volunteers had obviously just made a pot of tea and Robert momentarily stood in the entrance and watched the quiet scene of volunteers working and enjoying their tea.

He came back to earth when Joan Cramond, until recently an internee at Sime Road Camp, said, "He always turns up when I've just made a pot."

Robert grinned at the reference clearly made about him. "Years of practice, Joan."

"Yes, well it must be your turn by now to make a pot."

Mary Dyson looked up from where she was studying a list. "Neil's been and given us the names of internees that left last night.

I had a quick look and I think they must be KL internees. I've left the list on your desk.

Robert nodded at what she said and headed for his desk. "Mmm. I've just seen him. He told me."

Mary continued speaking as Robert moved over to his desk. "Before you look at those lists can you help with what we've got? David Leslie met some Army nurses bringing in evacuees when he went down to catch his ship home. He managed to get a list of the evacuees and sent them up to us before he left. We think they're from Taiping, although there's some mention of KL. Apparently, they shipped them down by army lorries. Poor devils, the trip must have been horrendous; it took them days. They've been hospitalised up at the old Royal Navy Hospital for assessment, as the General is full to brimming. One of them had the sense to bring the Japanese lists from the camp. By the looks of it the internees were mostly miners and estate workers, but I can't read the hieroglyphics against some of the names."

Robert walked back over to Mary's end of the large table that four or five ex- internees normally shared and sat down beside her.

"Have you got yourself some specs, Mary?" He took up one of the sheets on the table beside Mary as he said it.

Mary just shook her head. "I saw someone yesterday at the General and they have made an appointment for me to have tests on

Tuesday." She changed the subject. "I've told Paul that I am not leaving until I get some news of Brian."

Robert knew what she was referring to. Paul Kennick, who was supposed to supervise the work of the Repatriation Office; he had tried to persuade her to take one of the ships taking internees home. He started to read through the names as he spoke, "It's still early days yet, Mary. Half the camps in Sumatra are still being emptied never mind camps in China, Indo China and Thailand. Brian could be anywhere." He looked at Mary and then he returned to the lists; he felt more than heard her sigh. Quietly he said, "Keep going. Something good will happen, I'm sure."

Robert felt Mary turn away as Joan put a mug of tea beside him. "Don't you upset my friend, Robert Draper, or you'll know about it."

It was Mary turning back to face them both who said, "Come on, Bob, decipher what these hieroglyphics are saying."

Robert had been rifling through the dozen or so sheets of badly typed and handwritten pages trying to decipher the Japanese writing in the margins. "As far as I can make out, they are records of when internees entered hospitals, something about being fit to work, and this one…." Robert pointed to one name on the list, "It says he died but doesn't say exactly when or what was the cause. If I'm right, it looks as though he died around early September 1943." Robert picked up other sheets from the desk. "What camp did you say this is?"

It was Joan standing looking over Robert's shoulder who said, "We were told Taiping, although some of the internees seem to have come from KL."

Joan moved away from standing beside him and Robert settled back in his chair. "Give me a pencil and I will scribble what I think is being said on these sheets." Looking up, Robert added, "Have you had a look at the stuff Neil brought in?"

Mary shook her head. "No, I just had a quick look and then put the sheets on your desk."

Robert continued studying the sheet in front of him and adding pencil notations as he interpreted the Japanese language.

Mary broke into his thoughts. "Shall I give Neil's stuff to Keith for him to get started?"

Robert nodded as he asked, "Do we know how long this lot will be around?"

Mary who had moved to the next desk, shook her head before saying, "I am told they have been sent up to the Royal Naval Hospital for a few days while they are being assessed."

"Well, I think you and Joan should go and find them. Get them to tell you who died and when and see if it matches these records. If any of them were executed, we need to know the details. These records are incomplete. It doesn't look as though the Nips were too bothered about keeping accurate records. There must have been transfers out to other camps and yet there doesn't seem to be anything about this happening. We need to try and corroborate some of the information on these lists. You OK with that?

Mary nodded. "Keep me busy. I know."

"I was thinking more of keeping Joan away from me."

Mary smiled as she stood up. "Liar" As she went over to where Joan was working on another table she shouted back, "Paul has two new volunteers helping this afternoon. He didn't say who they were so I can't help. Oh, and your friendly American airman has been in earlier and left you a present in the back. It's all wrapped up and clinks."

Robert just nodded now deep in thought. He had just seen a name he knew.

Apart from a couple of short interruptions when some Sime Road internees came in to say that they were on their way home to Blighty the next day, and a brief phone call from Hugh Bryson, the Colonial Office person responsible for civilian repatriation, Robert worked on the Taiping list during the rest of the morning.

More than once he returned to the name he recognised – Jim Clemence. It seemed he had died of fever in early March 1945 having been based in the internees' camp attached to Japanese HQ in Taiping. Robert guessed that as a mechanic he would have been very useful to the Nips. But where was Melanie Clemence? It didn't look as though there was a women's camp at Taiping and anyway, she had probably been taken prisoner in KL. The latest KL records might help.

Robert knew that the KL internees had been shipped down to Singapore in small convoys over the last few days but he had not seen her name on the list of names that had arrived in the office so far. Mind you that was not entirely surprising. The desire to get internees out of the camps and back to their homeland was paramount and records didn't always matter despite Hugh sending out missives almost daily and Robert trying to get the various entry points to the Island covered by volunteers.

A short meeting at the Colonial Office the previous day had brought it home to him just how complicated the situation was, with a number of the Governments of the Allies insisting on spiriting away their countrymen direct from dozens of camps in the Malay States, Sumatra, Java, Borneo and Thailand. Only yesterday, at the meeting, he had learned of two new camps in Borneo and Celebes, and how some internees who had been based originally at Adam Road, on Singapore Island, had disappeared on the way to Japan in

1943. So far, he had not come across any records of those interned in Adam Road camp and what information he had been given was by word of mouth. Laz, a close friend and currently tucked up in a bed at the General Hospital, had been at the Adam Road camp for a short while before he became part of the forced labour that worked at the docks; he had been a useful source but as was nearly always the case it was often of people with first names only.

Later in the afternoon Hugh turned up with Paul Kennick, both fellow internees and colleagues in the Fatigues Office at Sime Road Civilian Internment Camp, together with two new volunteers one of whom had assisted in the Fatigues Office. After a short introduction to the impossible task in front of them Robert left the new volunteers with a couple of the regular helpers and went over and sat in a corner to talk with Hugh and Paul.

It was Hugh who kicked off by saying. "Sir Shenton is beginning to get back on track after his journey from Japan and would like to see you, Bob. He suggests 10 am tomorrow morning."

"Why me, Hugh?"

"Oh, I think just to thank you. Without you and Mary the office would be in chaos. I'm sorry I've had to drag Paul off, temporarily, to set up a new department in the Colonial Office but we're very short handed."

"Then I presume Mary ought to be there as well."

Hugh shook his head. "I think it's more than just a thank you. I don't know any more. It's above my pay grade. The meeting's at the Goodwood."

Robert just nodded. The hotel was close to where he lived.

Hugh continued as Robert sat down on a hard chair. "Any news about your situation yet?"

"I haven't heard yet, Hugh. I don't know whether I even have a job. I've been contacted by eight of the clerks who used to work at the bank and I've taken it off my own bat to get them to clean the place out and make sure the records are okay. I have an American friend who has managed to find me a whole pile of stationery and binders. Don't ask me from where and I don't want to know. Anyway, the clerks are copying the records as the originals are just about dust."

It was Paul who came in with," I'd be surprised if you get many more of your clerks turning up as the Nips seem to have removed most of the qualified Chinese from the scene. Harry Longfellow has just arrived back from India and the First Secretary has given him the task of getting to grips with what happened to the Chinese immediately after 15th February." Robert knew that he meant by the 15th February as referring to the surrender by the Allies in 1942; he merely nodded.

One of the volunteers came across to where they were sitting and interrupted them. "Do any of you know a Martin Kennedy? He seems to have caused the Nips problems."

Robert almost shot up off his seat. Martin Kennedy was one of the names on his list of people to find. "He was General Manager, Malaya Tin Mines. He went missing on 8ᵗʰ December 1941, up north of Kuantan."

"Well, I have just been told that he was shipped off to Thailand from a camp up near Khota Bahru. For some reason he was shipped off with some military."

"How do we know this?" Robert asked.

"The chap sitting over there is an Anglo- Indian, who was only interned in mid-1943 up in KL. He was telling me about fighting around the estate he worked on. Apparently, some Europeans were killed in a shootout and Martin Kennedy was wounded. He hid Kennedy and the Nips moved off and it was only later that Kennedy was captured by a Nip patrol. Mr Greeves … over there, thinks a local man betrayed them."

"Do we know what happened to him once he was up in Thailand?" Hugh asked having already muttered that he knew the name but couldn't place him. The volunteer shook his head and said he would continue talking to Mr Greeves.

The volunteer started to go back to his desk, but Robert stopped him. "I need to speak to Mr Greeves before he goes so ask him to stay. I won't be long."

The volunteer went off as Robert turned back to Hugh. "Have we had any internees from Thailand come down so far?"

Hugh shook his head. "As far as I know the Yanks have flown them out from Bangkok and on to Hawaii."

"It will take us years, Hugh, if ever, to trace everyone and maybe only those that are alive."

Hugh just nodded as he stood up to leave. "Oh, and you should know that I have my ticket to go home on the 28th so Paul will be in charge. Paul will give you the other news." "Don't forget tomorrow morning."

Paul and Robert watched Hugh leave before they turned back to continue their meeting.

"It's quite ridiculous Paul. We get half the story, half the time. It's not as though everybody doesn't know that they should be telling us."

Paul smiled back. Robert could see that Paul was uncomfortable. Finally, apologetically Paul said, "You should know that they're setting up a central records office in Kandy for the collection of all

POW and CIC names in this theatre. Hugh's argued against it but has been overruled. He's still arguing but he's wasting his time. Some Major General is to take charge. We've to continue collecting what we can and at some point, we will close down and our records are to be transferred to Ceylon."

Paul could see Robert was cross. "I know. I know. Nevertheless, the powers that be think this is the best idea despite Hugh, and I think Sir Shenton, arguing that we are far better placed. I don't know how long we have but I suspect at best a few weeks by which time most of the camps will have long dispersed and Kandy will have little to work with."

Robert just sat there shaking his head. In the background he could hear female voices and realised that Mary and Joan had arrived back from their visit to the Royal Naval hospital.

"Don't suppose you have any news about the POWS that were sent to Saigon," Robert said watching Mary talking to the new volunteers.

"Not a dicky bird. All I can find out is that the Yanks shipped out those that survived to Manila."

Mary had seen them talking in the corner and came across. As she approached Robert shook his head and she knew what he meant.

"Hullo Paul. Robert, I have lots more information about the Taiping camp, and I'll go back tomorrow with Joan. Some of them are being shipped out on Wednesday so we haven't long."

She was about to go and say something else but saw the look on Robert's face. "What?"

It was Robert who answered. "They're proposing to close us down in the next few weeks and centralise everything in Kandy."

Mary stood there. She looked hot and still very thin from her three years in the camp. All she said was "Oh", before she turned away and went back to her chair.

Paul got up from his chair. "You in tomorrow?"

Robert shook his head. "No, I've got things to do at the bank and a hospital appointment about my foot, as well as my meeting with Sir Shenton. Joe's in and Mary will be around as well. I want to check the KL records before I go, though."

"You ought to know that I will be going home in a couple of months. I agreed to stay and cover for Hugh until the First Secretary can get replacements for him and a few of the senior staff."

With that Paul left and Robert got up and went across to where Mary was now sitting working through some records. He sat down beside her.

"It was inevitable really."

Mary just nodded.

"Paul and I think Brian may have ended up in Saigon and from there we think what's happened is that the POW's have been shipped off to Manila and then the States. There is a request out for information on British servicemen based in that camp, but we have nothing yet. I'm seeing Chuck tonight for a drink so I will see if he can go through his channels and find out what happened to the POWs in Saigon.

Mary didn't look at Robert. She went back to reading the lists. "Thank you. Now go away and leave me to concentrate on these records."

Chapter 3

Airmail

Union and China Bank

Piccadilly

London

28 September 1945

Dear Robert,

What wonderful news to hear of your release. The evening before I received your letter, I had dinner with Peter and Ethel and we spent much of the time talking and thinking of you and our many friends stuck in camps in the Far East.

I am pleased to tell you that Peter has accepted my request that he take up the post of Regional Director for Singapore, the Malay States and Indonesia. We are trying to arrange for him to be with you sometime early in the New Year. Ethel will join him a little later as Peter tells me that you have told them that their former home is in a poor state, and he would want time first to find her decent accommodation. I think Ethel is also keen to have some time with their son, Geoffrey, who is still recovering from five years as a POW although I understand he is making good progress and anxious to take up a new career in the church. I know that Peter will be writing with all his news so I won't spoil what he will want to say.

Now to you. First of all, I am very pleased to confirm that you can hold the post of Assistant Manager for as long as you wish. From what Peter tells me you were indispensable in the days leading up to the surrender. Peter will sort out all the paperwork and send it on to you. He has said that he suspects that it is your long term wish to go into business and I would understand if this wish remained strong, but I earnestly hope that you will stay with us and assist Peter in building the bank back to its former glory. The bank will forever owe you a great debt of gratitude for your work in rescuing the gold from the Malay States.

Peter will correspond with you about getting the bank back into working order but if in the meantime you can get the basics organised, I know he will be most grateful.

I look forward to further letters from you with news of what is happening in Singapore as there will always be a part of me missing the daily life of the Island. I have told Peter that I intend to come out to the Far East sometime later in 1946.

With best wishes

Sir John Hutton

Grahame Kerr

Airmail

9 Condover Road

Sale

Manchester

26 September 1945

Dear Robert,

Thank you for your airmail of 7 September which we received a few days ago. We are very grateful for the time you have taken in sending us the news of Joyce. Until the Red Cross informed us in July that she was in Sime Road Camp we had no idea where she was, and our worst fear was that she had been killed in the fighting in Singapore. As you can imagine it has been a very difficult time for us these past four years with no news whatsoever.

I have been in touch with the Colonial Office and after much toing and froing they have put me in contact with a Repatriation Office who confirm that she has now been hospitalised in Colombo, undergoing treatment, and that she will be on a ship home in a couple of months. Her sister Jane is engaged to be married and they had planned to have the wedding before Christmas, but they have now decided to delay the ceremony for a while in the hope that Joyce will be able to attend. I cannot tell you how relieved we are to hear of Joyce being alive but of course we will not rest until she is home, and we can look after her. My wife has had a particularly difficult time these past four years as she and Joyce were always very close and the waiting to see Joyce is causing her great strain.

I hope that you are recovering from your ordeal in the camp, and we are very grateful for your letter. I would very much welcome further correspondence with you.

Yours sincerely,

Dr Michael Connor

Grahame Kerr

Airmail

10 Morrissey Gardens

Wimbledon

London

28 September 1945

Dear Bob,

I suspect you will get a letter from Sir John at roughly the same time as you get this one. First, Sir John has offered me the post of Regional Director and I have agreed to take on the job for only three years partly to mollify Ethel who would prefer to stay in England. The appointment is not quite the same remit as Walter's old job, but in my view, it offers a better challenge. Second, he has agreed, without any difficult, I should add to my suggestion that we offer you a permanent post of Assistant Manager. In fact, he said that he leaves it to me to decide on the appointment of senior staff and I am already dealing with the Staff Office regarding the recruitment of people. I'm sending you the contract you thoroughly deserve, by standard mail.

I know you will be sorting out some of the basics in Fullerton Square and I leave it to you to continue that work. Can I ask whether you will be able to go up to Penang and KL in the next few weeks

34

and find out the situation? I have no idea of the problems but if it was possible for you to make a preliminary visit to assess the major issues then at least I will have some idea of the magnitude of the problems.

Bangkok will now be the responsibility of Ken Lambton who Sir John has appointed to be the Regional Director for Hong Kong, Shanghai and Bangkok. I don't think you know Ken, but he was the manager of our Australia outpost for some years and was then in the Royal Navy from 1940 before arriving on our doorstep in Piccadilly having been demobbed in May. That leaves Batavia but I have been advised by the Foreign Office that the situation there is precarious to say the least, so I suggest we leave that problem until later.

You will need some funds to operate with and I am in meetings with officials from the Bank of England for funds to be made available in Singapore. The other banks are doing the same and you should hear from the Singapore Treasury in the next few weeks. I have given them your details.

Ethel sends her kind regards and asks that any stuff from Margaret Road that you can rescue would be greatly appreciated. She will be joining me on the Island once she is satisfied that Geoffrey is fully recovered from his five years as a prisoner of war. He's decided that he wants to go into the ministry and has been accepted for training starting in late October. I think Ethel just wants to mother him and Geoffrey is already finding it a bit too much but he's not going to get away from it. I've got meeting after meeting with various Directors and Bank of England officials about issues so I hope to be able to book a passage for just after Xmas by which time we should also have a decision about when the Island and Malay States will be allowed to use their own currency. I gather you are using some Allied service currency currently which unless you tell me otherwise sounds as though it only creates a great deal of opportunity for a black market.

I am writing to Henry separately. The lack of news about Arthur and Neecha and their boys is worrying to say the least. It does not bode well. We may never know the full story. It's all very sad. I just hope something good does emerge as I gather new camps are still being found.

Best wishes

Ps You haven't said anything about your injuries but in Henry's letter he has said you suffered badly with the Kempetai. Do you want to tell me?

Chapter 4

Finding lost friends and colleagues on an Island that is not really that big would seem a relatively easy task to undertake but Robert had found in the eight weeks since his release from the internment camp that every obstacle possible was put in his way. The problem was that everything was in transition, what with new people arriving on the Island every day from the camps dotted all around South Asia and people leaving for Europe or Australia as quickly as possible, anxious to get back to their homeland and families. Few people worried about the need to leave a record of the past three and half years.

It was frustrating in every way possible. Robert left notes in various places trying to contact someone only to discover that he had missed that person by a day and the person was now on a ship headed for Europe. Mind you the same could be said of people looking for Robert who was all over the place but in this case the problem was easier to solve. He had his home up in Tanglin and there was always the bank where a dozen or so of the clerks, who had worked with him before 15th February 1942, had now returned to work; and there was always the Repatriation Office.

Robert had set the bank clerks the task of cleaning the place out and copying all the files that had been found. Ju We Yin and Chin Lee, had made a good job of boxing all the files in the Loans Department in February 1942 so copying these files was easier than the copying of the cash transaction and account files that Mr Wuh and his staff had boxed rather hurriedly in the last few days before the Island surrendered. These files were in a poor state, mildewed and by the looks of it termites had had a feast. As Ju We Yin and Mr Wuh seemed to have vanished Robert put a much older looking Chin Lee in charge of the task of sorting the bank records out.

Old customers were now asking to take out money before they took passage to England, and Robert promoted one of the long serving clerks whom he knew well, to be responsible for tracing a customer's records and producing a statement. In most cases the customer wanted a balance to take with them back to Blighty and Robert was able to give them a letter to draw the majority of their funds on return to England with some Allied service currency to tide them over on the passage home. Few businesses were functioning sufficiently to see them needing a regular banking service and it was with some amusement that Robert was told one morning when he came into the bank that a Mr Hussain wanted to see him about a business opportunity.

Mr Hussain had been a customer for many years running a small timber business up near Bukit Timah and he had been a great help to the Camp Committee in Sime Road Camp in supplying timber for the hundreds of huts that had had to be built.

"Mr Lee, can I suggest that you contact Mr Hussain and tell him that I shall be very pleased to see him on Thursday next week before

I go up to KL. Ask if he has any written details of his business plans for us to study beforehand."

Robert could see Chin Lee frowning and looking a little circumspect about the suggestion.

"I know, Mr Lee. Mr Hussain is not good on paper. He used to get Kenneth Chen to help with some of his ideas, but I know he has one of his sons doing the paperwork now and from memory the son is well educated." Robert finished by saying, "You never know your luck," smiling at a Chin Lee who looked very sceptical.

It was that morning, 24 October 1945, when Robert did get some information that was important and urgent. He was just finished sending another letter off to Peter Connaught when the telephone rang. Picking it up he immediately heard the Texan at the other end say, "Finding you is a bigger task than trying to find Brian Dyson."

Robert immediately sat up. Captain Charles Henry Karpinski, Chuck, to his many friends was with the American Airforce based up at Kellang airbase. In the six weeks since they had first met, they had become great friends with Chuck involved in repatriating American POW'S and Civilian Internee's being found in Sumatra, Java and in a few cases the Malay States. Robert had got Chuck to assist with tracing several civilians and had raised the issue of Mary's missing husband. What little information Robert had been able to find out about Brian Dyson's unit was that they were captured in Johor in January 1942 and that the group had possibly been marched off to a camp on the East Coast of the Malay States and then they had disappeared. What he and Paul had also found out was that quite a few of the early groups of captured service men had been shipped off to other parts of Asia.

"I've got great news and bad news. What do you want first?"

Robert knew at once that Chuck had found Brian. "Give me the great news."

"He was in a logging camp in Indochina. Maybe forty of them including five Brits. He's on a hospital ship in Manila Bay right now. He's in a bad state. He had no tags, so they didn't know who he was until yesterday when one of his mates who was also in a bad way came round and identified him."

Robert sat for a moment not saying anything. He wanted to yell.

"Are you still there?"

"Chuck, I don't know what to say. It's fantastic news, I'm going to go find Mary now and tell her."

"Hang on a minute you haven't got all the news. You Brits are always rushing off before you have all the information."

Robert came down from the clouds. "Alright, alright. What's the bad news?"

"Well, there's two bits of bad news. First, the ship that Brian is on is now on its way to Hawaii not towards Singapore, and second, I'm being posted back to the States in four weeks."

"Bloody hell. That's not fair. We're a team."

"What do you mean "we're a team? As far as I can see it's been all one way. Booze, meals at the base and then looking for Sergeant Dyson."

"Come on, Chuck you've made a friend for life. You'll be able to have free holidays out here whenever you want. Anyway, what about that young lady I introduced you to in Bugis Street."

There was a chortle at the other end of the phone. "She, should I say he, was certainly different. I shall dine on that tale for years."

"Look Chuck how do we get Mary to Hawaii."

There was silence at the other end before Chuck came back. "I thought you would be at me about that. Look leave it with me. We have planes going to Manila most days and maybe my General will agree to a civilian going. From Manila there must be planes to Hawaii. It's a humanitarian request after all and the General is a great one for that. I should be down in the *Mata Hari* tonight, so I'll let you know what the General thinks."

Chapter 5

Robert went straight to the Municipal Building, about half a mile away. Ordinarily he would have sought out a rickshaw for the journey over Anderson Bridge and round the edge of the Padang, but he couldn't wait and when you wanted a rickshaw there was never one around. He limped as fast as he could drawing stares from the few Europeans and Allied soldiers walking across the bridge, but he didn't care. Looking across at the Padang on his right he could see it was better for its first grass cut in years, but it still looked a long way from its pristine state of 1941. The cricket pavilion looked as though it needed major repairs and, in the distance, around St. Andrew's Cathedral, he could see the grass had yet to be cut. The heat was building up and by the time Robert reached the steps of the Municipal Building he was sweating profusely. He clambered up the steps, briefly remembering that on these very steps was where he had seen the Allied forces led by their Generals being marched off to captivity in February 1942 and where he had witnessed the formal surrender of the Japanese Southeast Armed Forces to Lord Mountbatten only six weeks ago.

He topped the steps of the Municipal Building with the sweat pouring off him. Like all the released internees Robert was still woefully unfit and he had to stop for breath. The Malay policeman standing at the entrance looked shocked at the state of the man appearing before him and started to put his arm out to prevent him from entering the building and then recognising Robert he lowered his arms.

Robert walked through the entrance hall which was surprisingly empty and entered the room where the Repatriation Office was temporarily housed. Perhaps a dozen people were working at the long tables and those nearest looked across at him.

"Where's Mary?" he almost shouted.

Joan, who was sat at one of the tables, answered. "She's in the back making a drink."

Before Robert had a chance to move towards the back Mary came out having heard the noise and perhaps her name being mentioned. She knew looking at Robert's broad grin that he had news.

"Mary, we've found him. He's alive." Robert was almost shouting it.

Mary dropped the glass of water she had been holding and started to crumple with a couple of the volunteers immediately coming across and helping her up.

"If this is some sort of joke, Robert Draper, I will skin you alive," Joan said as she went across to help Mary into a chair.

"No, no. Mary, Chuck Karpinski up at Kellang base has been on the phone to me. They have traced Brian. He's on a hospital ship on its way to Hawaii."

Mary had started to sob, and Joan was now holding her. One of the volunteers came around the back of Robert and clapped him on the back. "Wonderful news, Bob."

Joan helped Mary to steady herself. "Come on love. Take a deep breath." She turned to Robert. "Now Bob, let's hear the news again."

****

The *Mata Hari* was not the place of old, but it was still Robert's favourite drinking hole. Everything looked as though it had seen better days but there was a warmth about the place. The waiters knew him, the bar staff knew what his tipple was and, on the occasions, he had had too much to drink they always made sure that he had a trishaw home. His uncle John, *Captain* as everybody remembered him by, had introduced him to the bar and it had become the starting place for a night out and for colleagues to meet after a day at work. In the short time the Japanese had attacked the Malay States and Singapore it had also been a watering hole and refuge for the younger members of the local defence unit.

Robert arrived with the place already quite full, a mixture of soldiers, a few sailors and just a few stalwarts from the old days who were gradually returning to their sanctuary. Chuck was with two other American army buddies drinking at the bar. Chuck saw Robert arrive and got up from his stool to welcome him.

"Hell, man you look hot."

Robert grinned back. "Chuck today is perhaps one of the best days in a long time. Trouble is I'm also trying to organise going up country in a few days and that's not been easy. Sir Shenton wants me to go with an official party for my protection because they think that the commies may be interested in me."

Chuck stopped what he was about to say and frowned. Then he spoke. "Hell, you want to avoid that. These guys don't play fair." As he said it, he turned to his two drinking partners and introduced Robert. "Matt, Ken, this is Bob Draper, recently released from internment and on a quest for gold." The two men stood up and shook hands with Robert; with Matt greeting him immediately with, "Yeah Chuck has been telling us that there is gold hidden somewhere." Robert grinned back at them, momentarily going a little red in the face, as he recalled a heavy drinking session with Chuck and him telling the tale of the missing gold.

"We just don't know if it's still missing. The people who knew where it was and who looked after it all seem to be dead. Who knows it could be a fortune or it could be just two pieces of silver."

Ken looked across to where Robert was sitting, drinking the glass of beer the waiter had produced without being asked. "You seem to get good service round here."

Chuck was smiling at Robert. "So, how's your Mary?"

"She's on top of the world, Chuck. She couldn't stop crying."

"Well, you better tell her to get her bags packed. The General has said she can have a pass to fly out to Manila on Friday. Tell her to give me a ring tomorrow and I will give her the details. The General agreed when I told him she had helped some American women to stay alive in the camp."

Robert raised his eyebrows. "I'm not sure about that part, Chuck."

"Just tell her that it's a thank you for looking after some of our women." As Chuck was saying it, he winked across at Robert and the other Americans at the table all laughed. "We're sending some nurses stateside so she will go with them. " Chuck waved an arm in the direction of Ken. "Ken here has a very friendly nurse who will look after her and get her to wherever Sergeant Dyson is."

As they were talking a Chinese waiter came across and whispered something to Robert in Chinese. The Americans watched, two of them smoking as the other finished off his beer. Robert stood up finishing his beer.

"Sorry gents but it seems that an old friend has arrived on the Island and needs to see me urgently.

Chuck just shook his head. "Some friend you are. We just sit down for a drink and now you're off. Will I see you before I go stateside at the end of the month?"

Robert grimaced. "I thought I would be up in Penang and KL for ten days, but Sir Shenton has insisted on me being part of an organised trip with the Army so how long I am stuck with them I don't know."

"I suppose we've laid on a plane," growled Matt with Robert shrugging his shoulders and saying he didn't know what the arrangements were exactly.

Chuck grinned. "We have to learn to share, Matt."

"I'm not sharing my women."

As he had been talking Robert had scribbled down an address and passed it over to Chuck. "It's a party off Orchard Road, officers only. I'm told the ladies are thoroughly disreputable."

It was Ken who started to laugh. "Where did you get this information?"

"The police know everything. I think it's a fellow countryman of yours who is holding the event to promote international relations." With that Robert left waving his left arm at them and heading towards the far end of the bar where a large Chinese man in a smart suit was waiting.

****

"That looks a bad scar on his face, "Ken said as the waiter brought over another round of beers.

"The *Kempetai* gave him a bad time. They tortured him trying to find this gold he talks about. He says they killed the two guys who probably knew where it was hidden but it seems they didn't squeal so Bob was the next best bet. Mind you I think it was a long shot and by all accounts he wasn't the only one questioned."

"So how much is at stake? asked Matt taking an interest.

"No one knows. Bob brought down $25 million bucks from KL with the Japs trying to get their hands on it, and he says there was more on the Island as well.

Matt whistled at the amount. "Hell, that's worth getting killed for."

"Bob reckons they got more than half off the Island around the 5th February 1942 on some destroyer which it seems made it to Perth. What happened to the rest is anybody's guess."

"When you're gone Chuck, I might just stay friendly with Bob. You never know he may want to share what he finds."

Chuck roared out loud. "Come on you bums let's go see what this party is all about."

Chapter 6

Outside the *Mata Hari* a large Chinese man was waiting for Robert; he bowed slightly before ushering him into the back of a waiting car. Robert had for weeks been asking around as to whether anybody knew the whereabouts of Kenneth Chen, one of the senior clerks who had worked at the bank before the Japanese captured the Island. He knew Kenneth Chen was involved with the Kuomintang, the Nationalist Party of China. The last he had seen of him was on the 6th February 1942 when Robert had offered to pay to get him and his family out of Singapore. The next he had heard was that he had been spirited away just as the Japanese had invaded the Island.

After he got into the back of the car he sat next to the Chinese man, who insisted on covering Robert's eyes, assuring Robert that it was for his own safety. Robert sat patiently trying to work out where they were going not really hearing any noises that would help him. For some reason he guessed they were on the road up the west coast of the Island, but it was guesswork really.

After perhaps half an hour, although it seemed longer with the Chinese back seat passenger refusing to talk when Robert asked questions, the car turned onto a mud road and then he heard the tyres on shingle or was it sand? The door opened and as he got out the scarf was removed from his face by a small Chinese man who had helped him out. He heard the door on the other side of the car shut and the large Chinese man came around the car.

The place was in darkness other than for two small lights over the porch of the large house he was facing. He looked around as he followed the large Chinese man up the steps of the house. It seemed as though the place was surrounded by jungle but just to one side, he thought he saw the glimmer of the sea. The air was sticky with the heat, yet Robert shivered. Shades of nights with the *Kempetai*. Thank God it was Kenneth Chen he was going to see.

The Chinese man spoke in Cantonese to someone as Robert swished away the buzzing mosquitos. The noise of the jungle close by was constant and he could feel the sweat running down his back. "Follow me, Mr Draper." It was only then that he saw the dark shapes of other men. The front door opened, and Robert was spirited into the house in seconds with the door closing behind them immediately. He was ushered into what was a large airless reception area with only one light, on a desk, where a man sat beside a telephone. There did not seem to be any overhead fans working. Robert could see that there was a revolver on the desk. Again, the large Chinese man, who in the dark shadows of the hall looked enormous, said, "Follow me".

The double doors to a lounge opened as if someone knew they were approaching, and Robert found himself in perhaps a small dance hall with men sitting on settees in various alcoves although it was difficult to see everything as most of the room was in semi darkness with just the lit embers of the cigarettes to tell him that men were sitting watching him. Robert followed his escort towards the well-lit zone at the far end of the room.

A beaming Kenneth Chen stood up from one of the settees as Robert approached and came to meet him. "Mr Draper, it is so good to see you again." He momentarily stopped when he saw the scar on Robert's face and saw that he was limping. "Mr Draper, you have been treated badly."

Robert smiled back at Kenneth Chen. "I am patient. I will get those that did this to me, Kenneth. I am just pleased that you survived the last few years." Taking a breath in the stifling heat Robert added, "Are your wife and sons safe?"

Kenneth Chen ushered Robert towards the settees. "They are well, Mr Draper. My sons are both grown up now and my wife enjoys good health."

The large Chinese man brought over a tray of drinks and offered Robert a whisky which he accepted. "I know you like a short in the evening Mr Draper and it is the least I can do having dragged you away from your favourite watering hole."

Robert raised his glass to Kenneth Chen who had refused a drink. "Here's to us surviving the next adventure, whatever it maybe." Robert looked around before saying. "I take it this is some sort of safe house?"

Kenneth Chen just nodded. "We are at war with the communists and there are no safe places anymore. Lai Tek and his comrades will not rest too long before they try something so we must be on our guard."

"You will not be returning to the bank, Kenneth?"

Kenneth Chen smiled almost wistfully. "No, Mr Draper. Those days are gone. I am now the Treasurer of the Party's funds in South Asia and there is much work to be done."

Robert looked suitably impressed. "Where were you during the occupation?"

"Often the best place is just under the nose of your adversary. I lived for most of the time near the Thai border working with Force 136, funding the agents we had in the towns and villages." Kenneth Chen stopped smiling as he lit a Chinese cigarette and sucked in the strong nicotine. "I suspect you do not even know about Force 136. It was a small group of men who organised the fighting from the jungle although they much depended on the help that my supporters could give with information, and with carrying supplies. The armed fighters in the jungle were mostly communists led by Chin Peng and Li Bo but the Kuomintang were much involved in the towns. I was trusted with the funds that were needed and I dealt with a source in

Singapore until he was killed by the Japanese without him betraying us. I even had to arrange the funding of joint action against the Japanese Army. It is wondrous what we will do to beat a common enemy although the communists arranged their own finances for those fighters living in the jungle."

Robert was beginning to realise what Kenneth Chen was leading up to. From nowhere the large Chinese man reappeared and without any ceremony he refilled Robert's glass. The room seemed to be getting even hotter if that was possible with no fans working and Robert felt that the temperature had gone up a notch. He could feel the sweat running down his back and his armpits felt very sticky and unpleasant. Somewhere in the room he could hear the buzzing of a mosquito seeking blood.

"The thing is, Mr Draper, the Kuomintang helped our Allies during the War, and it was agreed that we would be paid for our brave actions. Not all the money has been paid that we are owed for this service, and we are most anxious to have the outstanding balance. When the source stopped in 1943 there was many months of non-payment until Force 136 could arrange funds from India. We need this money to be paid for us to continue the struggle against the communists. I am sure you understand."

Robert started to say that he couldn't help, and that Kenneth should talk to Sir Shenton, but Kenneth Chen interrupted him by putting up his right hand. "Mr Draper, we are satisfied you do not know where the gold is hidden but I can tell you that we believe that there is more hidden on the Island. The Japanese always believed that there was more. We agreed with the British Government that they would deliver gold to us through Tan Choo Sin, who had a transport business, and we know that he died in a purge of Chinese industrialists in late 1942. We know that the Allies made a deal with the communists for them to be paid as well and we learned later that Tan Choo Sin was also responsible for delivering gold to them. That of course dried up when he was murdered. We know all this because we found the driver Tan Choo Sin used to deliver gold to Li Bo. He told us he was to deliver gold to Li Bo at a meeting of the MCP Central Committee, at the Batu Caves, in late 1942 but he hid the gold because there were many Japanese patrols near there and he could not get through."

****

Robert stood drinking his whisky. He said nothing just taking in the information. He did not know of a "Tan Choo Sin", so he said nothing.

Kenneth Chen continued. "The Japanese killed many of the Central Committee including Li Bo when they attacked them at the Batu Caves. Chin Peng, who was there, escaped. The driver told us that he hid the gold and then he hid from the Japanese and did not return to Singapore for many months. When he returned, he found that Tan Choo Sin had been arrested. He went into hiding again and we later found him.

As Robert digested the information Kenneth Chen stubbed out his cigarette and picked up another. "We are satisfied that he hid the gold on the route to the Batu Caves. It was many months before we were able to go to where the driver said the gold was buried but it had gone. Perhaps the Japanese found the gold, who know? We do not think so. Nor could we contact Tan Choo Sin as he was killed in the purge only weeks later. As Tan Choo Sin was gone we had no way of knowing who the source was, and we were without funds until Captain Davis of Force 136 contacted one of our agents." Robert did not ask what had happened to the poor driver; he just digested all the new information.

Kenneth Chen looked at Robert directly, "We have been looking for the gold ever since. Lai Tek or Chin Peng, it seems also do not know or the communists would not be searching for it on the mainland."

Robert knew that Lai Tek was the leader of the Malay Communist Party although rumours were circulating the Island that a power struggle was happening. "It could be that Lai Tek looks for other gold that he knows exists and only pretends to look for the gold that was destined for Li Bo?"

A Meeting Under A Banyan Tree

Kenneth Chen stopped momentarily to take a draw on his cigarette before continuing. "What makes you think that? It is not impossible. We know that the Central Committee never received the shipment. If what you say is true how would Lai Tek know where it was hidden? He would know that Tan Choo Sin was responsible for delivering gold to Li Bo but how would he know the delivery arrangements. In my later dealings with Force 136, I had to request that they bring extra money from India because the source in Singapore was no longer accessible." Kenneth Chen let this fact sink in before he added, "We are sure that you have not found where the gold is hidden otherwise why would you be asking about it. What we hope is that you may find someone through your enquiries that has some idea as to what happened to it. Whatever happens it is most important that if there is gold that it does not fall into the hands of the communists. Lai Tek does not worry us, but Chin Peng would do great damage with a large amount of gold."

Robert answered almost immediately. "I know that Maurice Levy and Ernest Beverley were involved in the original plan to fund the continued fighting against the Nips. They both died at the hands of the *Kempetai*. I am sure the Bishop of Singapore was also involved or had knowledge but when I spoke to him in Sime Road Camp, he denied knowing anything about the gold; anyway, why should he trust me – the camp was full of informants. He was with me in the YMCA but in a different cell and after many months the *Kempetai* released him; he was in a pretty bad way, but he does not seem to have betrayed Ernest Beverley or Maurice Levy, who died in the YMCA. I don't think Maurice betrayed anyone. I think that the Head of the Island's Treasury may also have known things, but he died on 16 February 1942. I saw what was left of him after the Nips had tortured him in the Municipal Building. He certainly never made it to Changi." Robert momentarily thought of Rachel Knowles who was involved in some way or other, but he said nothing about her.

Robert sipped the last of his whisky and then added, "It may be that what you had up to late 1942 was all there was on the Island."

Kenneth Chen made a bit of a face and said nothing. It was obvious he had thought through the issue many times and thought it was unlikely.

Robert watching Kenneth's expression said, "It is always possible that there was no gold being sent up to the Batu Caves. It was all a put-up job and there never was any gold."

Kenneth Chen laughed out quietly. "You and I both don't believe that. The Japanese certainly did not, and we think that they had an informant who knew a little but not enough. They made a mistake when they murdered Tan Choo Sin and failed to realise his connection to the gold."

Robert finished his drink. "Kenneth, I have always been honest with you. We worked well when we were in the bank. I also want to make the Island my home. What I'm trying to say is that I don't want to be piggy in the middle. God, I have even had Military Intelligence insisting that if I get new information that I must tell them first. I have been asking around because I want to ensure that the man or men who helped the Japanese are caught and to make sure that the Japanese who tortured us for the gold get their comeuppance."

Kenneth Chen lit another cigarette without making any comment and then signalled to someone in one of the recesses of the room. "I wonder if you remember Jai Mung. He tells me that you met briefly at the Kings Dock on 5th February 1942 when he went with his father, Jai Lee Kwan, to Australia, with the emergency gold shipment."

Robert turned to face a young Chinese man, perhaps in his mid-twenties. Robert spoke to him in Mandarin and Kenneth Chen laughed. "Your languages have certainly improved, Mr Draper. Perhaps something good did come out of the war. Jai Mung tells me that his uncle, Wu Tu, who you know stayed behind, had been told to work with Mr Levy, on preparing funds to be used in fighting the Japanese in the event of the Island falling. He also knew Tan Choo Sin well; he ran a transport business used extensively by the China Bank. Sadly, we have learned that Wu Tu died in February 1942 when the Japanese forced thousands of the Chinese wealthy to swim out to sea in the days after the fall of Singapore. In their haste to remove potential problems the Japanese removed possible links to the gold although perhaps Wu Tu preferred to go into the sea rather than be caught and tortured. We will never know."

Jai Mung looked at Robert as Kenneth finished speaking and made a resigned acknowledgment of what had happened to his uncle. He just whispered, "They made thousands swim out into the sea."

Robert spoke to Jai Mung. "Your father and you took a lot of gold to Australia. That is the property of the China Bank and will be coming back to Singapore at some point, surely. It's obvious to me that the bank is controlled by the Kuomintang. That money will be of great help to the Party."

Jai Mung shook his head. "The Australian Government impounded the gold when we arrived in Perth and then placed it in your bank vaults in Sydney. My uncle and I were then put in a camp with other Chinese. We were not made welcome and but for Mr Foley, our English manager, we would have had a very bad time. Until he was conscripted, he got us extra food and argued that we should be set free. It was only when Chang Kai Chek sent a delegation, and Mr Chen went with them, to Australia in August 1943 to meet General Macarthur that we were set free. We returned with Mr Chen to China. The gold is still in your vaults in Sydney."

Robert said nothing about Frank Foley. He had been one of the team that had got the gold out of Kuala Lumper just before the

Japanese arrived. Frank had worked for the China Bank and Robert knew that he would have worked hard to have his Chinese employers treated well. Robert turned to Kenneth Chen. "The gold boxes that went to Australia were clearly marked as the property of the China Bank. I helped to make the boxes. If the gold is still in our vaults, Peter Connaught, will I am sure want to return the boxes to their rightful owner."

Kenneth Chen stopped in the middle of sucking on his cigarette." What has Mr Connaught to do with this?"

"Oh, this is something you have not been told." Robert was almost pleased that for once he was ahead of the game. "Peter has been appointed as the Regional Director for Union & China Bank.

Even in the gloom Robert could see Kenneth Chen smiling. "That is an excellent appointment. I hope to see him again. I much enjoyed working for him. Now Mr Draper I think we can do no more tonight but be warned my superiors are determined to have what is owed to them." He signalled to someone in the dark recess to Robert's left. "Wie Chen will take you back to Tanglin Road, Mr Draper. As I said you are safe if my master's do not believe you have given the gold to Lai Tek or Chin Peng. I know you will always be fair in your treatment, but you must understand that this is a fight to the death between us and the communists and your gold could be very important in the fight to survive."

Robert shook the hand that had been proffered by Kenneth Chen. "Kenneth, it is not my gold. In some ways I don't want to find it, but I think it can help me in my quest to find who betrayed us." Robert turned and followed the large Chinese man out feeling as though the long conversation with Kenneth Chen was already being dissected by hidden people in the room.

As he got to the end of the room Kenneth Chen shouted after him. "Be careful when you go on your trip to KL and Penang, Mr Draper, for Chin Peng will know you are coming. If you need to speak to me again then tell the waiter, Zhu Yin, at the *Mata Hari* and he will organise another meeting. Good luck."

Sitting in the car, again with his eyes covered up, Robert went over the long conversation with Kenneth Chen and wondering how he knew about the trip to KL and Penang. Kenneth Chen had been very much in charge of proceedings; he was now someone quite important in the Kuomintang Party but even then, it was obvious that he was following instructions even saying at the end that he could not protect Robert.

At home he scarcely spoke to Chunggy, his houseman, who was wanting to tell him about various things that had happened during the day. He only half listened and, in the end, Robert said that he would speak to him in the morning and after a long shower he went to bed, with the fan he had procured, through Chuck, whirling away near to his face.

Chapter 7

Sir Shenton Thomas, looking immaculate, had put on weight even in the short time since his return from being an internee in Japan. Robert shook the hand proffered to him and said good morning before nodding a good morning to the First Secretary who was stood at Sir Shenton's side. Robert turned and went over and stood beside Michael Sanders, a police inspector who had been a fellow internee in Sime Road camp. He nodded at a few other people in the room whom he recognised, some who had accounts at the bank and others who he knew to be stalwarts of the business community before the war.

Sitting on a large settee to one side of Sir Shenton was Lady Thomas still not looking too well from her long illness in the Sime Road internment camp. Sitting beside her was another woman who Robert did not recognise. Robert briefly nodded across at Lady Thomas and the other lady. Looking around the room Robert recognised several people including the General commanding civil order in Singapore and a Colonel who looked extremely hot and ill-tempered who was responsible for the internment of Japanese soldiers. A Major and two civilians were standing some way apart from the General and Colonel. Robert said a quiet "good morning" to Michael Sanders as a Brigadier arrived with Captain Cassidy.

Captain Cassidy smiled across at Robert, and after he had been introduced to Sir Shenton he had then taken up his place beside the other military personnel.

Drinks were brought in by waiters as Sir Shenton started speaking. "Gentlemen we have several things to discuss. I have asked my wife and Lady Copeland also to be present as it may have relevance for the women who will be travelling with you, and I prefer it if we don't have to repeat the conversation." Robert couldn't see any other women in the room.

"I have had a number of meetings with individuals who want to visit the Malay States and I have agreed that it is now safe to send a party of civilians up to inspect the state of play in the peninsula." Sir Shenton waved at the Major and two civilians standing alone, and said, "We have already set up a programme called Operation Zipper which has been undertaking a preliminary review of the situation in the Malay States. Major Comber is an expert in security in the Malay States and will be advising the First Secretary and Brigadier Starling on the situation as your party proceeds north to Penang. His two colleagues, Mr Crombie and Mr Lewis have been looking at problems in Johor and will also be accompanying you."

Pausing for a moment he then continued, "Our initial thinking was that it would be safer to fly up to KL and Penang and the Americans had agreed to assist in these arrangements, but the rail line is at last open sufficiently for us to send your party with an armed escort up north although conditions will be quite basic, I fear. The rail journey will enable you to see more of the country and evaluate problems as you proceed. Arrangements have been made for stops at Gemas, Segamat, Taiping and Butterworth as well as KL. Arrangements are also in hand for civilian parties to proceed to Malacca, Port Swettenham and Khota Lipis to assess immediate problems. There are to be meetings with local leaders and members of Malay royalty. The First Secretary will also be conducting discussions with a Thai delegation about the return of part of the north of the Malay States that the Japanese seceded to Thailand in 1942. I am afraid there is no prospect of any visits soon up the East Coast to the Kuantan or Khota Bahru areas as the communists are causing severe problems and it seems there are still significant Japanese troops in the area. The Army has arranged to send more troops to take control so I fear it will be well into 1946 before we can fully restore order. Indeed, from what Major Comber tells me there are still groups of guerrillas and bandits roaming significant parts of the south of the peninsula."

Sir Shenton turned to the First Secretary. "The First Secretary will oversee the arrangements as they unfold in the Malay States, and he will be taking several officials with him to set up a civil administration in each of the provinces. I cannot emphasise how difficult the situation over the causeway maybe. I have the assurance of all parties who will be going that they feel able to cope with the probable difficulties. Pockets of Japanese soldiers are still surrendering and as I said the communists and Kuomintang fighters are causing unrest in large parts of the countryside."

Sir Shenton went on like this for a few more minutes before handing over to the First Secretary who outlined what he planned. He said he could not see how the trip could last for less than three to four weeks at which Robert made a face. The Brigadier then came in at that point to explain the security arrangements he had put in place for the trip and Major Comber was invited to outline what Operation Zipper had so far achieved and the current "no go" areas.

More drinks were taken around the audience who were wilting under the amount of information and the increasing heat in the room. Sir Shenton again started talking. "As I believe you all know General Moresby has set up a POW camp for the Japanese on Rempang Island. For those of you who do not know where that is it's about 20 miles south of us. He will be sending Colonel Wallace, who is responsible for the transfer of Japanese military to the island, with you to assess the importance of any Japanese prisoners who remain on the mainland and to hasten the arrangements for their transportation to Rempang." Sir Shenton had waved an arm in the direction of the very hot looking Colonel as he spoke. He then pointed at Mike Sanders. "Chief Inspector Sanders will be going with you to take up the post of Acting Superintendent of Police for Kuala Lumper, with the military title of Colonel."

Robert had been sitting through all these announcements and taking in the information. He was beginning to think he was at the wrong meeting when suddenly he realised that Sir Shenton was talking about him.

"It is vital that we get the commercial activities of the Malay States and Singapore operating as soon as possible and I have agreed that a number of civilians should be included in the group to assess what remains of the economic infrastructure and the banking arrangements for the peninsula. Each of the civilians I have authorised for the trip are therefore people I see as essential in assessing and activating the commercial opportunities." Sir Shenton looking directly at Robert said, "Robert Draper was an indispensable member of the camp organisation at Sime Road. Better still he became highly proficient in Japanese. He has been doing a splendid job working at the Repatriation Office down at Municipal Hall, but I am afraid that will be closing shortly. It so happens that Robert is a banker by profession and although he is more junior than I would normally condone for such an important mission I have been persuaded that his observations on the banking regimes up north will assist his colleagues in the various banks, in the next few months, to move forward much more rapidly. Sir John Hatton, the Chairman of Union & China Bank, with the support of other banks' directors has pressed for him to be included."

Robert found himself nodding as Sir Shenton continued, "His knowledge of Japanese could be very useful as I understand we have two or three thousand Japanese civilians housed on the racecourse in KL."

Sir Shenton paused for a moment and before he could continue Lady Thomas spoke up, "And what of Marjorie, Shenton."

Sir Shenton smiled across at both ladies, "I have agreed with the First Secretary and Brigadier Starling that Lady Copeland can go with the assessment group. There are also two other ladies to go with the group, a Miss Latimer who was Head Teacher of a school in Fraser Hills and Mrs Coady who was Head Teacher of a school in Penang. They were unable to attend today but will be briefed later today by the First Secretary. Both had to abandon their schools in December 1941, and they will be assisting local officials and the Army in assessing the situation. Miss Latimer and Mrs Coady will join you tomorrow evening." Robert didn't recognise the names of the two women although he later learned that both had been interned in KL. Finally bringing the meeting to a close, Sir Shenton addressed Lady Copeland. "You know it will be no easy trip, Marjorie, possibly even dangerous. I have talked to Major Comber about your specific mission, and he tells me that the circumstances are very difficult. Brigadier Starling who will be responsible for your security will always have the final say." Robert saw Lady Copeland move her head in the smallest of acknowledgements.

A Meeting Under A Banyan Tree

It was obvious from the look on several of the faces in the room that they had not a clue what the mission could be.

It was the First Secretary who ended the meeting by saying, "Ladies and gentlemen, we leave tomorrow evening. If you could be at the railway station for no later than 9 o'clock I should be most grateful."

As Robert moved to leave the meeting, he was waved over by Sir Shenton. "My dear chap, I was not sure at all about your inclusion, but Sir John sent a telegram which said it was imperative for the main banks to have an expert eye to assess the problems and not a military one. Barclays and Hong Kong and the Union are sending out new Directors, but they will not be in place until after Christmas and they need information. Could I thank you again for all your hard work over the past two months in getting the Repatriation Office organised. I am sorry that I didn't get a chance to see Mrs Dyson before she left, but I will write to her once she and her husband are back in England. I can only repeat that I am sorry that I have been overruled and the Repatriation Office is to close down, and all records transferred to Kandy." Robert just shook his head to show his disquiet at the decision and then confirmed that Mary had flown out on an American Air Force plane and was now in Manila maybe even on her way from there to Hawaii. He then left briefly saying to the First Secretary that he would be at the station the following evening, as Sir Shenton went over to talk to the ladies.

Robert caught up with Eric Cassidy who was standing a discreet distance from the Brigadier and the General who were talking animatedly with the Major; the Colonel was standing beside them just listening. The General's assistant who hadn't been at the meeting joined Robert and Eric Cassidy.

"What's all the fuss, Bodger? Robert whispered to Eric looking at the senior officers some twenty feet away.

Eric Cassidy, looking at the senior officers, whispered. "Clare here has just told them that the remains of the Nips 25th Army is marching down the west coast, full regalia the lot and we are likely to meet them. Apparently, they have marched down from Taiping giving the Allies no warning that they were setting off. General Itagaki signed off the surrender in mid-September with Lord Mountbatten but a large part of the 25th Army has remained in their barracks in Taiping. Anyway, they set off a few days ago leaving the few Allied troops stationed up there not able to stop them." Captain "Clare" Claremont having shaken Robert's hand, nodded at Robert to confirm what Bodger had just said.

Robert just shrugged his shoulders. It was obvious that there were going to be hiccups. "Can one of you give me a lift to the Municipal Building?"

Bodger grinned at the request. "You seem to have friends in high places. How can we refuse?"

Clare asked, all the time watching the senior officers for a sign that they had finished their discussion, "Why do they call you Bodger?"

It was Robert's turn to smile. "We worked in the Union & China Bank in London before the war, and shall we say that Eric was less than useful with a pencil and in adding up numbers."

Clare grinned at the comment, and it was Bodger's turn to make a face. Fortunately for him the senior officers finished their conversation, and this saved him from any further embarrassment. They waved over their juniors with Robert in tow.

Chapter 8

Robert spent the day before his trip to the Malay States organising everything for his likely four-week absence. Arriving early at the bank he spent the morning with the senior Chinese clerks going through the work being undertaken in the bank in preparation for it reopening after Xmas. The Island's Treasury had finally released some funds for use by the Bank and Robert was anxious that authority to use the currency was limited.

"Follow the procedures we have agreed, Mr Lee, no exceptions. Any business applications – there should be very few – then tell them there will be a delay in any decision until nearer Christmas. That will give us time to contact Mr Connaught. I got a telegram yesterday to say a Mr Nigel Renshaw is on his way from Durban. Mr Connaught has appointed him as an Assistant Manager. I don't know when he will arrive, but it should be soon. Either way you can tell him that he's in charge, but the rules are not to change unless there is authority from Mr Connaught." Robert stopped what he was saying. *"Shades of Walter Trehearne. I'm getting like him. I must be getting old."* Robert smiled to himself. How the circle had been completed.

Mr Lee and the two other senior clerks in the meeting sat quietly. They like Robert were still adjusting to the new regime. Mr Lee finally spoke. "What if there is a real emergency, Mr Draper?"

Robert smiled back at Mr Lee. "You know how Mr Connaught would deal with situations. Always presume you are in his place. If you do not have an answer to the problem, then delay making one until I get back or until Mr Renshaw can deal with it. These times are very difficult but in a few months we will all sit having a beer and laugh at how we had to solve the problems."

"What about Mr Hussain."

At that Robert laughed out loud. "I have written him a letter. It is on my desk. Please arrange for it to go to Bukit Timah today. I know he will understand."

Mr Lee shook his head. "He has said he will go to another bank if we do not help."

Robert kept his temper. "Mr Lee, I promise you Mr Hussain will not take his account anywhere else. First no other bank is open for business, certainly not until after Christmas. Secondly, and most importantly, if he did move his account, he would risk losing interest on the balance he had in it before the occupation." Robert stopped for a few seconds before adding, "He is a friend of mine and in my letter, I have promised him my full attention when I get back. His idea is to develop his timber business before others have a chance, but he must work on his supply chain. I have suggested he work on this part first and then we can sit down before Christmas and work out a business deal. With all the building work needed on the Island he will end up a rich man "Robert added as an afterthought , " He will be able to afford the many weddings he will have to pay for with three sons and a daughter yet to be married." The clerks started laughing at the comment.

In the afternoon Robert went to the Repatriation Office for the last time. Since Mary had left for Hawaii the Repatriation Office had started to run down its activities and Joan and two other volunteers had started packing the records which now came to many thousands of index cards. Robert had arranged with Paul that the Office should have a skeleton service for another ten days or so just in case there were new internees arriving and Joan had agreed to manage the transfer of the records to Kandy. One of the volunteers had agreed to escort the records to Kandy; he would break off his journey back home to Ireland.

The atmosphere in the Reparation Office was muted, even sad. Everyone knew that the link to the 15 February 1942 was finally broken and they, who had shared the struggles of the past three and a half years, would not see each other again. The time spent under Japanese control, some of it too horrible to speak of, was being closed and the records of the time in the camps were being parcelled up and sent to another land. Friends, colleagues, camp mates, and enemies were no longer real, they had become just a paper record. A few volunteers such as Joan would be staying on in Singapore because they had nowhere else to go; others were going to a land, Britain, that would be unwelcoming and strange for them. From the conversations it was obvious that some of the volunteers had stayed thus far because of the fear of the unknown.

Robert never one for speeches went around thanking everyone and insisting that they exchange anticipated addresses. Speaking to Joan he made sure that she would be okay.

"I'll be fine, Bob. I've got myself a small flat in Cathay House and I've got a job over at Robinsons starting after Christmas. If I can't stick it my sister in Christchurch has said I can go and live with them. I don't fancy that idea – I would be a fish out of water. Anyway, I've too many memories here. I've been here most of my adult life."

Robert nodded at what she was saying. "So say all of us. I'm staying too, Joan. If you need any help then you know where I am on Tanglin Road. You only need to ask. My friends, David and Susie Masters will be back on the Island shortly and they have a flat in Cathay House so you must introduce yourself."

"Thanks, Bob. I will." With that the two ex-Sime Road internees ended the conversation with their futures dangling in mid-air.

Late in the afternoon Robert went back up to Tanglin Road stopping off at Henry and Mona's house. They had arrived back only a few days ago and Henry was already back working at the station. Mona was in the midst of instructing a new Indian maid by the looks of it, at least by the fluster the poor maid was getting herself into.

"I'm off up country tonight, Mona. Can you keep an eye on things at my house? I should be most grateful. Chunggy is getting quite forgetful."

The maid brought through a tea tray as Robert sat with Mona and talked; they were sitting on the small veranda where on 8th December 1941 Henry and Robert had first learned of the Japanese invasion. Mona was nodding as she checked what was on the tray and then quietly showing the girl how it should be arranged. Turning to Robert she said "You need more help, Bob. Poor Chunggy must be close to 80 years old."

"Try telling that to Chunggy. He dismissed the gardener that I hired. Said he was lazy and did not do the job correctly. The trouble is there are snakes in the long grass, and I need to get rid of them."

"Leave it with me. When you return there shall be no snakes. I will work on him. He needs to be shouted at just as Mrs Lin Yuen used to. You are too soft."

Robert grinned back at her, enjoying listening to her voice. Mona always broke into her best sing song voice when she got demonstrative. Mona had spent, from what Robert had learnt so far, most of the war in Shimla in India, with distant relatives, having survived getting away from the fighting on Singapore, with the last convoy on Friday 13th February 1942.

Mona started a new conversation. "The boys are coming home. Brian should be here in about ten days and Martin just before Christmas. Our last letter from him said he was in Assam with his beloved mules. He says that if the Army was to continue to have mule trains he would re-enlist. Even says he wants to bring his favourite mule home with him. Imagine how embarrassing it could be for his father if his youngest son walks around here with a mule."

Robert was laughing as Mona said it. "I don't think Henry would mind as long as his sons are safe and well."

Mona stood up and adjusted her sari. "Dearest Bob, Henry has a position to think of. His sons must be sensible. Henry is the Acting Station Master."

Robert finished his tea. "Mona, I have to go and pack. If I don't get back before Brian arrives, please tell him I look forward to seeing him. It sounds like Martin may not be back before Christmas especially if he decides to ride a mule through Burma and the Malay States. While I remember, I have an American friend, based at Kellang. He has got me some rather good tins of spam and some rice. I asked him to send them up here to you, so it sounds like a perfect welcome home meal for Brian. He should be well used to spam and rice." Robert was still laughing, at the thought of Brian's face when he was given spam and rice after nearly four years away from his mum's cooking, as he limped down the drive onto Tanglin Road, turning right for the two hundred yards or so to Mrs Lin Yuen's old home.

Chapter 9

Airmail

Salisbury Crags

Tanglin Road

Singapore

27 October 1945

Dear Peter,

I am finally on my way up country as part of an official party to assess commercial and civil matters in KL, Penang and various other places. Sir John sent a telegram, presumably at your request, saying it was essential that the banks had a representative in the group to look into the commercial difficulties in restarting trading and this seems to have done the trick. The First Secretary is leading us. Mark Travers and John Craig are in the group and have asked me to send their warmest regards to you and they look forward to you being on the Island again. Mark is looking at the Grosvenor rubber estates in Johor and up towards Malacca so there may be some need for him to develop the good relations he had with the bank before the war. John, I understand has been asked to look at the road network and what improvements will be needed.

A Meeting Under A Banyan Tree

We have a large contingent of troops on the train protecting us as there are still significant numbers of Japanese troops roaming around with some of them being quite difficult. We were told a few days ago that a General Inoue has marched south from Taiping with a large part of the Japanese 7th Army (at least that's the latest information although I have also been told that it's part of the 25th Japanese Army.) All very confusing and potentially dangerous if they decide to be difficult. Apparently, we were in the process of trying to find rolling stock to send them down by rail but Inoue hasn't waited. (The other bit of confusion is that this General doesn't seem to have been on our radar and has appeared from nowhere.) Why he decided to march down the west coast is not yet clear, but the theory is he wanted to surrender on his terms. One thing for sure, there are a lot more Japanese around than the authorities anticipated. There have been hoards marching down to Clarke's Quay for transportation to Rempang Island where we have set up a POW camp.

I started the letter an hour ago and then I had to stop and lie on the floor because we have been shot at from the jungle. The train stopped for about thirty minutes and our escort deployed but Eric Cassidy just told me that they found no one just some empty cartridge shells. What life will be like for the next few weeks I suspect! Eric's in charge of one of the companies of soldiers who are with us. (They seem a tough lot!) He says he is not coming back to the bank so I think we can tell Sir John that the profits are protected from his inadequacies although to be fair he seems to be very efficient as a paratrooper.

I got your telegram about Renshaw and that is great news. Chin Lee is more than capable of managing the situation until Renshaw arrives as we are not open for business. I have left him with written instructions which leave him in no doubt what he should do in certain circumstances and I have told him to telegram you if there is a real emergency as I think I will be largely out of touch for the next four weeks. I hope Renshaw is prepared for a challenge!

I learned yesterday afternoon that two of our colleagues in Bangkok did not survive the internment in some camp based near Bangkok. You and Sir John may already know through the FCO. It seems Mr Sedgeley-Jones died in early 1943 and Stephen Marlow died of malaria in January 1945. The camp allowed families to be together which seems far more civilised than the regime endured at Sime Road but in this case Stephen and his wife and their child all died about the same time. Very sad news. I suspect you know both Mr Sedgeley-Jones and Stephen Marlow but other than knowing them by name I never had a chance to meet them. I will drop a letter to Sir John to confirm these details. My understanding is that Colin Reeve did survive, and he and his family are travelling back to the UK so hopefully you should be able to see them soon.

I met an Australian Repatriation Officer a few days ago who tells me that he has been to Batavia which is literally burning with renewed fighting between the Dutch and the freedom fighters. I enquired if there was any Dutch organisation responsible for tracing missing persons and he advised me that at this time the situation is too chaotic for any such work. What he did say is that there were three camps where domiciled Europeans might have been sent to from Batavia or if they were rescued from sunken ships, and that all these persons have now been transferred to Darwin or Singapore. I am fairly sure I would have picked up any information about our colleagues at the bank in Batavia if they had come through the Island on the way home so Darwin is the remaining option. I find it difficult to believe however that more than eight weeks after the camps were liberated, we have not heard if any of them had survived, or for that matter any news about Walter or Marjorie Trehearne. The same must be said about Gordon. None of the group he went with have been found in any of the camps in Borneo, Sumatra or Java. I think that we must accept the fact that Gordon and his colleagues were probably killed by the Japanese somewhere between the Island and Java. Gordon when I last saw him said that he thought they had left it too late to escape and that Sir Shenton should have released Christian from his duties at the High Commission much earlier. I think you told me once that Gordon only wanted a quiet life after what he saw at the Battle of Jutland. It now sounds like the poor devil may have ended up dying at sea.

The Island Treasury have now released funds to the banks although Hong Kong Bank and Barclays have no managers in place as of today and no managers expected before Christmas. The Mercantile have a retired Director arriving from Colombo soon to get things started. Good news - I found someone with some glass to repair the windows. A carpenter is repairing the furniture in Walters's old office – it looks as though someone used a chisel on the surface of the boardroom table. I have the clerks washing the place out and an American friend has found us some paint which Chin Lee and our clerks are putting on the walls to make the place at least clean. More good news. The electrician I hired has said that the safes in the vaults should operate if they are serviced; the wiring seems fine. We therefore need an engineer from Johnson and Smith – Would you know who to contact as they are based in London? We will need them to look at the safety deposit boxes as the Japanese have broken into around sixty of them and the keys to the other boxes are missing. It may be that the whole situation needs replacing as there is quite a bit of damage.

Anyway, I must finish now as I need some shuteye as I suspect tomorrow will be long and tiring. Eric tells me that the situation further up the track is fluid to say the least and will be for some weeks to come. Regards to Ethel and I look forward to your next letter.

A Meeting Under A Banyan Tree

Airmail

Salisbury Crags

Tanglin Road

Singapore

28 October 1945

Dear Sir John,

A short letter to say that I am on the way to KL and Penang to assess the damage to the banks. Sir Shenton tells me that your telegram was very persuasive! The situation is chaotic with Japanese still surrendering daily, there is a good deal of looting, and the communists temporarily control parts of the countryside particularly up the Northeast coast and in Johor. Mr Fraser, the First Secretary, is leading a team of around 30 hardy souls to assess the problems in getting the States up and running again. As I said your telegram seems to have worked and I am included in the party although I think from what Sir Shenton said it is not just because I am needed to assess how the banks could start up again but also because I speak Japanese which could be very useful as there are more than 3000 Japanese civilians at large and still being rounded up.

We arrived in Segamat this morning and the plan is for delegations to go off in a minute to meet various people to discuss what is needed to get the community fully functional. By the looks of it food is in severe shortage and there seems quite a few people who need medical attention. A local Indian chap I spoke to a few moments ago said that malaria has been very evident during the past year. Talking to one Malay it seems everything is in short supply although they don't seem to have had problems with the communists. Our soldiers did have a short confrontation with a small group of Japanese troops a few days ago and it turns out they were members of the dreaded Kempetai who refused to accept orders from their superiors and wanted to continue fighting. Fortunately, they had very little ammunition and were forced to surrender. I was talking to the civil administrator, over breakfast, who will be responsible for this area, and he is of the opinion that it will take years to get the place back to pre-1942 levels.

I had my last afternoon working at the Repatriation Office two days ago. I am sorry but I learned that Mr Sedgeley-Jones and Stephen Marlow died in the internment camp in Bangkok. From what I was able to find out Mr Sedgeley-Jones died in 1943 but his wife survived. The information I have is that she has been flown to Manila with some other sick internees about four weeks ago, but I have no further information on her whereabouts. Stephen and his family all died earlier this year. I cannot be certain but I think from malaria. Colin Reeve did survive and is on his way home with his family and if my information is good then they should be in England by mid-December.

I've just been handed a mug of tea by a Sergeant who is telling me that I have been delegated to accompany a Lady Copeland on some rescue mission, so I had better finish. Will be in touch with more information.

****

Robert sat in the back of the army jeep with Lady Copeland on his right. The Army had wanted her to be driven in a car they had procured but she had stubbornly refused saying she wanted to see everything. She had only briefly spoken to Robert to say "good morning" and then sat quietly in the jeep as it worked its way across Segamat.

After a few minutes she turned to Robert who had been watching a team of labourers pull down what had been a war damaged building. "Mr Draper, I asked if you would accompany me this morning as the army is not always the best when it comes to dealing with civilians and Lucy says you seem to be able to get on with the locals."

Robert turned, as the jeep swerved around an enormous pothole in the middle of the road, holding onto the bar in front of him. "I've no idea why you are here, Lady Copeland. However, if I can be of help over the next few days then I am happy to assist. I am rather in limbo until we get to KL. The last time I was here the Nips were flying up and down this road strafing anything that moved. It looks as though they haven't done much since to sort out the mess."

The jeep came to a halt just as Lady Copeland explained her purpose. "My granddaughter was at this school in January 1942. For some reason she was not evacuated. My daughter tried to get up here but was killed when the Japanese attacked her train. My son-in-law was in the Scots Guards and was captured at Dunkirk; he died in Stalag 3 in 1944. So you see she is all I have left. It is imperative that I find her."

The sergeant who had driven the jeep stood patiently beside her as she spoke and then helped her down when she put her arm out for assistance. Robert merely nodded at the news and then clambered out his side noticing the lorry behind with a dozen or so soldiers who were now being deployed around the school building – at least it had been a school by the look of the noticeboard that was lying against the wall. "St. Clare's Preparatory Boarding School for Christian Children." It had further printing on the noticeboard but it was indecipherable. As they walked towards the school entrance Robert could see that the building was in a very poor state of repair.

Inside the school Lady Copeland and Robert stood momentarily in the hall whilst three or four soldiers went through the rooms. Finally, the Sergeant nodded to Robert indicating that the rooms were clear. Walking into the first room on the left it was obvious that it had been an office, probably the headmistress's room. Some books remained on the shelves and a few files lay on the floor. A desk had been turned on its side for some reason. Someone had thrown ink on the walls, dust was everywhere, and there was buzzing over in one corner. One of the soldiers had gone over and merely said, "Something dead over here, ma'am, best to keep away. Robert bent down and tried picking up the files that were disintegrating as he touched them. "It seems to have been a school register, but it will be no help."

Lady Copeland just murmured something and then left the room with Robert limping after her. Each room downstairs told its own story although it was obvious that one of the rooms at the back had been occupied recently, probably squatters. Robert turned to the Sergeant at that point. "There're some houses down the lane. Could you get a few of your men to seal off the houses and keep the occupants there until I come down? If we leave it too long, they will disappear thinking there may be trouble." The sergeant nodded and went off to organise the task whilst Lady Copeland and Robert climbed the stairs to what must have been the dormitories.

They found nothing there of any consequence other than a few pictures on the walls to show it was a Christian school and in one room a very moth-eaten teddy bear lay on the floor. Lady Copeland was extremely quiet throughout the viewing of the rooms and eventually Robert said, "I think we can gain nothing from searching the school. We need to find some of the staff, some of whom would have been local. The people down the lane may be able to help." As he finished speaking, he could hear in the distance a train hoot. He smiled to himself. "I know where we are. We came past here on our retreat from KL."

Outside they stood in the sun for a few minutes feeling the heat and humidity building up. From close by they could hear monkeys screeching in the trees. The sergeant arrived back in the jeep to say that the traditional Malay houses had been sealed off and Robert, first looking at Lady Copeland, said they were finished at the school. He helped Lady Copeland into the jeep and went around the back of it before clambering in for the short journey. Lady Copeland seemed remarkably stoic just sitting there saying nothing.

At the houses Robert got out of the jeep noticing the guards had assembled the occupants on a small grass verge. He left Lady Copeland to be helped out of the jeep by the sergeant.

Robert addressed the group who seemed to be all Malay, in their tongue, greeting them and saying that Lady Copeland had come to look for her granddaughter who had gone missing in January 1942. He asked if any of them had worked at the school and could help. At first there was no answer and then one woman, perhaps in her forties, said she had worked at the school. Robert again asked if she could help this time saying that the child's parents had died in the war and all the child had left was her grandmother. He pointed as he was speaking at Lady Copeland who was now sitting on a stool that one of the soldiers had produced from somewhere. The ice had thawed and one of the other women went into the house and returned with a straw umbrella to shade Lady Copeland as the first Malay woman said in broken English that the Japanese had left everybody alone until the end of February 1942. They had then collected the teachers and the older girls and taken them away in a lorry, but she didn't know too where. One older teacher was allowed to stay with the 6 youngest children. They had been told to leave maybe a month later. She said that she did not think the Japanese had told them where to go.

Robert thanked the woman and turned to Lady Copeland and after explaining what the Malay woman had said, asked her, "I presume we are talking about one of the younger children?" Lady Copeland nodded and then said, "Emily would have been 9 years. Her friend Sara was the same age. Her parents are stuck in England trying to get passage to Singapore."

"What about the other four girls. I've heard nothing about this when I worked in the Repatriation Office other than about 2 missing girls up in Penang who died later in the Taiping camp."

Lady Copeland was clearly becoming quite upset. "I don't know, Mr Draper. I just don't know. Could the Japanese have taken them overseas and they could be traced through that route?"

Robert turned back to the Malay woman and again spoke to her in Malay. "The older teacher. Who was she?"

At that the Malay woman smiled and in broken English she said, "She was very kind lady. Very old. She came from Bukit Lingtang and lived many years at the school. She had been a holy woman at a church in Malacca."

Robert had no idea where Bukit Lingtang was, but a glimmer of an idea came to him. "Lady Copeland, what this lady is saying is that the teacher who looked after the children dressed as a holy woman. I think she means a nun. She had worked at the school and then retired. She knows she comes from a place called Bukit Lingtang but does not know where that is. She says she knows she worshipped at the main church in Malacca. So there is a possibility that she took the children off to Bukit Lingtang if she still has family there although I've no idea where that is. Alternatively, she could have taken them to Malacca for protection from the church; by and large the Japanese did respect the religious establishments. Unless you can think of anything else I think we need to go back to Army HQ and get a decent map; and ideally a Malay policeman with some knowledge of the country."

Lady Copeland looking very tired and hot, nodded and stood up. "Thank you, Mr Draper. Can we please go?"

Chapter 10

As they returned to the railway station Robert answered questions from Lady Copeland about what Robert believed had happened when the Japanese attacked Segamat in early January 1941.

"The situation was impossible, Lady Copeland. I spent 10 days escaping from KL and travelling south towards Segamat and down to the Island. We had to travel mostly at night, often under attack; sometimes we only managed a few miles because of the attacks. I can tell you it was chaos. We never knew whether the Japanese were in front of us or what. We were attacked by planes during the day so we spent most of our time hiding. We were shot at from the jungle but rarely saw who was shooting at us and we had running gun fights at least half a dozen times, half the time not knowing whether we were shooting at friend or foe. Our lorries broke down and we spent much of the day coaxing them to start again. We had little medical facilities for the wounded and no time to bury the dead. If the girls had tried to escape by train, then chances are they would have been badly shot up. Quite a few of the hospital trains never got as far as Segamat, never mind Singapore. Why the girls weren't moved earlier I really don't know." Robert looked at Lady Copeland directly, "You're Roman Catholic I presume from the looks of the school?"

Lady Copeland shouted her agreement over the noise of the engine as the Sergeant brought the jeep to halt beside the station entrance.

Robert said, "I can only think that the Bishop in Malacca advised the head teacher that it was safer for the girls to stay in the school. Things were pretty unsafe everywhere and the school was a bit out of the way. The situation then overtook the arrangements in the school."

As they got out of the jeep and walked towards the train carriages Robert added, "What the hell happened to the teachers and older girls? What camp did they go to? And why the hell separate them."

It was a very weary sounding Lady Copeland who turned as they climbed into the carriage and said, "You are very naive, Mr Draper," momentarily stopping Robert from climbing into the carriage.

When Robert did get into the carriage it was empty other than for two attendants preparing tables for dinner, Lady Copeland having disappeared through to the next carriage where a temporary screen had been put up to give the three women on the trip some privacy. Robert stood for a moment thinking about what Lady Copeland had said and then turning back he returned to the platform. He could see at the end of the platform the Sergeant who had looked after them talking to Eric Cassidy, so he headed for them.

Eric and the sergeant had finished talking by the time Robert had limped the length of the platform. Robert thanked the sergeant for all his help that morning and taking the hint the sergeant excused himself.

"Eric, have you seen Mike Sanders? We need his new powers to help solve a problem."

Eric laughed at what Robert said. "Sergeant Mackie has just been telling me what happened this morning. I suppose you want us to start searching the jungle for half a dozen kids and a nun."

"They're more important than some old fart's idea of getting us back to being great again."

"Well, we have had a bad morning."

"The Nips took the teachers and teenage girls away to God knows where. Nobody seems to have reported them missing. They have not been repatriated through Singapore to my knowledge. Six young girls have disappeared. It's a scandal."

"My dear chap in the greater scheme of things it's small beer. We have a General coming into Segamat probably tomorrow with thousands of very unhappy Japs. So far they have travelled most of the peninsula without being stopped. The Brigadier has mustered one battalion from the Indian 5th Army who are not happy because they were on the way to being demobbed. I have one company of

Para's and two Lieutenants, one of whom is going down with malaria, and a limited amount of ammunition because we expected further supplies to be available in Gemas. Raise the problem by all means with the Brigadier and First Secretary but don't expect too much help until we sort out Ionue. Even his boss, General Terauchi, having surrendered all Japanese forces in this part of Asia has so far not persuaded Ionue to comply with the Emperor's wishes." Eric let Robert mull over the information for a moment and then said, "Come on Bob let's have a beer and go through the information. Mike will be back shortly, and he's probably got a Malay policeman able to at least identify the kampong.

Robert just shook his head in despair at what Eric had said. "Lead me to the bar, Eric, I certainly need one."

Chapter 11

"Inoue should be here late tomorrow evening, or more likely mid-morning the day after," a very hot looking Major was telling the Brigadier and the First Secretary with a group of half a dozen or so interested persons in attendance. They were meeting in one of the train carriages with no fans on and the humidity soaring. Outside Robert could hear the noise of army personnel going about their business.

"He doesn't seem to be difficult; it almost seems like he is on a state visit. The troops have behaved themselves, even paid for some goats they killed. It's difficult to say how many there are but we estimate around 6,000 including a contingent of *Kempetai* who even the old General doesn't seem to like much. Colonel Wallace has stayed with General Inoue and is at pains to keep matters calm, but I think when they arrive the *Kempetai* are the ones to watch. The Colonel asked me to say that if possible, we should corral them off from the main force. Colonel Barrett has a contingent of troops following them down the road from Gemas, but they only muster a Company in strength."

Brigadier was nodding. "What have they brought with them?"

The Major knew what the Brigadier meant by the question. "Most of the troops have no weapons, at least no heavy stuff, from what we can see. They had a few small tanks, but they ran out of petrol and they have been abandoned. There are a few bren type carriers, but they seem to be carrying mostly troops that are unwell."

The Brigadier spoke to the First Secretary and although Robert could not hear all of what was said he saw the First Secretary nod. "Right, what we will do is accept the formal surrender of the Japanese 7th Army at a ceremony at midday, day after tomorrow. The First Secretary will accept the surrender. Frank, you need to get back to Colonel Wallace first thing tomorrow and tell him of our decision and make sure that Inoue understands that the surrender will be outside Segamat and not in the town. Make sure that Inoue understands that all his men must be unarmed, all weapons to be handed over to Colonel Wallace or Colonel Barrett before the surrender ceremony. We shall have to trust Inoue as we do not have the capacity to search 6,000 Japs; that will have to be done once we can ship them off to Rempang. Make sure Inoue clearly understands the surrender arrangements and that we will not tolerate any variation. For God's sake don't let them get a whiff of the fact that we have only one battalion of demob happy troops to corral them. Use the radio to advise us if there are any last-minute problems we need to be prepared for; Colonel Wallace is to instruct Inoue that the *Kempetai* are to be split up from the main force, say a mile or so behind. Colonel Barrett will have to manage them." Seeing the Major nod his understanding the Brigadier turned to those listening, "Eric, where are you? "

Eric emerged from the back of the small group who had been listening to the instructions from the Brigadier. "Sir."

"Eric, radio Colonel Keighley. He should be on the way with his battalion and tell him that he has a bit more time to get here but I would want him here by early tomorrow afternoon so that we have time to flesh out the plan. You need to take your Company up to support Colonel Barrett as its likely that he may need help in containing the *Kempetai.*" Eric nodded that he understood the instruction.

The Brigadier then spoke to the Colonel sitting in front of Robert. "David, this is your patch. Show me in the morning the best place to have this damn ceremony. It needs to be somewhere where we can load the Japs onto the trains that are on the way from Singapore. We will need food and water for the Japs we send down. Can that be done? Oh, and we may need some of your men to act as security for the trip down to the Island."

The Colonel replied obviously expecting to be told of the problems. "We are on it. I have C Company ready to go down with trains if insufficient troops are sent up with the rolling stock. I have been in contact with KL and they are able to assist with water barrels and rice for the trip and also for the temporary camp we will need to set up. I will show you the ideal spot tomorrow; it's beside the track, about a mile north of here." The Brigadier acknowledged what the Colonel had just said as the First Secretary took up the discussion.

"We have the problem of some of our party keen to be off to Malacca and now Mr Draper and Lady Copeland are keen to go somewhere called Bukit Langtang," the First Secretary said out loud anxious to be seen to be involved.

Robert spoke out, "Its Bukit Lingtang, sir, and we have found out that its south of Malacca by all accounts".

The First Secretary looked harassed at being corrected but before he could go further in the conversation the Brigadier spoke again.

"My problem is that I don't have spare troops to send off to other places you may have in mind. At least not for a few days. The 7th Army will need corralling whilst Colonel Wallace gets them entrained to Singapore. If the information is correct there are two trains on their way up with cattle trucks and we have a battalion of troops on their way from Kl. With 6,000 Japs to control and entrain we must expect to be here for a quite a few days," the Brigadier said. As an afterthought the Brigadier added," All predicated on the presumption that the Nips are cooperative."

Mike Sanders sitting next to Robert then spoke up. "I have seventeen police officers now available. We could be of more use. Bob Draper and Lady Copeland want to go to Bukit Lingtang and my map shows a road from here to the coast that goes near to the kampong and then onto Malacca. I can delegate some officers with an experienced sergeant to take Lady Copeland down that way. Mr Draper has kindly agreed to accompany her. The other civilians that want to go to Malacca can stay here for the next few days and go with us to Kl once you have dealt with the 7th Army; they can then travel to Malacca from there. Mr Travers has said he would be happy to miss the show with Inoue and he has an estate over towards the coast that he needs to assess; he's willing to go with Bob and Lady Copeland. All being well we can meet up with Bob and his group in about a week in KL."

The Brigadier had sat patiently whilst Mike Sanders explained what had been discussed prior to the meeting, and the proposed solution; the First Secretary saying nothing just preferring to watch the scene unfold. The Brigadier turned to Eric. "Do we have a spare lorry, Captain. "

"Superintendent Sanders did speak to me this afternoon about the idea, and I can make a lorry available with a driver if you authorise the trip. Sergeant Mackie has checked supplies, and we have sufficient petrol and stores available," Eric replied.

The Brigadier looked at the First Secretary who nodded his agreement. The Brigadier turned to Robert. "It looks as though you have the green light, Mr Draper. You must understand that you are going into country that is still very much unknown territory. Our troops have been through it but not as far I know with any thoroughness. It could still be live with Japanese troops trying to avoid the surrender arrangements – hell we had an incident in Johor only the other day with 200 to 300 Japanese troops causing chaos." The Brigadier turned to Mike Sanders. "I'm not aware of communist activity from here to the coast. Do you know of any?"

"I have no information of any activity. Sergeant Megat tells me that there was a Kuomintang force in this area during the war so it's more likely there are some of them still around but as you know they can be a bit unreliable at times."

The Brigadier sighed at what Mike Sanders had just said. "Mr Draper it sounds like you have a bit of an unknown trip ahead of you."

Robert smiled wryly back at the Brigadier. "It sounds almost as scary as what you might be facing in the next thirty-six hours. Having experienced three and half years of the unpredictability of the Japanese mind, I think I prefer a trip to the coast."

"Right young man. You take Lady Copeland and whoever off to Malacca. By the sounds of it you have landed the job of being in charge. Good luck and if all goes well we will meet in Kl in about a week."

The Brigadier turned to Eric. "Before you set off to support Colonel Barratt contact the Royal Navy at Malacca. It's a Captain Reynolds from memory who is in command. The Navy have responsibility for the port and the immediate area. Tell them of this group making its way across to his neck of the woods. I can't think what troops we have there at this time, but he will know. Right, is there anything else we need to do now?" Not waiting for an answer, he carried on, "If not, I need a long drink, ideally a strong one. Turning to the Colonel sitting in front of Robert, Brigadier Starling said, "I need to talk to you David."

Robert and Eric exchanged a quick word about seeing each other later and then Robert went off to find Lady Copeland, and to talk more about the trip with Mark Travers.

****

The Chinese guerrilla fighter, in jungle camouflage, emerged from the undergrowth less than fifty yards from where they were sitting. He had a Lee Enfield rifle held across his chest and he seemed not to be worried by the fact that half a dozen Malay police had grabbed their rifles and were pointing them in his direction. It was Sergeant Megat who shouted to two of the men to check the back of the lorry and seconds later they yelled that there were guerrillas sitting on the grass about fifty yards away, smoking.

A very hot and tired Lady Copeland, sitting on the small travel stool she had brought with her, continued drinking the mug of tea one of the police officers had brewed using the hot lorry engine as a cooker. She looked unperturbed by the commotion despite Mark Travers who had been sitting on the ground besides her jumping up on seeing the guerrilla emerge from the jungle and reaching for the revolver at his hip. Robert who had been leaning against a wheel and looking at a map he had laid out on the ground scrambled up but did not reach for his weapon. Robert after a few seconds took the initiative and walked forward and standing facing the guerrilla he decided immediately that it was best to play the situation coolly. He said to the man now standing only a few yards from them. "Welcome. Come and have some tea. I hope you are able to help us."

The Chinese guerrilla fighter came forward the last few yards and introduced himself as Zhu Pan Lee. Mark who by now was standing beside Robert whispered, "Kuomintang I would guess."

Robert turned to the police officer who had been making the brew and asked if there was a spare mug of tea and was handed one. Putting a large spoonful of sugar in the mug and stirring it Robert handed the mug to Zhu Pan Lee who had put his rifle down against a wheel. As he drank his tea Robert questioned him, all the time watching the Malay policemen who had not lowered their weapons and who were watching the undergrowth.

"Are you in contact with your headquarters?" Zhu Pan Lee shook his head and said that there was only six of them left and they were making their way to Gemas where they hoped to be given orders.

"I have a good friend, Kenneth Chen, who is one of your senior officers. He told me that they still had men in the jungle."

At Kenneth Chen's name Zhu Pan Lee looked at Robert with interest. "He is very important officer. "

Lady Copeland who seemed totally unconcerned about the new situation interrupted the conversation. "Please ask him about my grand-daughter, Mr Draper."

Robert nodded at Lady Copeland and turning to Zhu Pan Lee he told him the story of the missing children. Robert embellished the story by adding that Kenneth Chen knew of Robert's mission to find the girls.

Zhu Pan Lee finished his tea and without further discussion with Robert shouted at his comrades fifty yards away before handing his mug to Robert. He walked some distance towards his comrades shouting some more and finally getting a reply. He turned around and walked back to Robert. "There are white women at a kampong perhaps five miles from Bukit Lingtang."

As he came back to collect his rifle Robert asked him how far it was to Bukit Lingtang. Zhu Pan Lee shrugged. "Perhaps two days across the hills but by road who knows? The road is very bad and the bridge at the river is down. It is too deep for you to wade across. We blew up the bridge maybe a year ago escaping from Japanese soldiers." With that Zhu Pan Lee picked up his rifle and set off to where his comrades where now standing.

It was Sergeant Megat who said, "Get behind the lorry "to Robert, Mark and Lady Copeland as the guerrillas collected their rifles and picked up their belongings and set off walking away from the lorry without looking back.

Once they were out of sight Mark asked the Sergeant, "What was that all about?"

"Only four of them came out in the open and yet Zhu Pan Lee said there were six of them. Two must have remained hidden with their rifles trained on us. That is why my men remained vigilant."

Nobody said anything for a few seconds and then Sergeant Megat said, "I think we should go to the river as quickly as possible."

"What's the hurry if the bridge is down?"

"It may be repairable, Mr Travers; it is safer than sitting here. Zhu Pan Lee may have been assessing whether we could resist an attack. Even now they may be going to attack us. Come, we must move now."

It was some minutes later with Robert sitting in the back of the lorry with the Sergeant that he questioned the officer further. "Why were you suspicious of Zhu Pan Lee?"

"The Kuomintang fought bravely in the war, but they became used to robbing people in order to survive. Many people did help them, but they also had many bandits in their army. Zhu Pan Lee and his men would see us as having many things they need. I also think it is strange that they did not demand something."

"Perhaps the mention of Kenneth Chen was sufficient to scare them off. "

"Who knows, Mr Draper, but it is best if we put a few miles between us."

Chapter 12

For the hundredth time Robert swatted at something buzzing around his face. His face was sticky with sweat, his shirt stuck to him on his back and under his arms. He looked across at Lady Copeland and not for the first time he admired her stoicism. She must have been just as hot, but she never complained just continued to watch the men working on the bridge repair.

He turned away from looking at her and watched two of the police officers with Mark Travers and a few Chinese who lived in huts beside the river, dragging planks across what was left of the bridge. Mark had turned out to be surprisingly knowledgeable about bridges as he had served three years in the REME in Europe before coming back at the request of Grosvenor Estates to get them up and running again.

After a few hours working in the sweltering heat Robert had more or less collapsed so he had been delegated the job of keeping an eye out for trouble whilst a dozen or so men toiled away. It was back breaking work and made Robert think of his time in the hard labour camp at Pasir Ris. It was as he was thinking of the horrible weeks, he had spent just surviving in that death camp, that Lady Copeland spoke. "What happened to your face, Mr Draper? Do you mind me asking?"

Robert turned to face her at the same time taking in that more Chinese villagers from the kampong across the river were getting involved. "The *Kempetai* were anxious to get their hands on a large amount of gold they think was left behind in Singapore and they thought I knew of its whereabouts. Fortunately, they got a bit diverted in their search and I managed to survive."

"That rather sounds like you have an idea where it is."

Robert smiled across at her. "I have ideas but so far, they have come to nothing. The Kuomintang, Chin Peng and the British Government are also looking for it. We all think it is on the Island, so the search is a bit crowded. Nor do we know how much but by the keenness of the British Government I suspect it is a few million pounds."

There was some yelling as Robert and Lady Copeland continued talking and Robert could see that they now had planks across the whole gantry although it still looked very rickety. One of the officers came up to the lorry and said he had been told to make tea and Robert excused himself and went to assist in brewing up. This was their third day since they had set off from Segamat and it was impossible to say how far they had come although Robert by his own calculations put it at no more than sixty miles. The roads they had come on were almost continuous potholed and they had had to stop innumerable times filling in holes that could not be avoided. When they had reached the river, they were in luck; they had found a small kampong with Chinese willing to help to make the bridge safe to cross. Mark had got everybody working on the repairs but even then, they had been working for most of the day in the steaming heat. How Lady Copeland was able to manage the heat was beyond Robert.

Robert watched as the officers came up from the bridge to drink their tea. The Chinese sat down by the bank drinking water. Mark stripped to the waist and wearing a borrowed coolie hat took the mug Robert handed him. "I never thought I would need these skills again. Last time was in Holland eighteen months ago."

"Did you see much action, then?" Robert asked as he passed a mug of tea to Lady Copeland.

"I wasn't at D-Day but pretty busy afterwards getting roads and bridges repaired for the heavy vehicles. The big problem was making sure everything was clear so that supplies could get through to the front or everything ground to a halt. A bit hairy around Arnhem crawling under bridges defusing stuff the Germans had left behind, but I survived."

Lady Copeland looked up at Mark. "My nephew Ronald was at Arnhem. One of the men who didn't return."

Mark just nodded. "Tough times, Lady Copeland. Let us hope the commies don't make this country into a warzone. There's been enough war."

Robert asked, "Have you got much more to do?"

"I need to check that the planks are properly in place and maybe shore up one of the stanchions at the far end and then we can see if we can ease the lorry over very steadily. Fortunately, our driver is very attached to his lorry and will want her in one piece on the other side."

Robert and Lady Copeland laughed at Mark's comment as it was already a joke amongst the party how the army driver, Jahsingar Rup, was more concerned about his lorry than about anything else.

With a yell Mark got everybody back to work and about an hour later Jahsingar Rup gently coaxed the lorry over the thirty yards of planking with Lady Copeland, Robert, most of the police officers, and all the equipment from the back of the lorry already on the opposite bank. Apart from one hitch when the bridge yawed for a few seconds to one side and the lorry could have slid towards the river Jahsingar Rup got the lorry over the bridge to great yells of encouragement and clapping. He looked very pleased with himself and getting out of his cab he gently patted the front of the lorry.

It was Mark who said to Robert. "I told you he loves that bloody lorry more than anything." Robert grinned back, "Right, my suggestion is that we pack the lorry and get away from the river. There's too many mosquitos. Sergeant Megat says that the other side of the kampong looks good."

That night Robert went with Sergeant Megat into the kampong and sitting with the elders questioned them about the whereabouts of Bukit Lingtang. When they went back to their camp later they were able to tell Lady Copeland and Mark that the villagers knew of Bukit Lingtang which was perhaps fifteen miles away, near to the coast.

Chapter 13

To travel fifteen miles is not really a long journey but on a mud road with some of the surface almost non- existent it made for miserable travelling. The driving conditions were awful. The lorry seemed to have no springs and sitting for hours on hard boards or metal was painful and with the humidity soaring; for most of the morning there was also heavy rain. Every few hundred yards they had no option but to get out and help the lorry manoeuvre through or past large potholes and on one occasion they had to build up a part of the road that was sliding down into a large ditch.

For much of the journey they saw no one, only the occasional wild animal. They had been going for hours when they saw a road sign indicating an estate up on the left. Jasinger Rup stopped the lorry and Robert got out and spoke to Sergeant Megat and Mark who both emerged from the back of the lorry looking very hot and miserable.

Robert was pointing at the track as it left the main road. "It looks as though the track up to the estate hasn't been used for a while. The signs in Japanese so I presume it was one of the estates run by them before the war".

It was then that they saw the old Malay sitting under a makeshift shelter perhaps thirty or so yards up the dirt track. Sergeant Megat shouted to him in Malay. "Greetings old man. Does anyone live up at the estate?" The old man shook his head and mumbled something, and Sergeant Megat turned to Robert and Mark. "I think the old man said that all the people have left and that many of the buildings have been burnt down in fighting when the Japanese soldiers fought the guerrillas last year."

"Ask him if he knows of a Christian church nearby, "Mark said before Robert could ask.

After Sergeant Megat asked the question, the old man said nothing for a moment and then said, this time sufficiently clearly for Robert to be able to understand, that there was a place in Bukit Lingtang where Christians worshipped.

"Give me a couple of your smokes, Mark", Robert said and after Mark had fished them out Robert limped up the lane and gave the cigarettes to the old man. Turning around Robert shouted to Mark to get in the front, but Mark was already clambering in the back of the lorry.

Lady Copeland had sat in the front of the lorry throughout the journey, not talking, only occasionally showing irritation as a mosquito sought to land on her. Robert had already decided that she was made of the stuff that made empires. She had made no complaint throughout the journey which must have been very uncomfortable for her as by Robert's estimation she was in her early sixties.

A Meeting Under A Banyan Tree

As they entered Bukit Lingtang it was obvious that the Japanese had used it as a military station with a disused checkpoint at the beginning of the kampong. Jahsingar Rup stopped the lorry beside some Malays who were standing under an awning perhaps 50 yards beyond the old check point. Robert greeted them and explained that they were looking for a Christian church.

The Malays smiled and seemed to all speak at once before finally one elderly man waved them to be quiet. "The church was burnt down in the fighting but Father Dominic lives in a house by the river". He said that the father was very ill and many Indians had come from an estate a few miles away to pay their respects. "The house is perhaps a mile from here. You will not miss it; it has a large cross beside it."

"Are there European children with him?" Robert asked.

The elderly man shook his head. "None now. After the church burnt down the children went to live up in the hills. The father may know."

Robert got back in the lorry and explained to Lady Copeland what he had just learned. "I think we should find somewhere to rest here, Lady Copeland. If nothing else, it will give Jahsingar Rup a chance to rest. He must be exhausted. We can make something to eat and meanwhile Sergeant Megat can get more information." Robert could see the sergeant and his men walking about and talking to more Malays who had emerged from the huts nearby. Mark came around from the rear of the lorry and Robert explained what he had just learned.

"I just walked up to the Japanese check point. It looks like they collected labour from the surrounding villages and compounded them at the back before sending them off to work."

Robert pursed his lips at what Mark had just said. "From what I hear they took them off to work on the railway they built up in Thailand. There's no obvious work round here. It doesn't look as though many have returned; there only seems to be older men around." Lady Copeland had been helped down from the lorry by one of the policemen as Robert and Mark talked.

"Why can't we go down to see Father Dominic now, Robert?"

Robert turned to Lady Copeland. "The old man over there said that the house was the other side of a stream, and it was very bad area. I presume he means it's swampy. If we stop here and rest I can go down with Sergeant Megat and one of his men and get what information we can. The old man also said that there had been trouble the last few days, so I think it best if we stay in the village while we get our bearings. It is likely to be safer. He says that we are about 20 miles from Malacca and that Indian troops have been here and come every few days just to check out the situation."

"What sort of trouble? "Mark asked looking around.

"He didn't say, and I left it to Sergeant Megat to find out. I suspect it was guerrillas trying to get tribute and finding that these people have even less than them. They certainly look as though they are starving." At that Robert shouted at one of the policemen. "Do you think you could find us a place to rest for a few hours?" The policeman who was standing about thirty yards away talking to a Malay answered back that the village headman was offering his home and to follow him.

Robert looked at the state of the road. The rain was no longer falling but the road was covered in puddles and mud. "Jahsingar Rup, can you bring Lady Copeland up to the headman's house? We will walk and get a lie of the land." Robert helped Lady Copeland back up into the cab without any protest from her.

"Where are these estates you are supposed to be assessing, Mark? "

"From my instructions they are not far from here. Grosvenor bought out Collinson's who had three estates more or less adjoining between Malacca and KL. They were effectively abandoned in late December 1941 so God knows what state they are in. The Board instructed me to make an assessment and telegram what was needed. They have managers waiting to come out. Dead keen by all accounts but the last few days suggests to me that they will have no idea how difficult it will be. It will take years to get the trees back to full production and I doubt if even Grosvenor have that sort of cash."

While they had been talking, they had walked up the muddy road finally stopping near to the headman's house which was set back a little almost in a small square. To Roberts right, opposite the square, was what looked like a large community building that had been used as a market.

"It looks as though they have had it pretty rough these last few years, "Robert said as they walked through the square towards where the lorry was now parked. Robert stopped suddenly at a large post with chains attached to it.

"Dear God, this is an execution post."

Mark on hearing what Robert said walked around the post. "Poor sods."

The headman welcomed them into his home with Lady Copeland already sitting on a small stool produced from a corner of the room which was laid out with rush mats and little tables. For perhaps half an hour the headman talked telling them of the bad times they had with the Japanese taking away many of the young men, forcibly, after the men had refused to go unless their families were looked after. Robert asked about the execution post and was told that the Japanese officer had executed 4 men for constant disobedience, including his son. "They also executed a British officer who was caught when the guerrillas came down from the hills and attacked the Japanese camp near Malacca."

Robert asked whether white children had been in the village and the headman said there had been 4 children who lived with Father Dominic and an old nun who had brought them from Segamat three years ago. The Japanese had shown no interest in them until Father Dominic had given help to a wounded British officer a few months before the war ended. The Japanese had come looking for him and when they discovered that he was being looked after in the church they had burnt it down. "Sister Teresa helped the children to get away but died in the fire. Father Dominic was tortured by the Japanese but told them little." The headman explained all this in short sentences with little emotion and when he had finished Robert thanked him.

Robert explained what he had been talking about with the headman to both Lady Copeland and Mark who understood some of the conversation but constantly said to Robert that his Malay was still very rusty. Robert said to the headman. "Do you know where the children are now?"

The headman smiled at Robert. "They live with the Overseer at the Marivan Estate. It is perhaps good that you have come because the communists, if they know they are there, will kidnap them."

"How far is it to the estate?" Robert asked immediately.

"Perhaps one hour."

Robert turned immediately to Lady Copeland and Mark. "I think we need to change our plans. There are girls just an hour away and the headman is concerned that the communists may kidnap them."

Lady Copeland had been drinking some tea that the headman's wife had brought to her. "Oh, we must go immediately," she uttered as she tried to get up. The headman and Mark helped her to her feet as Robert explained to the headman that they must go at once to the Marivan Estate even though it was late in the afternoon and would be dark soon. Robert went to the house entrance and shouted to the policemen sitting outside, asking where Sergeant Megat was. "He has gone to see Father Dominic as he thought you were all too exhausted to do more and needed rest." Robert asked one of the officers to run and collect Sergeant Megat and tell him that they knew where the girls were hiding.

"Are you really able to manage another journey, Lady Copeland? You could stay here with a few officers and have a rest and Mark and I will go on and find the girls."

A very tired old lady smiled at Robert. "I know you mean well Robert, but I must come with you." She finished what she was saying as Robert heard shouting outside. Robert had not told Lady Copeland that the headman had said that there were only four European children. To himself he said, "I *hope to god her granddaughter is one of them.*"

Chapter 14

Marivan Estate had seen better days. As the lorry turned into the estate drive Robert immediately saw that there had been fighting – the sign for the estate was lying on the ground with what looked like bullet holes in it and just further up he could see by the lights of the lorry two graves at the side of the road. The headman had delegated a villager to direct them but in fact it had been easy to find the entrance to the estate.

The guide said that it was perhaps two miles further to where the estate workers had their village. Jahsingar Rup put the lorry into a low gear up the long twisting slope taking them back into the jungle with the noise of the night animals now becoming apparent. Thankfully the heavy monsoon rain had stopped.

At last, somewhere ahead they smelt smoke and saw a few lights, and suddenly they were in the midst of a village of perhaps sixty or seventy houses. People had come running out at the sound of the lorry and all Robert could really see in the flickering light were rows of eyes. Those surrounding the lorry were Tamils and Robert when he shouted greetings in English got a mixture of replies. It was Sergeant Megat and Mark when they came around from the rear of the lorry who took over and spoke to the hundred or so people who had gathered around them.

Sergeant Megat turned to Robert and said, "The children are with the overseer, and I have asked one of the men to go to his house which is up the hill and tell him that we have arrived and want to see the children."

Robert nodded and climbed back into the cab. "I think you should get out Lady Copeland. The children have been sent for." Robert saw an old lady take a deep sigh. "Robert, let us hope she is here. I cannot go on much longer." Robert took her arm and helped her out of the cab.

For a few minutes they stood beside the lorry with Mark in conversation with one of the Tamils, watched by a crowd of curious onlookers. Suddenly there was great deal of noise and girls' voices could be heard and then they were there in front of them. The overseer, a large rotund Indian of late middle age, came over to where Robert and Lady Copeland were standing and the crowd separated, watching quietly as events unfolded. The girls were dressed in saris and barefoot. But for the fact they were clearly European they to all extent and purpose could have been Indian. They were holding each other's hands and Robert could see that they were frightened. Lady Copeland standing on Robert's right had said nothing and it was one of the girls who suddenly ran forward.

"Nana, Nana."

The next few moments were chaos. The crowd was all over the place shouting their approval and clapping. Robert and Mark ended up at the side of the lorry jammed against it until finally Sergeant Megat standing on the cab step shouted for order. As the crowd dispersed Robert could see a girl in Lady Copeland's arms being hugged. The overseer brought the other girls forward and introduced them to Mark, Robert and Lady Copeland; a very tearful Lady Copeland, brought them into her little circle and somehow, they were all hugging each other.

Robert turned to the overseer who had introduced himself as "Mr Mitanthatra." "I think we need somewhere where we can sit down, or we will all collapse. Also, somewhere to stay the night."

The overseer nodded and immediately started giving out orders. Turning back to Robert he said, "There is a visitors' bungalow, perhaps a hundred yards up the road. It is clean and I will order some women to take up bedding now. Your policemen can sleep in the servant quarters. The women will bring some food as well although we do not have much. "

Robert nodded and turning he shouted over to Sergeant Megat who was talking to his men. "We have accommodation just up the lane." Mark had gone over to Lady Copeland and the girls to tell them of the arrangements and Robert saw that he was arranging with Jahsingar Rup to take them up in the lorry. Robert turned to the overseer. "Mr Mitanthatra, perhaps we could walk up the lane and you can tell me what has been happening here." The overseer nodded and together they turned and walked through the village and up the hill to the visitors' bungalow as behind them the lorry engine started up. By the time Mark caught up with them Mr Mitanthatra was well into telling Robert everything that had happened for the past four years.

At the visitors' bungalow Robert left Lady Copeland to take over inside and he and Mark set themselves up on the veranda. "God I'm tired, Bob. Offering a rescue service is hard work."

Robert grinned back at Mark. "I have some whisky left so I think we should celebrate tonight. Hell, I'm supposed to be assessing banks in KL and Penang and seeing when we can reopen."

"I thought you were a gold hunter?" Mark said immediately as he set out his bedding and hung his mosquito netting over a cross beam.

"Who have you been talking to?"

Robert could see Mark smiling even in the dark, with his teeth momentarily flashing white. "Eric can keep no secrets."

"Useless sod, "Robert said, laughing out loud. "Half of Singapore will be digging before long.

It was later in the evening when Lady Copeland spoke with Robert and Mark that they learned from her that two girls had died of fever on the march from Segamat in 1942 and the old nun had died the year before.

Chapter 15

The following morning saw everyone up early. A tired but very happy Lady Copeland wandered around with the children whilst Robert, Mark and Sergeant Megat had a meeting.

"The overseer says that the road into Malacca is good, and it should take us no more than a couple of hours. The British have set up a military camp down by the harbour. He says they are also promising some food aid but they have seen nothing here so far."

"Well, the quicker they get it to here and Lingtang the better. The poor sods have nothing. What we left them at Lingtang isn't enough to feed the kids for a day."

Sergeant Megat suggested that they set off as soon after breakfast as possible and Robert went off to see Lady Copeland to tell her to be ready to go in an hour. Mark went off to see the overseer and take notes on the state of the rubber plantation for him to send on to the owners of the estate which he found out were the London Merchant Company.

Robert, after telling Lady Copeland about setting off after breakfast also went to look for the overseer and found him in the old rubber curing sheds. "Mr Mitanthatra, can you help. There are graves at the entrance to the estate. Who were they?"

Mr Mitanthatra shook his head in the way all Indians do when explaining something. "Mr Draper, it was a very bad time. Many Australian soldiers died. The fighting was very fierce. The Japanese had tanks and they shoot many men. They would not let us bury the dead for many days; they took no prisoners; they just shoot them. We have buried many men above the tennis court." He waved his arm in the general direction of the Manager's bungalow which Robert could see about two hundred yards away. "Come, I will show you." As they walked up the hill Mr Mitanthatra explained that the two graves at the estate entrance were two prisoners who had surrendered a few days after the Australians had left retreating towards Singapore. "They were hiding in the plantation and some of my workers fed them, but the Japanese camped on the estate and caught them at the main road when the Australians tried to go after their comrades. The officer cut their heads off with his sword and made us watch. He told us that it was the penalty for helping them. He said that if it happened again, he would execute some of the workers."

Robert said little as they walked up the hill and just listened to the overseer. At the side of the tennis court was a grave with a cross. What looked like a couple of old army hats were attached to the grave? "We buried thirty bodies, all Australian, here in the February. The Japanese bayoneted the wounded."

As they walked back Robert asked about why the Japanese had burnt down the church. "We are a Christian community, Mr Draper. We have been here for nearly 20 years and Father Dominic has always been our pastor. We were at his service one Sunday in June last year and some guerrillas arrived with wounded men including a British officer. They were escaping from the Japanese. Father Dominic gave them food and some medical supplies that he had stored away. I think he must have helped them before because they seemed to know him. Before they could leave however the Japanese arrived and there was much shooting. Father Dominic and Sister Teresa got the women and children out and they escaped up into the hills and walked that way back to the estate. Many of the men were not here as they were working on defences being prepared by the Japanese over at Port Dickson. The guerrillas hid in the church and the Japanese set fire to it and shot anyone who tried to come out. Father Dominic, they beat him, and now he is very ill. We sent a message to the Bishop in Malacca but there has been no reply." The overseer said all this in halting English apologising that he had not spoken in that language for nearly 4 years.

At the bungalow they found everyone was packed and impatient to leave. The four girls were saying some very tearful goodbyes to the people who had looked after them and Lady Copeland with Mark's help was thanking the overseer's wife for looking after the children and saying that she would not forget them. Mark and Robert shook hands with Mr Mitanthatra with Mark promising that he would get in touch as soon as possible with the estate owners and explain the situation.

Sergeant Megat came over as they were saying their goodbyes. "There has been shooting in the distance, up in the hills. I do not know what it is about, but I think we should move now. The workers say the communists have been having some fights with Kuomintang in the past few weeks, so it is best if we move off. We do not want to be involved. "

Without more ado Robert and Mark got onto the lorry and it set off with Robert stopping the lorry at the estate entrance momentarily so he could check the two graves. "The poor devils were executed to frighten the locals. There's no information who they were though other than Mr Mitanthatra thinks they were Australian."

Chapter 16

Malacca was not as Robert remembered it. There was little civilian activity in the town but a great number of troops. Everything looked in a poor state with a great deal of filth and litter in the streets. Arriving at the dockside, having been directed there by the military police, they could see a number of small Royal Navy vessels as well as a hospital ship and a mine sweeper a few hundred yards out at sea but only an old merchant ship tied up at the quayside. Further out at sea there was a very large ship with an escort of destroyers and Robert learned later that it was a US battleship. The order and cleanliness around the docks seemed out of place with the dirt, poverty and hunger he had seen in the four days since they had left Segamat.

After a little misdirection they eventually were seen by a Royal Navy 0fficer, Captain Forrester, who explained that he was acting harbour master until the civilian authorities took over in a few weeks. As he was explaining the situation Robert could see a tender taking people out to the hospital ship. "We have a woman and four children that need to be taken to Singapore as soon as possible. Sir Shenton allowed the woman, Lady Copeland, to come and search for her grandchild." Robert, while he was explaining why they needed help, handed over a letter of credentials given to him by the First Secretary before he and his party had set off from Segamat.

"We have been expecting you. We received radio instructions about Lady Copeland. "The Captain looked at Robert, and then at Mark who had accompanied him to meet Captain Forrester. "The hospital ship is taking on some Europeans from a camp they have just found north of KL. It leaves in a few hours heading down to Singapore, so I think you are in luck."

It was Mark who said, "That's great news. Lady Copeland is not well. She's been overdoing it and the heat has completely exhausted her. The medics on the ship are just the ticket."

The Captain turned to a sailor standing to attention behind him. "Rennie, take a signal to the hospital ship now. Advise them to expect five more patients in the next hour. Ask Dr Millar to come over and see Lady Copeland and the four girls." Rennie set off immediately as Captain Forrester walked with Robert and Mark towards where the five women were sitting on a veranda of a bungalow facing the docks. After Robert had introduced Lady Copeland to Captain Forrester, he left it to the Captain to explain that he was arranging for them to be taken out to the hospital ship in the next hour or so. With that the Captain left saying he would arrange for food and drinks to be brought over.

Robert and Mark walked over to the lorry where the police officers were sitting quietly in the shade, smoking and generally resting. "Sergeant, it looks as though we have got rid of our ladies as the Captain we have just been talking to has arranged for them to be transported to Singapore on the hospital ship out there in the roads."

Sergeant Megat smiled back. "I have spoken to Sergeant Rananurtha at the police station, and he says that they are preparing for an American food ship coming in later today. He says that the Indian troops have found some Japanese soldiers, this morning, on an estate about ten miles from here so the country is still not free of them."

"There's some food being sent over for us, so keep your eye out. Mr Travers and I are going to have a wander around for the next few minutes." As Robert was telling the Sergeant about the food, he could see someone arrive at the veranda and he presumed it was Dr Millar. The girls still wearing saris and in bare feet seemed to have taken the last twelve hours in their stride but were now quite subdued. When Robert had talked to them for a few minutes he found that they scarcely spoke in English preferring to speak Malay or Tamil. He hadn't asked them about the last four years and what they had been through, and he left that to Lady Copeland and the medics. Two of the girls looked ill and he suspected that they had had bouts of malaria or were suffering from the lack of food on the estate. He suddenly realised that only three months ago he had been suffering from the same problems indeed the medics had warned him before he set off to Segamat that he should remember that he was still building up his strength and needed to take things one step at a time. *"Fat chance of that,"* he said to himself.

Mark and Robert walked through the checkpoint first asking the MP on duty whether it was safe to wander in the town. "No problems that I am aware of, sir. The poor sods are too hungry to be troublesome."

Robert just nodded at the MP and said they would just wander up through the old town and then come back. The heat was beginning to rise, and the two men realised as they walked just how much had been taken out of them over the last few days. Mark asked how Robert had become lame and Robert told of his time with the *Kempetai.*" They were convinced I knew where the gold was hidden in Singapore just because I managed to get a large amount out of KL."

"And do you ….?" Mark didn't finish the sentence, just left it hanging.

"No, but I have had time to think about it and thanks to information from various people I'm beginning to wonder whether it was ever just one amount. More likely different pots. One thing for sure there are lots of people interested in finding it. Sir Shenton has spoken to me about it, as well as Military Intelligence, and just before we left Singapore the Kuomintang got a hold of me. The only lot not to have contacted me so far are the communists and I suspect that's only a matter of time."

"You need to be careful, Bob. They're not a friendly bunch."

"I know, Mark, but neither are the Kuomintang. They both think they are owed for what they did in the war and Sir Shenton just wants it in the Government's coffers. The real issue is whose property it really is. I can't find any evidence that the Singapore Government or the UK Government ever paid the banks for the money. Everything was in such a rush at the end and Sir Shenton and the First Secretary were just keen to keep everything at arm's length. It all makes for interesting times ahead."

On the way back Mark asked if Lady Copeland had told Robert much about the girls' ordeal. "It seems that the six girls walked with the nun from Segamat staying at kampongs. It must have been a real ordeal and one of them went down with fever and died. One of the girls died later."

"Well, we know about Lady Copeland's granddaughter and her friend, whose parents are on their way to collect her but what about the other two?"

Robert looked at Mark as they came through the checkpoint. "From what I can make of their story their parents were missionaries in South China. They got the girls out in 1941 with a missionary who was coming to live in Singapore, and it was arranged that they go to the school in Segamat as the parents knew the head teacher. Doesn't sound too hopeful that the parents survived the fighting."

When they reached where Lady Copeland and the girls were quietly sitting eating sandwiches and fresh fruit Mark sat down and Robert excused himself and went looking for Captain Forrester. He had suddenly remembered what the Captain had said about those on the hospital ship being from a civilian camp north of KL. Hopefully the Captain had a list of names.

Chapter 17

It was sixteen days later. The 4th of December 1945 and Robert sat on the veranda of the Royal Hotel looking across the channel at Butterworth. Gone was the hundreds of sampans and dhows of 1941 and Robert could see only a few sampans about a mile away towards the north. Presumably the Japs had chased them off as they had used the channel as a submarine dock.

He mused momentarily that a lot of water had passed under the bridge since he had last looked at that view in June 1941. He wondered what had happened to his girlfriend at the time, Fran, for that matter what had happened to Fiona or to Marcus, who had travelled down from Bangkok, to see them. The last he had heard Fiona was on a train trying to get out of Thailand on the 6th December 1941 just before the Japs locked down the country. As for Marcus he suspected that he had ended up in one of the internment camps in Thailand. The only thing was he hadn't seen his name on the lists of released internees. Fran was a different kettle of fish. She had set off from Singapore two days after the Japanese had invaded north Malaya, on the *SS Martinique,* and he was pretty certain that it had got to Colombo even though it would have been at risk of being bombed on its journey up the Sumatran coast. There were plenty of ships getting through, the only thing was that the Japs had moved a naval fleet into the Indian Ocean so the journey would not have been easy. Still knowing Fran, she would not let a little thing such as a Jap sub or cruiser stop her from getting home; she was probably in charge of something by now.

As he sat drinking a cup of tea and enjoying a few minutes of peace he could hear in the background some loud voices; he recognised the voice of the First Secretary but not the other voices. Suddenly a group of people were standing in front of him.

"What's this I hear that you have met with Chin Peng, Mr Draper? When did this happen and why wasn't I told earlier?"

Robert realising that his few minutes of peace were gone stood up and faced the First Secretary. "I briefed Major Comber. He is, after all, in charge of intelligence."

"Major Comber has had to travel up to Perak this morning to deal with a problem. Before he left, he told me of your meeting. Why I wasn't told days ago is beyond me."

Robert realised he was not going to get away with saying that he had reported to Major Comber in KL. For some reason Comber had delayed telling the First Secretary and he seemed to be getting the blame. Robert drew a breath and said, "After Mark Travers and I dropped Lady Copeland off at the Royal Naval depot in Malacca, with her granddaughter and three other children, we travelled on the Port Swettenham Road, to a kampong where I have family and friends. Sergeant Megat got quite anxious as the kampong had been raided by the communists only the day before for food. We stayed maybe a couple of hours while I made arrangements for my uncle's family, to come down to Singapore as it was no longer safe for them in the kampong."

"Yes, yes, but when did you meet Chin Peng?" the First Secretary said getting exasperated.

"You did say you wanted to know the detail." Robert looked around at the audience of civil servants and military personnel. He smiled at the attentive faces and ignoring further agitation from the First Secretary he continued. "We left the kampong and took a back road which we had been told about, through the old Swinerton Rubber estate heading for the KL road with the intention of staying at the Moray and Moray estate where Mark was to set up shop. Just before we reached the KL road we were stopped by a tree across the road. There was no shooting, but it was an obvious ambush and Sergeant Megat got his men out and they set up a defence ring. Mark and I watched the front. We must have been there about 10 minutes and were just beginning to think that we should try and move the tree when two communist fighters, in army jungle outfits, emerged out of the undergrowth and walked towards us. They both had rifles slung over their shoulders, so they were not threatening. Sergeant Megat shouted that no one should shoot unless they did first. One of the fighters came up to the fallen tree and said that Chin Peng wanted to talk to me and indicated that I walk up the road towards a Banyan tree that was maybe a hundred yards away."

The First Secretary sat down in one of the chairs beside the chair Robert had been sitting in and waved Robert to sit down. "It looks like it is a long story, Mr Draper."

Robert just shrugged and sat down. "I asked why Chin Peng couldn't come down to speak to me. The fighter said that comrade Chin Peng was at the tree, and I must go there. Mark did say that I shouldn't go but it seemed to me that if Chin Peng wanted a fight, he could have started one ages ago and it was likely he had a few dozen fighters close by and if there was a gun battle we would come out of it badly. I stood up and put my gun in my holster and walked over to the tree blocking the road and clambered over it. I could hear Mark and Sergeant Megat shouting in the background, but I just kept walking down the middle of the road and the two communists got in behind me."

"What the hell did they want you for?"

"Oh, come on First Secretary. You know why. Everyone knows I am looking for the lost gold. They're no different than the Kuomintang. They want to get their hands on it, and they think I may be getting close. Anyway, Chin Peng was sitting on a log under the Banyan tree. There were maybe six or seven other fighters there, all armed with Lee Enfield's. One of them had a fire going and he brought me a drink as I sat on the log opposite Chin Peng. It was very civilised now that I think about it."

The First Secretary shook his head. "I can see why Hugh Bryson says you can be an exasperating man. Here you are having a meeting with one of the most dangerous men in the Malay States and you make it sound like a tea party."

"What else could I do? I couldn't exactly say to him that I was arresting him. I just told him that I had expected the meeting as it had seemed to me that everybody wanted to know about the gold. Before he even asked, I told all that I had found out so far."

"What! You had no right."

"I can't see that I had any option. He would probably have known if I was lying. Anyway, as I have told Military Intelligence, for that matter Sir Shenton, my only interest is in finding who helped the Japanese in their search for the gold. We both know that there was more than one traitor operating in Singapore. What about Heenan? Geoffrey Blackmore told me once that Military Intelligence reckoned there were three or four traitors in the military, or in the civilian ranks working in the Colonial Office. A good friend and some colleagues died without saying anything but no thanks to someone who knew about the gold and passed information onto the Japs."

The First Secretary fidgeted for a moment and then asked, "How did the meeting end?" He chose not to respond to Robert's point about traitors.

"Ah. That's when it got tricky. Chin Peng wanted me to tell him when I found it, but I avoided saying yes and said that there may not be any gold, just empty boxes because someone else has got there already. I told him that he should look within his own organisation as it seemed to me that things went wrong after the Japanese raided the Batu Caves in '42. After that, Force 136 had to bring gold in from India. He became very quiet when I suggested that the problem might be within the Malay Communist Party. He immediately ended the meeting and shouted at one of the fighters and told me that his comrade would escort me back to the lorry. When I got back Mark said that he reckoned that there was at least twenty hiding around us."

"It seems to me that you were very lucky, Mr Draper."

"I knew they would contact me. The thought of a large pot of gold lying around is too enticing. They weren't likely to kill me as that would dry up the information. Better to keep an eye on me. Chin Peng gave nothing away, but I think he will now leave no stone unturned about what happened with the gold that should have been delivered to the Batu Caves. I suspect he has always been suspicious as to how the Japanese knew that the MCP were meeting at the Batu Caves and my information merely confirmed this." Robert started to smile as he finished what he was saying, "The tea wasn't very good though."

The First Secretary just shook his head in exasperation.

"For about five minutes after I got back to the lorry, we could see a group of men at the Banyan tree. Then they just melted into the jungle and Sergeant Megat got up from where he was lying at the side of a ditch and shouted at some of his officers. They moved the tree to the side of the road, and we set off again. It was quite late by this time, getting dark."

"How long did the meeting last?" one of the military officers standing behind the First Secretary asked.

"I should think about forty minutes. Oh, I did say to him at one point that we all thought he was in the Perak Province, and he did smile for once."

The First Secretary stood up. Looking down at Robert he said, "You were very lucky. Mr Draper, Chin Peng is a very dangerous man. He could easily have killed you."

Robert shook his head. "I had months of care and attention from the *Kempetai*. I no longer worry about such things."

"Mr. Draper, I want everything you remember down in writing by close of play. Captain Stonwick has a clerk who can type up your report. Don't think this is the last you'll be hearing on this matter. You should not be interfering. The gold is not your affair." With that the First Secretary got up and set off for his next meeting and Robert sat quietly pondering his next move.

Chapter 18

"I gather you had a difficult meeting with the First Secretary," Brigadier Starling said wryly to Robert as they sat having breakfast on the terrace overlooking the water, watching a large US Navy ship slowly come into sight.

Robert had come down for breakfast late and been waved over by the Brigadier who was sitting with Captain Stonwick who Robert had met the previous afternoon when he had given his handwritten report to him for typing. Captain Stonwick just nodded at Robert as he sat down.

Robert said good morning before saying, "The First Secretary is rather precious about the gold as I suspect he was involved in the original decision to create a bank for funding a guerrilla war in the Malay States. He certainly would have known about it but he got out of Singapore before the surrender. Just bad luck he ended up in a camp in Sumatra. I can only presume that the Nips didn't put two and two together and realise who he was." While Robert was saying this, he nodded at the waiter who had brought tea and toast. He shook his head when he was asked if he wanted a cooked breakfast.

"I couldn't care a damn about the gold, Brigadier Starling, I just want the bastard who betrayed us. Many men died because of the betrayal."

The Brigadier who wasn't much older than Robert smiled back at the hard language Robert used. "The man who betrayed you may not have had any option. It's often the case that you say more than you intend to under interrogation."

Robert shook his head. "The Nips responded to new information they kept getting. I am convinced that they had someone on the inside who didn't have all the information but just enough to set them off on another round of torture. I know now that they had one of the main links to the gold in their hands and executed him with other Chinese industrialists, but at the time they didn't realise who he was. That's the complication; the chain was broken and whoever was betraying us had to start again or gave false information for their own purpose.

"How did they know about the gold in the first place?" Captain Stonwick asked.

"From what I have learned so far, they obtained information from someone in the military or maybe from a senior civil servant in the Colonial Office who was part of the circle of people who first started to consider how to fund a guerrilla war using the Kuomintang organisation. If what I've been told is correct there was no discussion with the communists until later about them being a part of any organised resistance. At the beginning the understanding was that they would independently harass the Japs. The Japs clearly had a good deal of information which enabled them to go hunting from

16th February 1942 for gold and for possible troublemakers, but it wasn't by the looks of it coordinated and as they searched for the gold the distributors of the gold were being killed off largely by drowning off the beach in Singapore, or they were in hiding. Chin Peng seemed to confirm that this was his understanding when I spoke to him but then again, he didn't give much away. The only time he did seem agitated was when I suggested he should look inside his organisation as the betrayal could be closer to home."

Robert changed the subject. "Captain Stonwick. You told me yesterday that Eric Cassidy had been called back to Singapore as he had been reassigned to a posting in Aden. Would it be possible for you to give me his address as I would like to keep in touch with an old colleague from the bank?" Captain Stonwick just nodded.

Brigadier Starling got up putting his napkin on the table. "Good talking to you, Mr Draper. Good luck in your search. I wish you well but be careful. You are making powerful enemies. I've little doubt that Major Comber will want to see you again in the next couple of days. Come on, Leslie, we have work to do." With that he set off into the hotel interior with Captain Stonwick in tow and with Robert signalling to the waiter that he wanted more tea and toast.

It was later that morning as he worked on a report to Peter Connaught and the other banks' directors in London that an Assistant Manager of the hotel came to see him. "Excuse me, Tuan, but a Lee Pan Zin has asked to see you. He says he was a clerk in the Union & China Bank in Penang. He is in the foyer."

Robert looked up from where he was working. "I will see him here, Mr Kwan."

"He is not dressed as a clerk, tuan. "

Robert made a face at the comment. From what he could see most of the men in the streets of Penang were in a bad state. "Take him into the garden, Mr Kwan. I will meet him there."

****

A few moments later Robert walked into the garden and saw Lee Pan Zin standing with Mr Kwan.

Lee Pan Zin bowed to Robert and immediately apologised for his appearance. "I was forced to work in one of the labour camps, many men died, sir. "

Robert looked round and saw a bench nearby. "Let us sit over there, Mr Lee." "Thank you, Mr Kwan. I will take over from here."

Robert looked at Lee Pan Zin. "Do you need a drink, Mr Lee?" Seeing him nod Robert waved over a waiter who had clearly been told by Mr Kwan to keep an eye on things. "Mr Lee do you want a tea? I intend to have one. Do you need something to eat? Seeing Lee Pan Zin nod to both questions Robert ordered tea and biscuits."

"Now Mr Lee. I never met you as I never worked at the Penang branch so I will have to ask you some questions. Tell me about your time at the bank. Who was the bank manager?"

Lee Pan Zin answered immediately, "Mr Barwick."

"Who was your chief clerk?

Lee Pan Zin again answered immediately, "Wai Lee. He died from wounds in the bombing."

"There was a Chinese senior clerk who was sent up to work in the bank for long periods to help Mr Barwick. What was his name?"

Lee Pan Zin smiled at the question. "I think you mean Kenneth Chen."

Robert was satisfied with the answers and as the tea and biscuits arrived, he asked Lee Pan Zin to fill in the details of what had happened after the Japanese arrived. He knew that Peter Connaught and Kenneth Chen had managed to get some of the gold out of Penang on the last ship before the Japanese had landed on the Island but nothing after that.

"The Japanese shot many men in the streets. They killed wounded people in the hospital and then they made us bury the dead. I worked in a gang who had to put out the fires and clear the damage from the roads. Then they rounded up many Chinese and Malay leaders and marched them off to the other side of the Island. They never returned. Lai Pin and Du Song Yuh were taken."

"Who were they, Mr Zin?"

"They were senior clerks in the bank."

Robert nodded at what Lee Pan Zin had just said although he had not heard of them before.

"I am very sorry, Mr Zin. It sounds like a very bad time.

Lee Pan Zin nodded and took another biscuit having already consumed three ginger snaps.

"I hid, Mr Draper. I hid in my mother-in-law's house for many months and when a neighbour in the next house died, I paid his widow to take his identity. He was about my age. For a time, everything okay then Japanese tell us that all able-bodied men must report for work and they marched us off to the train station. Many days in wagons with little water. Many of us died. Then we had to march through jungle with much equipment and build a railway. Only a few come back to Penang. My wife dead when I return a few days ago."

"I really am very sorry, Mr Lee. It sounds as though you did well to survive the past three years."

Robert explained that Peter Connaught had been promoted and would shortly be on his way from England to take charge and that he had asked Robert to make a preliminary assessment of the situation. "Mr Connaught will want to get the bank up and running as soon as possible but the branch on Rangoon Street has been destroyed. It will be at least a year before he will be able to operate as before. I had a look around yesterday and it seems to me that Barclays will be able to open fairly soon but the other banks will not be operating for some months. What I can do is contact the new Barclays manager and recommend you for a position but that may not be until the Spring when I think most banks are hoping to become operational."

Lee Pan Zin nodded dejectedly. "Thank you, sir."

"In the meantime, I think Mr Connaught would want me to help you. So can I hire you to trace other employees and it maybe that we will need you for other tasks until a manager can be appointed."

Lee Pan Zin started to cry. He got down on his knees. "Mr Draper, I cannot thank you enough."

Robert bent down and took Lee Pan Zin by the arms and pulled him back on the bench. "Right, Mr Lee, I will give you some money and you should go off and get yourself cleaned up and buy some new clothes. Report here tomorrow morning and I will make another tour with your assistance as two sets of eyes are better than just one about how we can get the banks working again. I am leaving on the train tomorrow evening, so we have a lot to do." Robert took from his pocket some of the service money in circulation at the time and handed it over to Lee Pan Zin and watched him put the last of the biscuits in his pocket. "Here, have some more money. Try and buy some food although God knows there's not much about."

Chapter 19

Chunggy welcomed him back almost with an air of difference. Robert felt quite put out. He was much more used to Chunggy getting very excited when he returned after being away from home for a while. Invariably Chunggy would drop his "r's" and his words would get jumbled up, but not today. It took Robert a while to figure it out and then he remembered that he had asked Mona to keep an eye on Chunggy. He started to laugh at the thought of the diminutive Mona coming round and disturbing Chunggy's routine. He purposely went out into the garden and sure enough it looked as though someone had been working very hard during his four weeks travelling in the Malay States. There was even some new fencing blocking off the view of Chunggy's little house.

He could hear someone in the undergrowth adjoining the next garden and he shouted "hello" and a little Chinese face poked its head out of some bushes about twenty feet away. Robert greeted the little man in Haken and asked if he had done the work in his garden. The little man nodded and said that there had been many snakes, but all were gone now, and the police had been around and taken away the stray dogs that lived in the ruins of the house next door. Robert thanked him and said that he should continue to clear next door's garden. The little man nodded and disappeared back into the bushes and Robert turned round and wandered through the garden just getting his thoughts together before he went off down to Fullerton Square.

When he went back in the house Chunggy had put a mound of letters for him on the desk he used in the upstairs lounge together with a jug of fresh juice and some little caraway cakes. He was forgiven apparently! Robert sat for a few minutes rifling through the letters mostly from internees now far away in other lands, telling him that they had arrived safely. Peter had sent him two airmail letters and he quickly read them learning that two more managers were on their way from England and that Peter was booked to come out by plane on 7th January, possibly with a colleague and the new Director of Southeast Asia, Barclays Bank. Robert momentarily worked out that his report on the state of the banks should be in their hands before Christmas, so it gave them a little time to plan. Chunggy had left him a list of people and telephone numbers who wanted to speak to him when he got back from KL and Penang. There was also a message from a Miss Rebecca Masters at South Asia Shipping to say that they had arranged to pick up his family from Malacca and would bring them down before Christmas. He smiled as he read the note. David's stepdaughter seemed to be working for his Uncle John's old outfit; she would have enjoyed writing the note. There was no letter from the Connor's but a letter from Sally Cheeseman, one of Joyce's house mates, to say that she was frozen in a very cold Suffolk, but it was lovely to be with her family.

Finishing his drink, he took the last of the caraway cakes and stuffing it in his mouth he set off downstairs. Chunggy came through from the kitchen. "Thank you for the cakes, Chunggy. You've made a great job of the garden. We must keep the gardener on and get him to clear the garden next door. I think we should buy the plot as at the moment it's a worthless piece of land and the Reeves won't be returning by all accounts. Chunggy looked very pleased at what Robert had just said and then surprised Robert by saying, "You must get car, Mr Draper. You too important to just get rickshaw."

Outside in the drive a rickshaw was already waiting for Robert, and he just smiled. He hadn't asked for one, but Chunggy knew that he would have to go into Fullerton Square. As he got into the rickshaw, he shouted across to Chunggy who was standing on the front steps. "There's a present for you on top of my suitcase. Nothing much but I know you said you wanted a new one."

The bank was quiet when he got to it. Not open yet for regular hours but the notice on the front door indicated that customers should telephone a number and make an appointment. The new security guard Robert had employed before he left opened the main doors for him as soon as he knocked, and he entered a bank that smelt clean. The clerks had obviously enjoyed painting the walls and bringing the building back to life. He noticed that glass was in the windows as he was greeted by a number of the clerks. There was a couple of workmen doing something with the marble centre table that had been damaged.

Chin Lee emerged from the cashiers back office with a young European man. "Mr Livingstone, I presume," Robert said addressing the European as he went across to the hall towards them. "Good morning, Chin Lee. You have done a wonderful job. The place looks almost new."

Robert shook hands with the European who said, "Nigel Renshaw. You must be Robert Draper. "

"Bob, please." Robert turned to Chin Lee and shook his hand and said again, "Well done."

Turning to Nigel, Robert asked, "Where have you bedded down?"

"I'm using one of the offices in the Loans section as they are still decorating down here and in the vaults."

"Have you time for a meeting or do you have other arrangements?"

Nigel shook his head. "I've been here ten days and have just tried to get my head round the complexities. Chin Lee seems to have everything in hand and is even organising some basic services for some of our old customers. I've taken on the discussions with the

Treasury concerning the limits on money and getting a hold of currency."

Chin Lee who had gone off, as they talked, to speak to the workmen returned and said, "If you wish, Mr Draper, you and Mr Renshaw can go to his office to talk, and I will ask Kwan Shu to make you some tea."

"It sounds like we're not needed, Nigel." With that they went up the stairs to what had been Robert's old office when he had first come to the bank in 1940.

"I got a letter from Peter this morning to say that he is on his way on 7th January; he's flying out so he should be here around the 11th. I sent him a report on the state of the KL and Penang buildings. Penang is a rebuild job, but KL might get away with a bit of paint and a repair job to the deposit boxes. A bit like here. Mind you I couldn't find more than half a dozen of the clerks in KL in the five days I was there. It seems the Japs really did make life miserable for them, even sending some off as forced labour in Thailand. Penang is in an even worse state. We have no building to speak of and the Japs seem to have liquidated any of the English-speaking Chinese they could find. I managed to find one clerk who used to work for us, but he was in an awful state, poor chap. Spent better part of three years working on building a railway through the jungle."

Nigel sat listening as Robert outlined the problems and then said, "Mr Connaught, in the letter he sent me said that you were probably only going to work for us for a short time and then you are planning to go into business."

Robert nodded. "I was left a legacy just before the Japs arrived and also by the looks of it a business, well more of a charitable trust. It should keep me very busy, and I have a friend who wants me to go into partnership with him although I think my ideas may now be a bit different. I don't see myself selling pineapples, rather more property. Anyway, I will do my best to help you and Peter to get the bank back on its feet.

"What was it like in the Malay States? I've heard reports that it's pretty lawless."

Robert didn't answer for a moment preferring to drink the tea Kwan Shu had brought up to them. "I think it will take around a year to get things operational again, but it will never be the same. Anyone who thinks they can just come back and carry on as though nothing ever happened is living in cloud cuckoo land. It will need a lot of investment to sort things out and I suspect the old country has not got the money nor for that matter the energy. The real problem is the political makeup. The communists are not just a nuisance they are a force to be reckoned with. China is all set to have a hell of a civil war and that's likely to affect us all. Here in Singapore, I can't see us getting away with it either. I think we're going to have to listen to the other races more and collaborate or we will sink. The Dutch walked back into Batavia three months ago as though it was the old days and look at the mess they're in."

"Mr Connaught, when he wrote to me last week said that we must concentrate on developing the commercial side." Nigel said it almost like a question.

Robert nodded. "I can't see that you will be able to compete with the Hong Kong or Barclays. Far better you compete with the small banks like the Mercantile, in a niche market. Even then I suspect in this changing world the small bank may get swallowed up."

Nigel got up and walked round. "I understand that Sir John has arranged for Martins Bank to be associated with our Manchester branch, whatever association means. "

Robert who didn't know this information said, "There. That's the way Sir John sees us surviving in this brave new world. Right well I had better be moving. I have a meeting with the First Secretary at two o'clock. You got some decent digs?

Nigel said he was living with two other bachelors up near Kellang airbase but hoped to move out to new accommodation shortly. "Too bloody noisy with great big planes flying twenty -four hours a day."

"Without the Yanks providing, Nigel, I think we would literally starve. Chuck, a friend of mine, told me before he left for the States that they were flying in fresh milk and food for the children every day, from Australia. Four years ago, we had everything. Now we are dependent on hand-outs, and it will be that way for a while." With that Robert shook his head and set off leaving Nigel to go through some papers on Robert's old desk.

****

Robert sat that night in the upstairs lounge finishing reading the letters and notes that had been waiting for him on his return. The last airmail he came to was from Clive Sewell who had written to Robert, it seemed, just before Robert left to go up country. He sat for a while taking in the news hardly noticing Chunggy appearing and refilling his whisky glass. Finally, he picked up his pen and taking a fresh airmail letter from his drawer he started to write.

Dear Clive,

It was wonderful to read your letter. So much has happened in the past four years, so many questions unanswered. I enjoyed reading of your trip on the Tenedos. It certainly doesn't sound like a holiday. It doesn't bear thinking about what would have happened if the Japanese fleet had spotted the ship. From what you say the lookout spotted them and a bit of quick thinking by the Captain and you managed to evade the Japs in the islands off Timor. To then see a Jap submarine must have been terrifying; we may never know why you were not torpedoed. I can only think that the Japs knew that the gold was on the ship and were calling up support to get the Tenedos to surrender. From what Peter has told me the Captain had orders to scuttle the ship with the gold if it looked like you were going to be captured. You don't say how long this went on for although Peter does say that the Australian Navy turned up at some point and saved the situation only for you to be strafed as you approached Darwin harbour. It makes the escape from KL seem tame.

I'm sorry that your relationship with Monica didn't work out. I'm afraid the war has got in the way of many things. If Joyce had got away on the 12th February who knows we may have been able to make it work although I suspect she would have wanted to reside in England and I am very much camped on this Island.

I was up at KL about three weeks ago. The place is a bit of a mess but at least standing. I had difficulty in tracing any of the clerks or the Mukerjees; Mulhandra Singh was put into a forced labour battalion, and I understand died building a railway in Burma. Only Mr Mukerjee is alive but in a frail state; Mrs Mukerjee died in 1943. The bungalow up at Racecourse Road is in a sorry state. From what I can see the Japs used it as an officer relaxation centre with a number of Chinese and Eurasian girls. I hope that Peter pulls it down as the memories of what went on there is too horrible to contemplate. Try as I might I have been unable to find any trace of

Mrs Clemence. Jim died in a camp in Taiping in 1945 and I think Mrs Clemence ended up in a camp for women near Khota Lipis but there are no records, only the memories of the few women who survived and they are certainly not consistent. We may never know. Fred Samuels died fighting the Japs on the Island. I think it must have been on the 14th February. I'm told his unit was rushed over to Keppel Road to shore up the Malay Regiment and that there was literally hand to hand fighting. There's no record of him having been taken prisoner.

Stuart survived although not in the camp I was in. He in fact was in the same unit as Cedric fighting over towards the reservoirs and Cedric died of his wounds a few days after the surrender. Stuart used his brains and lied and said he was a mechanic so the Japs put him in a camp on Adam Road on the Island and he worked with a friend of mine, Laz, who I can't remember whether you met? The Japs put them to work repairing engines for the Jap army and repairing the ships that had been sunk in Kings Dock. Thankfully both survived. Stuart is back in Australia and Laz has only recently been released from hospital and has set off home on the SS Empire Trooper. I missed seeing him off which is a great shame.

Frank was with you on the Tenedos so you know that part of the story. From what I'm told by Jai Lee Kwan, Frank was furious at the Aussies locking up Jai Lee Kwan and his son, but he got nowhere. It was only after Chang Kai Chek's delegation visited

MacArthur in 1943 that strings were pulled and they were released. Their gold is still in the Union's vaults in Sydney and the Australian Government is unwilling to have it released. I saw Jai Lee Kwan's son a few weeks ago, who has returned now to the Island; he is working with the Kuomintang Party, and he was still very angry saying he would not forget the treatment. Kenneth Chen is now something important in the Party. Sadly, I think Abilash died in early 1945 when the Japs were forcing the male population to dig trenches in preparation for an invasion by the Allies. I think that is all the news from this end.

Anyway, I hope all is well in Manchester and the Boddington's is as good as ever. Please keep in touch.

Chapter 20

Robert sat between David Masters and Leanne Masters at the dinner table. Christmas Day with friends and family was a day that many could only dream of, a few months ago. Robert had managed to get an enormous turkey from his American friends at Kellang airbase and Henry had found fresh vegetables from another source and the meal was augmented with a large chicken from Chunggy's secret supplier. The result was that there was ample food for the gathering. Mona had borrowed tables from the church and had set them up outside in the garden where more than twenty family and friends ate and drank and thanked God, they had survived the war.

David Masters had arrived back in Singapore only a few days before, with his wife, Susie, after a long spell in hospital in Colombo although Susie's daughters, Leanne and Rebecca, had come back some weeks before to work at the South Asia Shipping Company in Rebecca's case and Leanne was now at the General Hospital having completed her nursing qualifications in Colombo. Alex, Susie's son, who had been interned with his stepfather, David, for three years in a camp in Sumatra, had after a great deal of persuasion from Robert sailed to Ceylon in October and from there, with again a little persuasion, this time from David and Susie, onto London, to take up the offer of a student place at LSE.

A still not very well David sat quietly, watching the crowd in front of him talking and enjoying their freedom. "So young man I hear you have been extraordinarily busy. Henry was telling me that Sir Shenton and the First Secretary are worried you are going to find a mound of gold and not tell them."

Robert smiled at David and then said in a grave voice above all the noise from guests, who were getting into the spirit of the party, "Not now David. There may be prying ears listening in on our conversation. Let's just say I am in demand."

Leanne who had been half listening as she watched her sister talking animatedly to someone she couldn't see, turned to Robert. "I didn't hear all what you said to daddy. Did you say you are in danger?" She sounded quite concerned.

Robert laughed off Leanne's concern as he took another fork of food. Finishing the mouthful of food he replied to a patient Leanne, "I told the First Secretary that if I do find some gold it will go towards the surgery to get my face sorted." Robert turned to David. "You can imagine what reaction that got. Fraser has absolutely no sense of humour. He took it so seriously and said he would me have arrested, even though the gold according to the Government doesn't exist and if it does it is not the property of the Singapore Government and is probably the property of the China Bank."

David Masters, looking pale and thin, laughed at what Robert was saying as in front of them people refilled their plates from the buffet that had been laid out. It looked like Susie and Joan Cramond were organising fresh bowls of salad with the help of a very harassed young Indian maid. Henry was going around doing a sterling job with bottles of wine and refilling glasses. Robert saw Brian emerge from behind the house with Chunggy carrying more food. Over the noise David said something about Robert having the dark art and it was Leanne who said, "Well I don't like the thought of you being in danger. You need to be careful."

As they sat enjoying the extended lunch under the makeshift canopy that Brian and Chunggy had set up the day before, Robert could see Chunggy in the background now helping Mona to carry out a giant frozen ice cream that had been delivered only an hour before from Kellang airbase. Robert started smiling to himself over his negotiations for the giant turkey and the ice cream which to everyone's amusement had turned up also in the shape of a turkey. As far as Robert could make out Chunggy now helped by Brian was using a hammer and chisel to break up the frozen turkey. It had taken a bit of persuading Chunggy, who seemed to have entered into the spirit of the day, that he would be needed at the party and Robert suspected he had only relented when Mona descended on him a few days ago.

Leanne who had disappeared for a while returned and sat down beside Robert. "So what surgery are you to have? " She knew that Dr Morton was treating Robert because she had seen Robert at the hospital only a few days before. Since her return to Singapore Robert had seen her and Rebecca on a number of occasions trying to help them get the Masters' flat in Cathay House habitable for David and Susie, and he had taken the girls out to parties.

Robert looked at her. "Dr Morton has suggested I go to the States to have some surgery on my face. He has also recommended that I have my toes broken and reset but I've told him that everything will have to wait until after the War Tribunals starting in March as I have been asked to give evidence at some of the trials. In fact, Neil Forsyth, Rob Scott and I have been invited over to Rempang Island to see the war criminals they have so far collared. There's also quite a few in Changi prison and Neil and I saw them yesterday. They're mostly the ones being sent to Japan for trial."

Leanne was shuddering as Robert was telling her about the Japs. "Horrible. What they did to you and daddy it's just too horrible to think about. I'll never forgive them." Leanne turned to face Robert fully. "Can I change the subject, Bob. I want to ask if you know of any property where Rebecca and I could stay. The flat in Cathay House is too small for all of us. Anyway, we want a place of our own and I have permission from Matron to stay in private lodgings."

Robert nodded at what she had asked. "It so happens I have a trust property that needs a lick of paint, at the east end of Beach Road. The property next to it is bomb damaged and will need a good deal of repair. I may buy it if the price is right so there will be some noise from the builders, but the trust property is lovely although it is rather large. You might be better off if you get a third person to share. It will work out much cheaper for you rent wise."

Nigel Renshaw came over as they were talking. "Bob, I'm not interrupting anything am I. I just wanted to thank you for getting me an invitation. Great party." He was looking at both Robert and Leanne as he spoke.

Robert laughed at Nigel. It was obvious that he wanted an introduction to the attractive brunette on his right. "My pleasure Nigel. We couldn't have you sitting in your room with a tin of bully and a warm beer. Oh, you two haven't met. Nigel Renshaw meet Leanne Masters. You two have a natter while I try some of the amazing turkey just being served up."

When Robert left later that evening there was still a dozen friends sitting dotted around the garden enjoying the cooling breeze, quietly talking. After the meal Henry had said a few words to the gathering and then sprung a surprise. "Now ladies and gentlemen, I think it is incumbent on our LDC leader to have the last word. More so because he has managed to find us two amazing turkeys." Robert was suddenly the centre of attention with three or four loud voices shouting "hear, hear" and most of the guests laughing at Henry's remark. It was something that everyone present wanted to share, a moment of reflection about the past four years. Even those like Nigel who had been spared the trials and tribulations of the past four years on the Island wanted to be part of the remembrance.

Robert got his feet and looked around the friends and family who had somehow ended up at Henry and Mona's house. He started by saying "I haven't anything prepared, I wasn't expecting this." He paused for a moment and looked around. "What I want to say is that I am so happy to be here today. Somehow, we have survived these past four years. I am so happy that we have Brian back safe and sound. I gather Martin will also be here in the next few days. From the few minutes I have had with Brian it seems that both he and Martin had some hairy moments in the Burmese jungle and it's just wonderful to know they are safe. "There were murmurs of" hear, hear" as Robert continued. "The same must be said of David and Susie, and their two lovely daughters who by all accounts are already helping greatly to get us back on our feet. For those of us who did our time in the camps I think all I can say is that we survived but let us never forget the friends we left behind. Nor indeed the friends that we lost trying to escape from the Island nearly four years ago." Robert continued looking around and speaking about each of the families and friends present until all of them had been included. Robert could see Henry giving Mona a hug as she whispered something to him; she was crying.

"Can I ask you to raise our glasses to our friends who are not with us. To those who we may see again and those who we will always remember." Robert looked around his friends as he raised his glass. "I have no family, but I have the next nearest thing, some wonderful friends." Leanne standing next to him squeezed his arm.

In later years when Robert thought back to what he had said he cringed at the sentimentality but at the time it was just right. He meant it and his friends, who believed in him, who supported him and who loved him, respected the words he said. But Robert being Robert had to have a final word.

"To Brian I only add that we have had too many holidays and now we have to get down to some hard work because life will not be the same. Many changes are coming, and we have no time for friends swanning off for hula hula holidays." At that Robert sat down with David and Leanne asking what he meant. There was a hoot of laughter from Henry and a smiling Brian. With much laughter Henry and Brian, by now shaking his head, spent the next few minutes explaining about the time they were in the LDC and how Robert had told Brian he had been on a holiday with hula hula girls and how Brian had believed him when in fact Robert had been in KL being bombed and strafed by the Japanese air force.

Chapter 21

Robert stood on the tarmac at Kellang airbase beside Henry and Mona along with a crowd of perhaps fifty very excited people peering through the mesh fence that separated them from the runway. It was very hot with the sun beating off the ground and with little humidity. The women looked cooler in their floral dresses and large shady hats, but the men looked decidedly less comfortable in their suits. The crowd could see the plane circling and coming in over the sea and gradually grow in size so that they could at last make out the markings on the side of the fuselage. For many of them it so exciting to be so close to the large plane.

Peter was one of the first off the plane, almost bounding down the steps and shaking hands with the senior steward before setting off for the hangar which served as a terminal. He heard Henry shouting from the fence, perhaps fifty yards away, and he looked across and waved. "Come on let's go inside and wait for him to go through customs," Henry said to Mona and Robert.

Henry and Mona set off inside, but Robert took his time knowing full well that it would be at least a half hour before Peter had collected his luggage and was through customs. Inside the building Robert saw a soda stand had been set up by some enterprising American and he went off and bought himself a soft drink. Finishing his drink, he wandered across to where Henry and Mona were waiting with a crowd that had grown to perhaps a hundred people. As they waited, they could hear another plane taking off. At last people started to emerge through the arrival gate and excited people ran up to welcome them. Peter emerged looking older and greyer but still Peter. Mona couldn't wait and hitching up her sari she ran the few yards between them and hugged him much to Henry's amusement. Peter and Henry just shook hands grinning like two Cheshire cats. Finally, Peter turned and looked at Robert. "Well young man you have been in the wars." He shook Robert's hand giving it a good squeeze.

Robert had hired a car from the Australian dealership that had just opened for business on Hill Street on the pretext that he may buy it but as he didn't drive Henry got in the driver's seat. Mona was chattering away to Peter as Robert got in beside Henry leaving Peter and Mona to get in the back. Henry smiled at Robert both knowing that any conversation with Peter would have to wait. "We've put you up at a hotel on Orchard Road for a few days until you decide what you want. The Goodwood has just closed for urgent repairs and Raffles is still being used as a repatriation centre, " Henry shouted after they had been driving for about ten minutes and Mona had momentarily run out of steam. "Robert managed to get us this car as all our cars have disappeared." Peter nodded as he listened to Mona who had started up again this time chattering about the boys and what they had done since they had got home, in Brian's case four weeks ago and Martin on the 28th December.

Going down Serangoon Road Peter leant forward and tapped Henry on the shoulder. "Any chance you could just drive round by the Padang and over Anderson Bridge on the way, just for old times."

The two in the front laughed at the request but it was Mona who said, "They had bets you would ask to go round that way."

In Fullerton Square, Henry pulled up beside the Fullerton Building, opposite the bank. Looking across they could see that the doors were open with a resplendent Mr Gupta standing outside in a uniform and turban. Robert turned to Peter, "You can go in you know, boss. I think they would be very disappointed if you don't."

Peter looked at a very different Robert from the one he had known four years ago. Getting out he just said he wouldn't be long; Robert waited a few seconds and then got out of the car and followed him, with Henry and Mona trailing behind. At the doors to the bank, Mr Gupta came to attention, at Peter's approach and said, "Welcome back, sir", with the most enormous smile.

Peter said thank you and walked into the building to be received by a crowd of clapping people. He was quite overwhelmed. So many faces he recognised, so many who looked older. For the next few minutes, he went round shaking hands and just talking to clerks who he had worked with for years before the war. It was after this had gone on for quite a few minutes that Colin Worriston, himself newly arrived only the week before, clapped his hands. "As a newcomer on the block I don't want to spoil the party, but we will all get a chance to meet and talk to Mr Connaught tomorrow night. I know that the Prestons' and Mr Draper want to spirit him off to have a rest after his long flight. Do you want to say anything, Mr Connaught?"

Peter quite overcome by the welcome just said he was looking forward to working with them all in making a success of the bank and with a wave of his arm he let Robert lead him out of the bank into the sunshine. "You so and so. I didn't expect that."

"You would have done it for me. Anyway, they couldn't wait to see you. Some of them would have stormed the hotel if we hadn't brought you in."

"Now you're going over the top," Peter said as he helped Mona get back in the car before sliding in beside her. "Anyway, where did you get this open top. I should think even Sir Shenton doesn't rate this model."

Henry laughed and replied for Robert. "You are talking to Mr Big, Peter. He's the future. He's buying real estate all over the place. Half the Island think he's found the missing gold and using it. Certainly, the First Secretary does."

Robert waved arm in the air and shouted above the noise of the car engine starting up. "It's not true, Peter. I've bought three bomb damaged properties for a song. The other properties are owned by the Lin Yuen Trust. "

Mona not to be left out added her pennyworth. "Bob got us the most enormous turkey for Christmas flown in from America and a giant turkey ice cream."

Peter started to wilt under the barrage of information with the car slowing to a crawl in Chinatown. "I need a drink. A strong one after the last hour"

"All arranged, "Henry shouted back as the car speeded up out of Chinatown and made its way towards Tanglin Road.

As they got out in the drive of Henry and Mona's home Peter turned to Robert. "Have you arranged meetings for me?"

"From tomorrow in the bank with Colin, Nigel Renshaw and Mathew Craig. Laurie Tomlinson should arrive on Monday. The bank staff have laid on a party for you tomorrow night at the *Mata Hari.* I think Colin wanted something a bit more splendid, but the staff wanted something a bit more informal and the *Mata Hari* has just been refurbished which is more that you can say for most places."

As they sat on the balcony looking out over towards the Kings Dock, Robert finished what he was telling Peter. "Sir Shenton has invited you to a dinner on Saturday evening. The rumour is he will be announcing his retirement." Looking at a smiling Henry, Robert added, "The Chief Station Master and his lovely wife will also be attending the reception."

Peter turned to Henry and to Mona who had just returned from the kitchen. "This is great news. Thoroughly deserved. "

The little Indian girl came in with a tray of drinks and Henry poured large scotches into three glasses. Mona's drink was already on the tray. Picking up the glasses he handed them round. "Here's to the future.

Chapter 22

Singapore in the first half of 1946 was still very much an Island in turmoil. Since the Japanese had capitulated in August 1945 more than 250,000 Japanese troops had surrendered in the Malay States, Singapore, Sumatra and Borneo with the majority of them being accommodated at one time or another, on Rempang Island, about twenty miles south of Singapore. As many of the Japanese were transported via Singapore this caused great concern when civilians saw large numbers of Japanese marching through the city. More than six months after the formal surrender of the Japanese army small groups of Japanese soldiers, on occasions even groups of some hundreds, would emerge from the jungle causing a great deal of alarm.

The turmoil made it necessary to have large numbers of Allied troops stationed in the Malay States; troops that really didn't care about the situation in the Malay States or Singapore, the war was over, and they just wanted to go home. The Americans were seen in ever greater numbers with a large air force unit based at Kellang aerodrome, and often an enormous naval presence.

The small British community were now dependent on American resources and definitely no longer top dog. The Chinese community was large but muted, still recovering from the terrible losses it had suffered at the hands of the Japanese whereas the Indian community was highly vocal demanding that Britain agrees to independence for India.

Chaos always creates an opportunity for factions to take advantage of the situation and in these first few months after the Japanese surrender the communists rapidly grew in confidence causing disruption whenever they could and generally trying to intimidate the dispirited resident population.

The Island was still showing a great deal of war damage caused by the fighting in 1941-1942 and it was only very slowly that commerce was able to start up; the many shops or thousands of little factories that were dotted over the Island had nothing to sell or make.

Robert therefore spent a great deal of his time in the early months of 1946 helping Peter Connaught to get the Union & China Bank to become operational although he no longer worked for the bank as an employee. Peter recognising that Robert was now happier working independently had asked him to help the new managers as they arrived to settle into life on the Island and later on, he asked him to go up to KL and Penang to assist the new managers in getting the bank trading again. Preparation for the Military Tribunals dealing with war crimes occupied Robert's time with him to be involved in the trials of Captain Ishiguru, Colonel Sumida and Sergeant Sato.

It was just before Robert had to give evidence at the War Crimes Tribunal that Robert had sat with David Masters one Sunday morning in his garden and they had agreed that David was not up to going into partnership with Robert as his health was still very poor; Susie had privately said to Robert that she doubted that David would ever be able to work again. What they did agree was that David would be a great ambassador with all his connections and Robert was thankful for this help.

It was in March 1946 that Robert received an invitation to a garden party to be held by the Sultan of Johor at his palace over the causeway. David and Susie had also received invitations and Robert arranged for them to go with him. He certainly needed the break as he had been preparing for the trials of Ishiguru and Samida starting the following week and he was feeling exhausted. It was therefore on a beautiful late hot sunny morning that Robert in his new car driven by his new driver, Bin Lau, had set off to the function at the Sultan's Palace with David and Susie, and Leanne, sat in the back. Susie had told him that the Sultan disliked single men attending the functions and she suggested that Leanne should partner Robert who thought this was an excellent arrangement.

Bin Lau drove the car towards the causeway leading to Johor with Robert sitting quietly and the three in the back chattering about everyday life. The sun was particularly hot with the ladies wearing hats to keep the sun off and at Susie's insistence David was sitting between them under a parasol that had been procured from Chunggy. Robert presumed it must be an old one of Mrs Lin Yuen.

It was as they approached the causeway that Bin Lau spoke. "I'm sorry boss but I think we need some petrol. There's a garage just up on the right. I'll stop and get a few gallons. I'll only be a few minutes."

Bin Lau was the son of one of the bank's clerks who had worked with Robert in Fullerton Square and when Bin Lau had turned up looking for a job Robert knew instantly that this was somebody he could trust. Better still he could drive. Robert just nodded at what Bin Lau said and turned to say something to those in the back.

Bin Lau only a few minutes later stopped and indicated to go right waiting for a gap in the traffic. Robert looked across at the garage which he had never noticed before. It had seen better days and as Bin Lau drove in behind another car that was preparing to leave from one of the two petrol pumps, he saw an old sign, *"Causeway Garage. Proprietors: Jai Shu Lai and Tan Choo Sin"* leaning against the shop wall. If they had not stopped for petrol, he might never have seen it.

"What's wrong, Bob?" he heard someone say. The voice seemed miles away. The question was repeated, and this time Robert turned around and answered.

"I've just seen a name that I've come across before. Excuse me a minute." Robert got out of the car and walked over to the shop. He came out a few minutes later and walked back to the car.

Bin Lau finished filling the car with petrol and got back in the car. "All done, boss. "He stopped what he was about to say and looked at Robert. "You Okay, boss?"

"Tomorrow you and I are coming up to this garage. I think I have been looking in the wrong place".

It was Leanne who leant forward and touching Robert on the shoulder said, "Let's go, Bob. I have a feeling it's about the gold you're always looking for. We're late as it is."

The Party at the Sultan's Palace was a wonderful affair with dozens of friends also at the luncheon and a setting overlooking Singapore Island that was difficult to take in. Robert forgot for the rest of the day what he had seen and immersed himself in the surroundings and with his friends.

****

Bin Lau parked the car at the side of the garage. It was late morning, and the sun was beating down with a drowsiness in the air that suggested rain later. Robert noticed when they arrived that the sign was still leaning against the shop wall.

Grahame Kerr

On the way up to the causeway Robert had suggested that Bin Lau should go into the shop and browse the few items on the shelves and then make some casual enquiries as to whether the business had been owned by Tan Choo Sin and whether any of the workers who worked there, had worked for him during the occupation. Robert had put Bin Lau fully in the picture with regard to his investigations just in case there should any threats and Bin Lau had merely shrugged after Robert had given him the story. "We just have to careful, boss. Both the communists and the Kuomintang are as bad as each other."

As Bin Lau walked into the shop Robert strolled around the back of the wooden building that served both as shop and office for the business to find a large repair yard with workshops opposite the back of the shop. Behind the workshops he could see what looked like workers houses, each built on stilts with washing hanging from trees and two or three small children playing in the dirt under one of the houses. To one side of the repair yard Robert could see a number of lorries parked. The workshops were busy, but no one approached him as he walked towards the end of the yard. He walked slowly watching the mechanics repairing three cars including one with an official number plate. When he reached the end of the yard, he half turned to walk back but then he stopped. Hidden away at the side of the building he saw a car; standing next to the car was a Chinese driver smoking a cigarette. He had his back to Robert who turned around immediately and walked back the way he had come.

Bin Lau was already back at the car gesturing at him. When he got close enough Bin Lau said, "Shee Yang Chen is in there, sitting in the office, with the manager. Do you know him?"

Robert nodded. "I know him. He has made it big since last September buying up property and a godown near the Roche Canal. He seems to have a lot of influence with the Chinese community and the High Commissioner has invited him to attend the security committee he has set up to deal with the communist problem. I was invited to the last meeting. Quite a few are asking where he got his money." As Bin Lau drove off towards Singapore city Robert added, "I saw his car. For some reason it's hidden behind the repair workshop. Let's get out of here and have a think about it."

About half a mile down the road Robert said, "Turn back towards the causeway and see if there's somewhere where we can watch the garage. When Shee Yang Chen goes, we will go back." Bin Lau just nodded and turned the car back at the next junction.

It was perhaps twenty minutes later that they saw Shee Yang Chen leave, being driven towards the city.

"I find it a bit of a coincidence that we should see Shee Yang Chen at this garage, Bin Lau", Robert said, "especially with his car hidden away. I would like to know his connection to Tan Choo Sin. I'm already suspicious, as are a number of people, as to how he managed to become such a successful businessman during the occupation." Bin Lau just nodded.

They waited a few more minutes watching customers drive in to get petrol and one car drive round behind the garage presumably to the repair workshop.

"Let's try again, Bin Lau. This time I will go in. You get ready to leave quickly. I just have a feeling about this place."

About ten minutes later Robert walked into the garage whilst Bin Lau stood beside the car which he had parked away from the pumps. A Chinese attendant had come across to ask if he wanted petrol, but Bin Lau said that they didn't need anything.

The inside of the garage shop was old with shelves that looked as though they had housed everything for every conceivable emergency, but they stood largely empty now. What stock there was looked as though it had been there for years. A middle-aged Chinese woman in traditional black was at a small counter serving a Malay truck driver but Robert quickly looking around ignored them and walked over to the little office where he could see an old man working with the accounts.

"Jai Shu Lai?"

The old man looked up and shook his head. "Jai Shu Lai is dead. What do you want?

"His name is on the board outside as the owner. If he is dead who owns the business. I want to speak to the person who owns this business. I know that Tan Choo Sin is dead."

"Jai Shu Lai and Tan Choo Sin both died in the war. The Japanese killed them."

"Then who owns the business now?"

The old man looked at Robert saying nothing, just sucking at his cigarette.

Robert spoke in Cantonese. "Look, I either get his name now or I call the police and have this place raided." Robert had not a clue for what, but he would worry about that later.

"Shee Yang Chen takes an interest."

"You mean he owns it."

"He paid Tan Choo Sin's widow some money; Jai Shu Lai had no family."

"When did he buy it?"

"Just after the Japanese killed Tan Choo Sin."

Robert moved round the little office intending to look through the little internal window into the shop. As he was asking his questions, he saw photographs that were hanging on the wall behind the door he had come through. Robert peered at them more closely as he asked the old man, "Do you still have workers here who were employed when Jai Shu Lai and Tan Choo Sin were in charge?"

The old man shook his head. "No. They came from Jai Shu Lai's village in Hainan and returned there after the war."

"Were you here during the war?"

Robert turned back to the old man as he said it and saw him nod at the question. "One of your workers was killed when he delivered a parcel to the Batu Caves in 1942."

The old man stubbed out his cigarette and took another from a packet on the desk. He said nothing just taking his time lighting it before he answered. "He died with others when the Japanese killed them."

"How do you know this?"

"I have been here many years. I was told." As he said this the Chinese woman came into the office and in Cantonese asked what was going on. Before the old man could answer Robert said "I have come to find a man."

The Chinese woman looked puzzled at first and then said to the old man in Cantonese, "Say nothing or Shee Yang Chen will be angry."

Robert said back in Cantonese, "You will find my anger to be as great. Now tell me about Lai Tek and Shee Yang Chen. And tell me who told you that the driver was killed at the Batu Caves?"

The old man got up hurriedly and started yelling. A customer who had come into the shop started shouting what was wrong and why was there yelling. Then the Chinese woman skittled off to the back of the shop starting to shout. Robert realising that nothing more could be gained turned around; he hurried out of the office and through the shop into the bright sunlight. He could hear more urgent shouting at the back in the repair yard and signalling Bin Lau he ran across to the car. "Let's get out of here. We have found a hornet's nest.

Chapter 23

"Mr Draper," the military policeman shouted down the corridor of the Justice Building. Robert stood up and followed the soldier into one of the court rooms now being used as a military tribunal. Briefly looking around as he limped into the room, working his way towards the table and chair that had been set aside for witnesses, he saw that cameras and recording equipment had been set up on his left behind two officers who were seated at two desks Over to his right he could see a number of Japanese officers sitting ringed by military police. The MP stopped at the table and ushered Robert behind it and asked him to remain standing.

Robert looked in front of him and saw a panel of five men, four in uniform and a civilian, a lawyer, he presumed, on the left of the group. The Brigadier chairing the panel asked him to take the oath and then invited Robert to sit down. To Robert, who had never been in a court before, it all seemed very strange, and he was still getting used to the surroundings when one of the officers sat at the desks stood up and addressed him.

"Mr Draper, good morning" Seeing Robert nod the officer continued. "Mr Draper, I am the prosecuting officer on these matters, and I will be asking you questions and Major Dennis, sitting on my left, may at some point be asking questions on behalf of the Japanese officers in court today. Would you please address your answers to Brigadier Lowther and the panel. There is water for you on the table but if you should need more or need a short break, please make such a request to Brigadier Lowther. The members of the panel or their legal adviser may also have questions at some point. As Robert looked at the prosecuting officer, he could see a name plaque on his desk with "Major Balfour." Behind Robert was a small audience and when he had looked around on sitting down, he had recognised Rob Scott, a fellow internee.

The questions at the start were merely confirming the early events before the Island surrendered on 15 February 1942. Robert confirmed that he had worked at the Union & China Bank in Fullerton Square and had been the Team Leader, at least that's what Robert called himself, of the Local Defence Unit based in Tanglin from January 1942. Asked about when he had first come to the Island he explained that he had been on the Island exactly two years at the time of the surrender.

"Take us through those early days after the surrender, Mr Draper. What was your involvement?"

"I wasn't involved in it too much. I became a fatigues organiser on the 16th February and with two other internees I collected mattresses and mosquito nets and other such goods for the women internees. I was given a permit by the Japanese to go and collect goods and we were given a lorry. We were all required to be registered with the Japanese on the 17th. In the building next door to be precise. All Europeans had to register at the Municipal Building or at Raffles Hotel. It was when I told the registration officer that I was a banker that things went wrong. I was immediately taken into another chamber for interrogation. It was a room at the other side of the central committee chamber." As Robert looked at the panel, he waved his right arm in the direction of the next building.

"Tell us what happened, Mr Draper."

"A guard pushed me into an outer room, and I sat there for an hour or so. I tried speaking to Ash Cooper who was sat over to my right, but a guard hit me on my back with his rifle and told me that I mustn't talk. Ash, I think he was injured because he didn't turn to me when I spoke to him. There was also another man in front of me, but I didn't see his face. I think it was Mr Springfield from the Overseas Mutual Bank but I can't be certain and when I later enquired no one had seen him since he entered the Municipal Building on 17th February, nor since. Ash was taken out about half an hour later and then the man in front of me a little later. I haven't seen Ash since the 17th February; he wasn't in any of the camps on the Island because I was responsible for the collection of all the names of internees. In fact, we collected the names until late last October using a room in the next building.

Major Balfour was nodding at the information. "Thank you, Mr Draper. Now tell us about your interrogation. Who conducted the interview?

Robert answered, "Captain Ishiguru of the Kempetai Military Police."

"Do you see him in this room?"

Robert looked across at the Japanese officers, perhaps a dozen of them. Some of them had earphones on but Captain Ishiguru was sat looking totally disinterested. Robert pointed him out.

"Are you sure this is the man?"

"I am."

"Thank you, Mr Draper. Now we have a typewritten statement before us which I understand you prepared in Changi prison when you were interned. It is on the table in front of you. Please look at it and tell the panel if this is your statement."

Robert looked at the typed document on the table which went for about twenty pages. He looked at the signature on the last page; it was his. "Yes, this is my statement."

"Mr Draper, it would assist the panel if we could examine in greater detail the actual interrogation in the Municipal Building; your statement does detail what happened and that the guards hit you a number of times with their rifle butts and that you saw Captain Ishiguru signal them on a couple of occasions to hit you. The reason for the interrogation was because Captain Ishiguru was looking for gold. Is that right?"

Robert took that as his cue and reiterated what was in the statement and added that he had been hit perhaps a half dozen times, on one occasion being concussed by a blow to the head. He remembered that he had been dragged back onto the chair but as he had said in his statement, he couldn't remember how many men had helped him onto the chair. Robert then reiterated the range of questions that had been put to him and that Captain Ishiguru kept warning him that unless he gave the information the Japanese wanted that he could forfeit his life. From a question from Major Balfour, Robert explained about Captain Ishiguru warning him that he should take no notice of the noise from the man in the corner, under a large committee table, who was moaning and obviously in a great deal of pain.

Brigadier Lowther interrupted and asked Robert, "How far were you from this man?"

"About fifteen feet, sir. He was on the far side of the table. He seemed to be wedged down the back and just kept moaning, more like a whimper."

"Could you see him, Mr Draper, to identify?"

Robert shook his head. "As I said in my statement, I think he had a bald head, but I only saw the top of his head when the guards threw me out into the corridor."

"Is it likely it was the same man who sat in front of you before your interrogation?" Major Balfour asked.

"No, it wasn't the same man." Robert continued after a pause. He noticed as he momentarily stopped speaking that at least two of the Japanese officers seemed to be asleep. "I spoke to Geoffrey Blackmore about three weeks later and he said that two senior Colonial Government officers, the Head of Treasury and the Head of the Mint had both gone missing, and when I described the man under the table as having a bald head Geoffrey said he thought it was probably Lawrence Charters, who was Head of the Mint. I understand from subsequent discussions with Geoffrey that both men were not seen again, after the 17th, and I have found no record of them in other camps.

Major Balfour asked, "Who is Geoffrey Blackmore?"

"Geoffrey was one of the senior assistants to the Governor and was for a time the leader of the Civilian Internment Committee in Changi."

Major Balfour continued his questions, "Mr Draper, why would these men have been of interest to the Japanese?"

Robert looked a little surprised at the question and then answered. "The Head of the Mint would have been keeper of the plates for printing new money and presumably the Japanese would have liked to get their hands on them so they could print money. As for the Head of Treasury he was responsible for all the currency held by the Island and by the Malay States. He would have some idea of the amount of gold that had been on the Island at the time of surrender and what had been shipped out."

"In your work did you have dealings with these men?"

Robert shook his head. "No. I only knew of them. When I assisted in boxing all the gold on the Island, towards the end of January 1942, I remember numbering the boxes and giving a tally of the boxes to Mr Levy, of the Hong Kong Bank, who was charged with coordinating the collection of the gold on the Island for shipment.

"Why Mr Levy and not the Head of Treasury?"

"Mr Levy told me that Mr Carragher, the Head of Treasury was unwell, and the First Secretary was short staffed so had asked the banks to help. Mr Levy ended up with the job of collecting the gold in one place. At a meeting of the banks, it was decided that I should be involved because I had been able to get the gold down from KL and had a good understanding of the problems in shipping a large amount under war conditions."

A Meeting Under A Banyan Tree

"Do you know how much was involved, Mr Draper?"

Robert smiled across at Major Balfour and then said, "I was a banker. I wanted to know the size of the problem and the value. I did do a tally of the amounts held in each box as we collected from the various banks, and I know that it came to more than forty-seven million Straits dollars and that there was also more than two million in US dollars. The money was piled in boxes in the vaults and corridors of the Union and China. I was not privy though to the arrangements for getting the gold away to Australia. I managed to get down to the Kings Dock on 5th February to see some gold being loaded onto tenders to go out to the *HMS Tenedos,* but I did not count the boxes. In fact, I arrived about halfway through the operation as I had been working with the LDU up in China Town, from memory, removing bomb damage. I only learnt of the decision to ship it out at the last moment and had to get down to the docks in a bit of a rush. I had really gone down to say goodbye to colleagues who I knew were going with the shipment. I did say later to Mr Levy who was there that I had thought there was more bullion than had been put on the tenders and I remember that he had just said that it must be my imagination and not to get involved."

"You say in your statement that Captain Ishiguru seemed to know that gold had been left on the Island. Did he accept that you did not know of its whereabouts?"

"No, sir. He said at the end my interrogation that he knew where I was, and he would check out what I had said. I just kept telling him that as far as I was concerned that all the gold had been transported to Australia and that I was too unimportant to know of any hidden gold. He said he did not believe me because I had been in charge of getting the gold out of KL. That was not actually true. It just so happened that I was Acting Manager of our branch in KL and I managed to get what gold that was left in KL out with a small reserve company of soldiers. The Japanese somehow knew about the gold that had been kept back on the Island. I will always believe that they had inside information." Robert gave the Tribunal more detail about the gold that he and colleagues had managed to get down to Singapore just before the Japanese had captured KL and how it had been mainly gold coinage.

Brigadier Lowther interrupted the proceedings. "I think we should adjourn at this point, Major Balfour" With that the panel rose and exited to the left through a doorway that had been opened for them by an MP. Robert stood beside the table feeling exhausted after hours of giving evidence, not sure what to do next and then an MP came up to him. "Follow me, sir. We have a room for you."

After a lunch of tea and some sandwiches supplied by an MP, Robert returned to the court room and resumed giving his evidence.

"Tell us more about what happened after your interrogation in the Municipal Building."

"I collapsed outside on the steps and two internees helped me across the road and I was looked after by friends from the Tanglin LDU. I started a fever and don't remember very much for the next two to three weeks. I do remember that we were placed in a temporary holding camp in a local jail and then we were marched, about 2500 of us, up to Changi prison. I was wounded on 8th February in my left arm, and it caused some discomfort for some weeks and that plus the beating I had from Captain Ishiguru's men and then a touch of fever and really those first few months were all a bit of a haze."

Robert stopped at that point and Major Balfour looked up from where he had been sitting. "Please continue."

"The *Kempetai* came for me again I suppose about two months after I had been in Changi. They took me with two other internees to the YMCA on Orchard Road. One of the two men with me was the General Manager of the Shell installation; I knew him slightly as the bank dealt with their account.

"I was made to strip, and I was put in a cell. I think now although I didn't know it at the time that all the people in the cell where people Captain Ishiguru was interrogating about the gold."

"Can you tell us who was there?"

"Maurice Levy was there. He was a banker with Hong Kong Bank. Rachel Knowles. She was the wife of a Chinese pharmacist.

Both of them had been badly beaten. Maurice was so badly beaten around his face that I did not recognise him at first. In fact, I think he also had a broken arm and in the time I was in the cell with him he was unable to speak and I am not sure he was conscious for much of the time. Not that we were allowed to talk; we just managed a few whispered words when the Indian guard was outside the cell. It was obvious that Maurice was dying. He was unable to take food and water and was unable to move. They dragged him out of the cell not long after I was put in the cell, presumably for more interrogation. He never returned after the second day. Rachel Knowles was stripped to her pants. Her face was swollen and badly bruised, and her chest and arms had cuts and swellings. One of her hands was crusted in blood and I think they had removed her nails. On the third or fourth day the man opposite who kept swaying and muttering to himself, he didn't return, and I later learnt from Rob Scott, who has given evidence to you already, that he was the chief officer in the Assay Office. There was a man next to me who I never saw properly because we were not allowed to turn round, only to look straight ahead. He was also taken out at the end of the second day and never returned. I couldn't identify him but Geoffrey Blackmore when I spoke to him some time later suggested it could have been someone called Ronnie Millar who worked in the Colonial Office; I understand that he was to do with intelligence work and often was the link with the communists and the trade unions on the Island."

"Your statement deals with the days of interrogation. Do you wish to add anything about the ordeal?"

"Just to say I think I was one of the lucky ones. The others in that room clearly did not survive. Nor did Ernest Beverley, or Jai Shu Lee, the Chief Clerk at Hong Kong Bank. Patrick Freebody at the Mercantile, he died later at the hands of Colonel Sumida who took over the task of looking for the gold. There are others as well."

Brigadier Lowther interrupted Robert. "Try and deal only with events as they concern Captain Ishiguru. We will deal with Colonel Sumida at a later point."

Major Balfour continued, "What were the conditions like in the cells? You say you could not converse with your fellow inmates?"

Robert shook his head. "You were stripped to your underwear or a pair of shorts. You were made to sit on a rope netting about four feet off the floor. As I said you were not allowed to move or turn your body. You peed and defecated through the netting. The heat in the cells was overpowering as was the smell. There were flies all over you, but you were not allowed to move or remove them. We had an Indian cell warder who had a lathi stick which he used to hit you with if you moved around or spoke. You only whispered when he was out of the cell perhaps for a few seconds. The only person I ever managed to whisper to was Rachel Knowles."

"How long were you there?"

Robert shrugged his shoulders. "I can't be certain but at least two weeks, probably a bit longer. I was interrogated a number of times, certainly four times and at one of them Sergeant Sato ripped out the toenail from my big toe of my left foot; he used pliers. In doing so he broke my toes, and I will now have to have surgery although Dr Morton at the General has said that I must not pin my hopes too high on being able to walk without a limp. Captain Ishiguru at the last interrogation lost patience with me and told Sergeant Sato to deal with me. Sergeant Sato slashed my face with the pliers he used to remove my toenail."

One of the panel members said something to Brigadier Lowther and getting a nod from the Brigadier he turned to Robert and asked, "Did all these interrogations take place in the YMCA building?"

Robert nodded. "As I said in my statement the interrogations were always in the YMCA gymnasium. As I explained I was usually hung by my wrists from poles fastened to the wall but on the last occasion I was strapped to what I think was a hobby horse. The type they use for vaulting."

The officer nodded his thanks to Robert.

The prosecutor asked further questions about Robert's interrogations and then said, "Did you have further contact with Captain Ishiguru?"

"No, sir. I presumed he was transferred to another theatre of war and Colonel Sumida took over. I did not see Captain Ishiguru again until I went to Rempang Island where a number of us recognised him as a member of the *Kempetai*. He was pretending to be a Japanese infantry officer, but the military authorities were suspicious. I was invited along with Mr Scott and Superintendent Forsyth and a number of other internees to assist with the identity of possible war criminals. We just happened to be there on the day they pulled him out for questioning, and we were able to identify him."

Brigadier Lowther came in at that point. "It's getting late in the day, and we are having to deal with a great deal of noise from outside. I will adjourn this hearing until tomorrow morning. Mr Draper you remain on oath, and I ask you not to discuss your evidence with other parties this evening. Robert nodded at the Brigadier and stood up as the panel departed. The MP signalled for Robert to follow him, and an exhausted Robert walked out into the corridor where the prosecutor was standing talking to some military men. "Well done, Mr Draper. Your evidence has been very clear. I suggest you go home and have a stiff drink. Be here for nine tomorrow morning, please. The Brigadier wants to see if we have less noise if we start earlier."

Robert just nodded and went out into the sunlight where a journalist from the *Straits Times* was standing on the steps. "When this is all over would you be willing to be interviewed." Robert as he walked down the steps towards a waiting taxi just shouted back, "When the times right."

Chapter 24

Robert was picked up by a military jeep and driven to a new venue for the Military Tribunal and arriving at Changi Prison he felt even more *deja vu* than two days earlier when he had given evidence in the building next to where he had registered with the Japanese authorities on 17 February 1942, and where he had his first encounter with the *Kempetai*. The Tribunal chair had stopped proceedings before they had even commenced the previous day and insisted that it be moved to another venue because of the level of noise of traffic going down past the Justice Building. Who had thought up the idea of Changi Prison he did not know but Robert did know that the prison still held a large number of the Japanese men who were accused of war crimes.

On the way to Changi, he had seen squads of Japanese soldiers, many stripped to the waist, working on clearing war damaged sites. As he sped past them, he thought of his visit to Rempang Island four weeks ago. There he had seen thousands of Japanese troops building their own huts, cutting back the jungle to make vegetable plots, and digging endless long ditches as latrines. What had surprised him had been how few Allied troops there were around.

"They can't go anywhere, Mr Draper. We have given them garden tools and told them to get on with growing their own food, apart from us bringing in rice and medical supplies for them," the escorting officer had merely said to the question. Robert when he walked around one of the camps that had been built so far had been astonished at how the Japanese troops just seemed to accept their lot.

"Can't say we have even been involved in any disciplinary issues. Not that five officers and a few NCO's could do much," said the Major who was now taking Robert, Neil Forsyth and Rob Scott on a tour of one of the camps. Learning that all three spoke Japanese he had agreed to take them on a walk around and it was then that Robert saw Ishiguru along with other *Kempetai* officers being escorted by a Sergeant and Corporal to the Administration building for questioning.

The Major saw Robert and then Rob take an interest in the Japanese officers. "We are fairly sure these men are *Kempetai* as they seem to have false papers".

"I can't speak for the others but the one at the back is Captain Ishiguru. He speaks excellent English and was in charge of the YMCA on Orchard Road." Robert said it very quietly almost under his breath. Ishiguru had by now seen both Robert and Rob, but he made no sign of recognition and walked past them as though they did not exist.

The Major put his arm out to Rob as he started to say something. "Leave it for the Military Tribunal, gentlemen. Your identification was very fortuitous. I shall make sure the information is passed on. We intended for you to see a group of soldiers we are suspicious about and that's where they are going now, to an identity parade. Ishiguru is on our list of wanted criminals but with 150,000 prisoners on the Island; it's like finding a needle……." The Major didn't finish what he was saying and instead said, "One of our other visitors is also looking out for him for his crimes up at Taiping so hopefully he identifies him. At this time, we have thirty-one officers in the bag for the Tribunals in a few weeks' time and I think Major Drummond has around a hundred non- commissioned ranks identified as well."

Robert and Rob just nodded their heads in acknowledgement at the numbers as they watched Captain Ishiguru disappear into the Administration Building, both momentarily thinking of past events. The Major realising the importance to both men of seeing their old torturer knew they needed to be diverted. "Come on gentlemen, I think you have seen enough of this camp. It's far too hot out in the sun so let's go and complete the identity process and then we can have a drink. If you wish I can give you another short tour later. I know the Colonel also wants to brief you about military tribunal procedures before you leave the island. "

As they walked back to the Administration Building the Major said, "I think you have already met Colonel Wallace, Mr Draper. He tells me that you had a bit of a brush with Chin Peng. Nasty piece of work from what I hear so you did well to come away intact."

Robert said nothing and it was Rob Scott who said, "If you're ever in trouble Major make sure you're near Bob. He has a charmed life. You're guaranteed to survive." Robert just stayed in deep thought, saying nothing.

****

Changi administration block was not ideal for a tribunal hearing, but they had cleared out the old refectory and set it up as a temporary court. Robert when he was finally ushered into the Tribunal just followed the MP almost in a dream; he smiled to himself when he saw that the panel's table was placed roughly where his bed had been.

The panel were already in the room waiting to commence proceedings. Brigadier Lowther spoke to Robert as he went behind the witness table. "Mr Draper, I understand you were an internee in Changi Prison."

"Yes sir, I slept here, approximately where you are sitting."

The Brigadier nodded his head at the information but did not follow up on this information and instead addressed all those present, "The proceedings in the Municipal Building were unacceptable because of the noise from the traffic. I insisted that we move, and they have at short notice supplied this facility which in fact is probably better as it requires less transport of prisoners." With that he signalled to the MP Sergeant standing to his left. "Bring in the prisoners, Sergeant at Arms."

As Robert watched the Japanese officers were marched into the refectory; he saw that they were chained at the wrist. They stood in two rows and two MPs went round and with a key undid the padlock at one end and then pull the chain out of the loops on the cuffs attached to the officer's wrists. All this took a few moments with none of the Japanese showing any emotion. As he watched the scene he saw Rob Scott and Neil Forsyth and Brian Preston enter and sit on chairs in the visitors section.

Major Balfour stood up and saying "good morning" to Robert he then proceeded to ask more questions for a further hour before addressing the chair and explaining that he had completed his questions of Robert. He asked Brigadier Lowther if he or members of the panel had any questions of clarification before the defence had their turn and for a few moments Robert answered more questions.

One of the panel members asked, "Mr Draper, you said that after the Japanese guards took you into the wet room waiting for transport to take you to Outram Road gaol you were there for perhaps an hour or so with two other internees."

After Robert had nodded that this was correct the panel member had asked if he knew who the two men were. "Yes sir, when I was in Outram Road I learned that they were Captain John McRae and Simon Jackson. Both were executed. "

"Was Captain Ishiguru involved in the executions. "

Robert shook his head as he answered. "Not that I am aware of. That is why I did not give further information in my statement. Colonel Sumida carried out both executions in front of all the prisoners about a week after I was there."

"Were these executions to do with the missing gold?"

"No sir. Captain McRae was a ship's captain working for South Asia Shipping Company. He captained the sister ship to my uncle's. He rammed his ship into a tender of Japanese soldiers who were landing at Port Swettenham where there were thousands of refugees waiting to escape. I never spoke to the captain but it is my understanding from a survivor I met and who ended up in Sime Road camp with me that he rammed the ship into the tender because the Japanese soldiers were shooting at the poor people on the dockside and they would have killed hundreds of women and children." After a pause Robert said, "The other prisoner was an old man who lived on Adam Road and was well known for standing on the Padang on Sunday mornings and arguing for change. A bit like Speakers Corner in London, sir. He refused to bow to a soldier one morning and was put in the punishment box and when he was released, he told a Japanese officer that the Japanese were on marked time and that the Allies would make them pay. He was sent to the YMCA and from there to Outram Road." Robert started to say more but Major Balfour intervened.

"Do you know if Captain Ishiguru was responsible for the state of the two prisoners you have just brought to the attention of the court, and for their execution?"

Robert paused for a moment and then said, "Captain Ishiguru was the officer responsible for the YMCA. All interrogations would have been carried out under his instructions. But he would not have been responsible for any interrogations at Outram Road gaol. I know the two prisoners when they arrived at Outram Road were in a very bad state and were put in ground floor cells which were the ones normally used for prisoners facing execution. However, I did not see the executions as I was down with fever for a few days after I was interned in Outram Road and I was housed in the hospital wing for about a week to ten days and not required to do *tenko* when the executions would have occurred."

At that point Major Balfour put down the papers he had been holding. Addressing Brigadier Lowther, he then said, "That is the case for the Allied Services Prosecution, sir. Unless you have further questions, I propose to pass the questioning of Mr Draper over to Major Dennis. Seeing Brigadier Lowther shake his head, Major

Balfour turned to Robert, "Thank you for giving your evidence so clearly, Mr Draper. He then pointed to the defence counsel on the next table to him. "Major Dennis may have questions for you.

Major Balfour sat down, and Major Dennis stood and without looking at Robert he addressed the panel. "Captain Ishiguru has asked me to say that he does not recognise this court. He has always done his duty according to the oath he took when he joined the army and that he has no questions of Mr Draper." With that Major Dennis sat down.

Robert watched Brigadier Lowther confer with his colleagues and the panel's barrister before he turned to address the court room audience. "We are satisfied that we have sufficient information in order to reach a decision. We will retire now." Turning to the Sergeant at Arms, Brigadier Lowther said, "Take the prisoners back to their cells and when we return bring only Captain Ishiguru. The MP said, "Sir" and stood to attention as the panel walked across to a door almost behind where the row of cameras and journalists were situated. Robert remembered as he watched them that it was the room were Geoffrey Blackmore used to hold meetings away from prying eyes.

Outside in Yard A, Robert saw Rob Scott and Neil Forsyth talking to a group of other civilians and he walked across. Brian had disappeared off back to the city, presumably. "Well done, "Neil said with Robert just making a face. Rob clapped him on the back and said something similar and then introduced him to the other members of the group some of whom Robert now recognised as internees from Taiping camp whom he had seen at the Repatriation Office last September. "You were the last of the civilian witnesses," Rob said as Robert came round from nearly two days giving evidence.

"Come on, Bob. I'll take you home," Neil said a few minutes later as Robert was talking to a Taiping internee called John Travis. "Yes, I remember Jim Clemence. The Nips used him as a mechanic. All he worried about was where his wife was. I seem to remember that he somehow found out that she was shipped off with other women to a camp up near the Slim River but nothing more. Jim died in March last year. He just withered away, poor sod. "Robert thanked the internee for the information and turned to Neil. "Yes, I'm coming. I've had enough of this place."

As they walked out to where Neil had a car waiting for them, he told Robert, "Rob is staying to hear the verdict and will ring us I would be surprised if it takes them long. Did you learn anything from your conversation with Travis?"

Robert had discussed with Neil about people who were still missing and how he had failed to trace Melanie Clemence. "Travis obviously didn't know that the camp Melanie Clemence and the other women were taken to up near the Slim River was a death camp.

All of them seem to have died within months of going up there. Jim wouldn't have wanted to live without her so in a way it's fitting."

On the way to Tanglin, Neil told Robert that he was off to Blighty for six months after the trials. "I need to see the family back in Scotland, but I shall be returning. David Turton will act up so I've told him to keep an eye on you as your bloody gold mission is causing people to lose sleep. Leon Comber is yelling blue murder about your interference in intelligence matters."

Robert who was sitting just enjoying the air as the police driver sped the car through the traffic turned and grimaced across at Neil. "The more I delve the murkier it gets, Neil.

****

Robert attended the War Crimes Tribunals for another three weeks giving evidence about Colonel Sumida and Sergeant Sato knowing that his evidence was crucial to finding them guilty.

Captain Ishiguru was sentenced to death and executed in Changi prison in May, about eight weeks after the hearing, and Colonel Sumida was also sentenced to death, but the execution was delayed a short time as the Australian Government wanted to question him on other alleged war crimes. Sergeant Sato was hanged in Changi prison only days after he was sentenced. Rob Scott when Robert had had a beer with him, at the reopened but very dilapidated looking Raffles, said that the Australian Government had wanted to question

Sumida about atrocities against Australian troops but that it would have no effect on the sentence.

Robert completed his contribution to the War Crimes Tribunals in May 1946, proceedings he would remember for the rest of his life.

It was June1946 and Robert was taking his time adjusting himself to the traumas he had been through at the War Crimes Tribunals. Reliving the time with the *Kempetai* was something that would not leave him too quickly. He had had little time to deal with the information he had learned at the Causeway Garage more than eight weeks previously other than to send a note to Kenneth Chen to say that he had more information and then to have a quick meeting with Major Comber the day before the tribunal hearings had started, a meeting that had ended up being very difficult.

Robert was being driven down Bras Basrah Road a few days after the Tribunals, in the mid-morning. The heat was building up and Robert could feel the sweat starting to make the back of his neck wet. He was on his way to look at a property that he might be interested in buying for himself. Bin Lau realising that he was exhausted left him to his own devices, although to be fair Bin Lau was also very tired having only returned two days before from a trip to Hainan Island.

As the car sped down Bras Basrah Road Robert suddenly saw the Major he had met on Rempang Island some months before and had Bin Lau stop the car so that he could speak to him. The Major was pleased to see him and congratulated Robert on his contribution to the sentencing of Ishiguru, Sumida and Sato. "Spotting Ishiguru when you were over on Rempang Island was just the ticket. We knew that he wasn't kosher, but we had no evidence and no one else seemed willing to admit that he wasn't who he said he was. Apparently, there's a real market in false papers so we are having to double check all the suspects and as you can imagine there's quite a few. We're shipping a large number of POW's back to Japan next week with a few senior officers who are for a show trial in Tokyo. We've been told by the UK Government that they want all POW's to be processed and sent back to Japan in the next few months, so I think we are likely to miss a few that deserved a stretch in prison."

Robert asked, "So what happens to you?"

"I'm here today to see what's in store for me. I'm due a bit of leave and then a posting to a nice quiet spot but knowing the Army, after two weeks leave, I will be posted to somewhere where there's a lot a flies and hot sand. Anyway, I'm not likely to be posted until most of the Japs have been posted home."

Robert pulled out his notebook and wrote his telephone number down. "Give me a ring when your next on the Island and we can have a beer."

It was as the Major said goodbye and continued walking up the road and Robert had turned to go back in the car that he saw Kenneth Chen getting out of a car that had just drawn up on the opposite side of the road. Kenneth waved him across and as Robert limped over, he noticed that two Chinese bodyguards had immediately stationed themselves at either end of the car. Kenneth Chen seemed pleased to see him and they shook hands. Kenneth ushered Robert round to the other side of the car, onto the pavement where there were no passers-by at the time.

"My apologies, Mr Draper, I was being driven down the road and saw you talking to the officer. I had just arranged to send a message to you that we must meet as your note said you had new information. I only got your note a few days ago."

Seeing Robert looking puzzled at the comment, Kenneth Chen continued, "the communists have been very tiresome the last few weeks and have tried to remove me. So, I have had to take precautions." Kenneth Chen waved at the two bodyguards as he said this.

Robert raised his eyebrows at the statement. "Kenneth, I am no longer surprised at what is happening; why should I be after all we have been through in the past few years."

Kenneth Chen just nodded as he continued talking, "Your note said that you may have discovered something about Lai Tek, Mr Draper."

"I sent you a message, Kenneth, because I discovered that Lai Tek worked for Tan Choo Sin up at the Causeway Garage before he became a trade union leader and then later the Secretary General of the Communist Party. He failed to turn up at the Batu Caves in 1942 but you know about that and it seems that it was one of Tan Choo Sin's drivers who was supposed to deliver a gold shipment to the Central Committee." Kenneth Chen nodded at this last comment.

"I am sorry that I have been rather preoccupied by the War Tribunals, and I only learned about Lai Tek and his connection to Tan Choo Sin the day before the Tribunals started."

Kenneth Chen drew out a cigarette from a packet in his shirt and lit it. "It is of no matter. It took some time to get the information to me as I was in hiding from the communists. They have been particularly difficult these last few weeks."

Robert wiped his brow and moved closer to the building a few feet away in order to get in the shade. "It seems a bit of a coincidence that the gold disappeared at that point."

Kenneth Chen nodded that he understood the point being made by Robert. "It is our view that it was only a small amount that was to be delivered to Li Bo."

Robert shook his head. "I am beginning to question that; I think you may be wrong. We know that the MCP and the Allies did a deal for the MCP to work at harassing the Japs and I know that the agreement including payment for their services. A bit like your agreement. What was the reason for all the MCP commissars to meet up at the Batu Caves? To me it looks like a set up. Lai Tek never arrived at the Caves so that must be suspicious. Only he and Chin Peng survived. The MCP is decimated of its senior officers. Very suspicious."

Kenneth Chen said nothing, he merely continued to look at Robert without any expression.

"Lai Tek would have known of the gold shipment to Li Bo because that in my opinion was the reason the Central Committee thought they needed to meet- so everybody could be paid. Did you know that Lai Tek had worked for Tan Choo Sin?" Kenneth Chen gave no indication that he knew so Robert continued, "I don't think so. It would have been easy for Lai Tek to have persuaded Tan Choo Sin to let him go with the delivery. After all he would have been going to the meeting. Tan Choo Sin would have no reason to be suspicious as he would have known that Lai Tek was involved with the communists. On the way to the Batu Caves Lai Tek could have persuaded the driver to hide the gold maybe because there were many Japanese patrols. On the way there they get separated or maybe they agree to separate because of the difficulty in getting through. If the driver had told Tan Choo Sin when he got back to the garage that they had to hide the gold it would have been useless information as they couldn't get to the spot where the gold was now hidden. Lai Tek then comes along and hides the gold in a new spot before you can get there. When your men interrogated the driver what did they learn. Very little from what you have told me. He admitted he had hidden the gold and gave you a location and that was all."

Kenneth Chen had gone very quiet as Robert outlined his theory. "It is an interesting story Mr Draper, but it cannot be. Lai Tek stood to benefit in terms of prestige if the gold was in the hands of his Party. I know that the Japanese were less rigorous in checking Tan Choo Sin's lorries because he delivered Japanese goods. The gold should have been easy to hide. We used the system often."

Robert shook his head." We know that Lai Tek failed to turn up at the Batu Caves. It would not have been difficult to persuade the driver that they had to take precautions if they encountered extra patrols." Robert repeated some of what he had just said, "He would have known that Tan Choo Sin is to transport gold to the Batu Caves for the Central Committee meeting. Tan Choo Sin would have known that Lai Tek was going to the meeting. It's obvious that Lai Tek was able to scrounge a lift."

Kenneth Chen had been looking at one of his bodyguards who was waving for him to hurry up. He turned to face Robert." If Lai

Tek took the money, I am not aware that he enjoys wealth now. If there is more gold, then why did Lai Tek not hold back and get more?" Kenneth continued with more thoughts, "Tan Choo Sin was merely responsible for the delivery, but he would have known the source. I only knew that gold would be delivered by Tan Choo Sin on an agreed date to a location near Tan Choo Sin's workshops in Ipoh; I never knew the source."

Robert realised that Kenneth Chen had given him more information than he probably wanted to. So, Tan Choo Sin must have known who held the gold or had a means of contacting the person who held the gold. To Robert, as he stood trying to avoid the searing heat of the midday sun, it seemed to him that Kenneth Chen was no further forward in finding out where the gold was. He knew that Tan Choo Sin was the link but he had not known that Lai Tek had worked as a mechanic at the garage before he became involved in the communist party.

After pausing momentarily and thinking through the conversation Robert said, "The Malay Communist Party would only have benefitted if Lai Tek ever intended them to get it. I think he betrayed the MCP Central Committee to the Japanese because it was to his advantage. It's obvious to me that he was playing a double game perhaps always was. He seems to have been able to travel round the Malay States without any impunity which suggests to me that he had an understanding with the Japanese. I bet you anything he never told the Japs that he was delivering gold just that a meeting had been arranged. He expected that they would kill everybody at the Batu Caves meeting leaving him free from suspicion because he had a driver who would say that they couldn't get through the checkpoints. What he didn't expect is for that firebrand, Chin Peng, to escape. You did tell me that when you got a hold of the driver he told you that he had been forced to hide the gold until it was safe to deliver it, but he never disclosed that he was with Lai Tek. You said when you later went to find it, that it was missing. If he was delivering goods for the Japanese, then they would not have been interested unless he was off the approved route. He must have been told that the Japanese would be more likely to search the lorry on this occasion and Lai Tek persuaded the driver to hide the gold. I came to the conclusion last October that as only Lai Tek and Chin Peng had survived that it had to be one of them who was involved in the missing shipment."

Robert stopped what he was saying and watched Kenneth who just continued smoking his cigarette and thinking through Robert's ideas. Robert could see that Kenneth was wrestling with the scenario and decided to continue with his thoughts. They had been standing talking now for well over ten minutes and the bodyguards were getting quite restless.

Robert continued. "Whoever stole the gold had to have at least one accomplice and transport, particularly if it was larger than the usual shipment as it may well have been as it was to pay all the elements of the Central Committee. My guess is that the driver Tan Choo Sin sent to the Batu Caves knew Lai Tek well and he might have been promised a cut if he said nothing, only he was caught by your men later and I presume didn't survive. We will never know for certain.

Watching Kenneth's face Robert thought he saw it go a little tighter. Robert repeated the information. "He was a trusted courier who would have known Lai Tek, perhaps he was even a friend. He would have taken his advice when they encountered the Japanese patrols. He would have felt reassured that an old workmate was coming with him on the dangerous journey. What I am no longer in any doubt about is that the Japanese were told that Tan Choo Sin was a risk to them, and they removed him only weeks later as part of the purge of Chinese industrialists, not knowing that he was a link to the gold. It is obvious that Lai Tek betrayed Tan Choo Sin to remove him from the picture. Perhaps because Tan Choo Sin became suspicious."

"Who else knows about your ideas?"

"Major Comber, and I have sent a message to Chin Peng."

Kenneth Chen took his cigarette from his mouth and gasped. "My god, Mr Draper, what have you done? When did you tell Major Comber and Chin Peng?"

"Two days ago. Just after the last Military Tribunal I had to attend."

"Why did you wait so long?"

"I needed to do some checking up on another person. As I said I think that Lai Tek was playing a double game and I wanted to check on that possibility. I say again, I cannot see how he was able to move around the Malay States for nearly four years. He was too well known. He must have had Japanese approval. Otherwise, it doesn't make sense."

Kenneth Chen stood looking at Robert as he finished smoking his cigarette still taking in what Robert had just told him. "What did Major Comber say? Am I allowed to know?"

Robert shrugged his shoulders. "Major Comber was furious. He said that I should not be interfering in these matters, but it was clear that he did not know about the Causeway Garage or about the gold going missing. He only knew about the massacre at the Batu Caves."

Robert continued, "When I went to Tan Choo Sin's garage, I discovered that Shee Yang Chen is now the owner of the Causeway Garage; he bought out Tan Choo Sin's widow in 1943. Tan Choo Sin's partner Jai Shu Lai was arrested with Tan Choo Sin and presumably executed with Tan Choo Sin. Shee Yang Chen was one of the mechanics at Tan Choo Sins garage. Where did he get the money from?"

"So" Kenneth Chen was not looking at Robert as he took out a pair of dark glasses from his breast pocket, unfolded them, and then covered his eyes. He said nothing else waiting for Robert to continue.

"In 1943, Shee Yang Chen was a mere mechanic at Tan Choo Sin's garage. There are photographs of him and Lai Tek with Tan Choo Sin and the other employees on the wall in the garage office, presumably from the early 1930's."

"You have been busy, Mr Draper. This is very important information. Shee Yang Chen is now a very important man. He is an adviser to the Singapore Government on many matters. Major Comber would be very angry that a man he deals with has past dealings with Lai Tek."

Robert started to laugh. "God, Kenneth you are holding your temper. Shee Yang Chen is involved with your lot. I've found out that he gives funds to your Party and he's even attending Kuomintang meetings. I think he and Lai Tek are a team. They're playing you all off against each other for their own gain. Did you know that they both come from the same village near Saigon?"

At that Kenneth threw down his cigarette. He said emphatically, "Shee Yang Chen comes from Hainan."

"No, Kenneth, he does not. They both come from Saigon. Going by the names at the bottom of the photographs in the garage, Lai Tek and Shee Yang Chen even had different names back in the early 1930's. Of one thing I am certain – it was them in the photographs. I got my driver, Bin Lau, to go to Hainan whilst I was at the War Crimes Tribunal, to find old employees of Tan Choo Sin. Shee Yang Chen got rid of them in September last year and paid their passage back to Hainan. They told Bin Lau that they knew Lai Tek and Shee Yang Chen had to leave Indochina very quickly in the late 1920's and they got jobs with Tan Choo Sin because he needed mechanics, and that Shee Yang Chen was good at it but Lai Tek was not interested and went off to work with the trade unions. Only the two old office workers remain from Tan Choo Sin's days, and it turns out that Shee Yang Chen sent for them sometime in the 1930's and he got them jobs with Tan Choo Sin. Bin Lau tells me that the garage is now closed and has been for a few weeks. Have you seen Shee Yang Chen in the past few weeks?"

Kenneth Chen did not reply. Instead, he turned to the bodyguard now leaning against the rear bumper of the car and shouted that they must move on, and then he turned back to Robert. "You have given me much information and I must decide what to do with it. If what you say is correct, then my Party must take action."

"Kenneth, all that I have told you about the gold is written down and I have a copy in a safe place, and should anything happen to me then I have left instructions that it be sent to the newspapers."

Kenneth Chen said nothing as one of the bodyguards opened the rear door for him to enter the car. Robert stood on the pavement as Kenneth Chen wound down the car window. "Major Comber will put a restriction notice on anything you have, Mr Draper."

"'I've thought of that Kenneth. The report is lodged outside of the British Government's sphere of influence and for that matter, the Kuomintang's."

Robert crossed the road, as Kenneth Chen was driven off, and flopped down into the car, next to Bin Lau.

"Boss, that looked a difficult meeting."

"I think I have really stirred the pot, Bin Lau. Let's forget looking at that property for now. Take me to the *Mata Hari* and let's have a drink and go through what I've just learned."

Chapter 25

It was two evening's later; Robert had invited Henry and Peter to have drinks and supper with him. Mike Davison had also been invited having arrived back on the Island after only a few months living in a cold, war damaged England that Mike and his family could not stand. He said on arriving for supper that living in England was not like home.

Robert was back in his home just before his friends arrived having had a difficult meeting with Major Comber who had demanded they meet concerning the Causeway Garage which had been burnt to the ground early that morning.

Sunni, newly promoted to houseboy, brought in drinks on a tray and he nodded at Robert when he was told to make sure that there was plenty of ice and then go and relax in the kitchen. Sunni just smiled at Henry as Mike and Peter talked about the large fire that had occurred up near the causeway.

Robert poured a large scotch into his glass and helped himself to some of the nuts that Chunggy, now promoted to head houseboy, had brought in earlier. Bin Lau had then taken Chunggy off to the Chinese Mission for his weekly get together with his old pals.

Robert interrupted Mike and Peter. "I can tell you a good deal about the fire. I've had my ear bent by the First Secretary and Major

Comber on the subject but anything I say is to remain between us. The First Secretary is threatening to bring charges against me under some act or other if anything gets out."

Both Peter and Mike who had been standing by the open doorway that led out onto the upstairs veranda turned round and came and sat on the settee with Henry already there, getting out a cigarette from the silver case that was now a permanent feature in his chest pocket. Both Mike and Peter declined the offer of a cigarette and Henry didn't offer Robert one.

It was Henry who got in first. "There's a communique out asking for persons who see Shee Yang Chen to inform the police immediately. Is that something to do with the fire? The back of the garage is beside the rail line, and we had to stop all services for four hours." He was watching Robert as he said it, almost smiling at Robert's look of angst, and taking his first drink of Robert's best whisky. Robert just groaned. Henry seemed to know more but was holding back.

"Come on tell us all, then, "Peter said sitting back with Mike beginning to wonder what it was all about. He had no idea who Shee Yang Chen was.

"It's all David's fault for inviting me up to the Sultans palace for lunch. On the way there we needed petrol for the car, so Bin Lau stopped at the Causeway Garage and there it was – an old sign that said that Tan Choo Sin used to own the garage."

"Ah," was all Henry said and then he and Peter filled in a bewildered Mike about a gold shipment going missing, a massacre at Batu Caves in 1942 and Tan Choo Sin being a probable distributor of gold for the Government. Robert sat patiently as they told Mike the story with some embellishment.

"Ah," said Mike as the penny dropped. "That's the gold you were tortured about by the *Kempetai.* I remember you in the camp saying you knew nothing, but nobody believed you."

"Great. What it is to have friends. And furthermore, there's no guarantee the gold that went missing at the Batu Caves is the only gold there is. I still think it possible that there is more."

"Do you know where Tan Choo Sin got the gold?" Peter said taking up Robert's point.

"I don't, but knowing Maurice he would have had more than just enough for 1942; he would have planned for a longer campaign with the nationalists. One shipment to the MCP would not have used up the horde. When I was at the garage I saw a photograph of Maurice shaking hands with Tan Choo Sin in, I think, 1933, maybe '34, at some grand event at the garage. There was bunting, the lot. The picture was in the office of the now burnt down shop. That proves that Maurice had a connection with Tan Choo Sin."

There was silence between the friends all comfortable with each other and able to speak their minds freely. Eventually it was Henry who said, "Well go on update us. The suspense is killing me. All I promise is not to say anything knowingly. What I say in my sleep I cannot account for."

Robert got up and refilled the glasses as he told them about his visit with Bin Lau to the garage and the events since then. "I'm surprised that Shee Yang Chen and Lai Tek didn't get in touch with me or whatever. They must have soon realised who had been asking questions, certainly I am pretty distinctive what with my scar and a limp. Anyway, when I saw Comber and told him what had happened, he went ballistic. He said he would have me arrested. Then the First Secretary came in on the meeting and said that I may have compromised a security arrangement. Neither of the sods let on whether Lai Tek or Shee Yang Chen were involved with the intelligence services. Anyway, what I found out was weeks ago, before the War Tribunal hearings, so it is old news. It seems both Lai Tek and Shee Yang Chen have gone missing and now the garage has gone up in flames. Whilst I was at the Tribunal Hearings, I sent Bin Lau off to find some of Tan Choo Sin's old employees and what they told Bin Lau suggests that they were involved in some way with the gold that went missing on the way to the Batu Caves. All Comber said this morning was that Shee Yang Chen is now incommunicado whatever that means. He didn't say whether he knew where Lai Tek was."

Nobody interrupted Robert and he continued, "Anyway I saw Kenneth Chen a couple of days ago. Well, more it was that he saw me. He was not pleased either. He said that I had caused a problem that was totally unnecessary, but he clearly wasn't fully in the picture, and he went white when I told him that I had found out that Lai Tek and Shee Yang Chen where not from Hainan and came from the same village, somewhere near Saigon. Not pleased either when I said that I had found out that Shee Yang Chen was a mainstay of party funds for the Kuomintang. Comber this morning wanted to know if I had anything to do with Shee Yang Chen's disappearance suggesting I was in cahoots with Chin Peng. About the only thing I wasn't accused of was setting fire to the garage."

Mike couldn't keep quiet any longer. "Dear god, talk about a nightmare. I came back for a quiet life and walk into this. How did the meeting finish?"

"I told him he was an idiot." At that Peter groaned. "I told him that Chin Peng was onto Lai Tek already. I haven't seen Chin Peng since last November and I don't want too again. When I saw him, I said it had to be an inside job and if you think about it, it can only have been Lai Tek or Chin Peng who betrayed the Central Committee and for that matter took the gold. Both survived the massacre at Batu Caves, the rest of the communists were killed. The fact that Lai Tek and Shee Yang Chen worked for Tan Choo Sin is strong evidence of the gold never reaching the communists; those two were playing a double game. My money is on Lai Tek planning the whole thing. I simply sent Chin Peng a note to say he should look at the Causeway Garage."

"Why did you do that?" asked Peter.

"Because Lai Tek clearly double crossed his Party and had dozens killed as well as Maurice and Ernest Beverley and other innocent people. He deserves to pay for his crimes. What I haven't worked out yet is the connection to Rachel Knowles."

"What about Rachel?" asked Mike. "I knew her before the War. Her husband was a chemist who ran a people's pharmacy up in Bukit Timah. Rachel and Mary got together a few times to help at a clinic where Rachel's husband worked with sick children."

Robert looked across at Mike. "She was in the YMCA with me. She died there."

Mike said nothing, and looked around before he said, "What happened to John Kwai Knowles? Does anybody know?

Nobody answered as Sunni arrived with some hot food which he put on a table at Peters side. Sunni left without saying anything, returning seconds later with more ice just as Peter said, "The Knowles used to help the Bishop and the Beverleys with some church activities. Ethel got dragged in sometimes. They did a good deal of charitable work. There's a connection there."

Robert got up and moving towards the food he motioned for the others to help themselves. Chunggy had made his stock dish of chicken curry with various side dishes. Over food it was agreed that no one knew what had happened to John Kwai Knowles and Robert said he would make enquiries.

"Just be careful, Bob. You're in enough trouble already," Henry said pouring himself a beer.

"I agree with you, Bob. It makes sense that there was more gold and the remainder is still out there," Peter said and then added, "How do we know that there's no gold left at Tan Choo Sin's and it just hasn't been found yet?"

Robert shook his head. "I am certain that the gold was never stored at Tan Choo Sin's. Tan Choo Sin merely delivered it. Kenneth mentioned that his link was a man who worked at Raffles College but he didn't give me a name. I have found out that there was a lecturer called David Abadi who was Jewish who worshipped at the synagogue on Waterloo Street. That's the probable link with Maurice. Anyway, I suspect Chin Peng burnt down the garage although they would have had a good search first. I don't think the Kuomintang did it as they are more into subterfuge than arson."

Henry was greatly enjoying the conversation. He couldn't resist saying, "Why not the British Government, to cover their tracks."

There was silence from his three friends as they took in the unthinkable.

It was Mike as they worked through the information who said, "In my view you should make yourself scarce for six months, Bob, at least until the hullaballo has died down. Lai Tek could be after you for revenge, and Shee Yang Chen has plenty of resources to make life difficult for you if he comes back. God what a mess, even the Kuomintang could go after you if what I have understood you to say that it looks as though Shee Yang Chen and Lai Tek took the money in '43 and then promptly swapped sides."

Henry raising his eyebrows at what Mike had just said added, "And Comber could get very nasty if Lai Tek was giving him information and Bob has scuppered the connection."

"When were you planning to go the America, Bob, "Peter asked putting down the bowl of chicken curry he had been eating.

"Anytime. Dr Morton has it arranged for me to go in late August for the preliminaries and then as I understand it, they should operate about a week later."

"Well go now. There's a temporary Catalina service out on Thursday, to Hong Kong. Be on it. Fly onto California and have a break before your surgery."

"What have you in place to cover your business interests?" Henry asked taking up Peter's line of thought.

A suddenly very tired looking Robert said, "I have most things in place. The Hussain Brothers know what I want and will do it at the two properties they are working on. Bin Lau will step in when necessary. David is capable of doing little things and giving Bin Lau advice."

"Where the hell did you find Bin Lau? He suddenly seems very important."

Robert nodded at the remark from Henry. "His dad worked for me in the vaults at Fullerton Square. Peter will remember him. Anyway, he turned up a few months ago and asked for a job. I always trusted his dad and I can't see why I don't trust him. He is pretty disparaging about the corruption in the Kuomintang and he certainly isn't interested in the communist movement. From what we have talked about he is a keen supporter of David Marshall."

Both Peter and Mike groaned. It was Peter who said, "He will have us all paying double taxes."

Henry, a long-time friend of Peter, laughed at him and said, "Maybe but it may kill off the communist mantra if the taxes are used to develop the Island and the Kuomintang won't be able to get their noses in the trough. Anyway, it's decided Bob, you get off the Island on Thursday. If need be, we will take you to the plane and stick you on it," all the time watching Bob's face and laughing at the various expressions that seemed to cross Robert's face as he thought through the decision.

"It presumes that there is a spare seat, "Mike said.

"Oh, there'll be a spare seat in First Class and Bob can afford it!"

"Well. Can you get everything in place, young man, "Peter said suddenly taking on a more serious tone the like of which Robert had not heard since January 1941 sitting in Walter Trehearne's old office and being told to stop interfering.

Robert nodded. "A few 'phone calls and it can be organised. I'm seeing David and Susie tomorrow night for dinner so any last-minute things can be settled there, not that I can give David much to do. He's just not up to it.

With that the rest of the evening was spent talking about Mike and his wish to set up his business and Peter telling them of the chaos over in the Dutch East Indies where he was trying to drum up business.

Chapter 26

When Robert set off for America it was almost eleven months since the Japanese surrender. Not a year since the war had ended and yet so much had happened. The Island was still very much battle scarred with shortages in food and basic services. The Indian population still rioted in support of independence for India and religious difficulties between the different Indian communities was becoming evident.

Brian who was down in Singapore for a short break from sorting the mess out in the KL railway station, left by four years of war and neglect, came with him to the Catalina departure shed. There was little conversation between them with Robert suffering from a combination of trepidation at leaving the Island and at the chaos he knew his mission for justice had caused. Bin Lau drove them over to Seletar having had coffee earlier with Robert, sitting in the garden getting last minute instructions, and with Chunggy hovering around anxious that Robert had everything he would need.

In the 40 or so hours since his meeting with Henry, Peter and Mike, Robert had had nothing but meetings and lengthy telephone calls arranging or confirming arrangements he wanted to have in place. He chose not to answer a message from Major Comber that he was wanted for further meetings with him and the First Secretary. Instead, he scribbled a note to Comber to say that he was travelling to the USA to have his long-planned surgery and hoped to be back before Christmas. At the departure lounge he asked Bin Lau to deliver the note.

Peter telephoned just before he left for Kellang to say that the Australian Government had at last agreed to the release of the gold held in the Union and China Bank in Sydney. Peter said that he was wondering whether holding back the gold had been a ploy on the part of the British Government and not the Australian Government, to make the Kuomintang compliant with some arrangement the British had in place with Robert caustically replying that it certainly couldn't be anything to do with Lai Tek and Shee Yang Chen as they seemed to be very cosy with the British Government. Robert's parting words were that he was pretty sure Lai Tek had been side-lined by the Communists since mid-1946 with Chin Peng more or less taking over and any information Lai Tek could have passed on to Comber would have been useless.

The night before he left Singapore, Bin Lau had driven him over to Cathay House for dinner with Susie and David Masters. David was thrilled at being asked to do something to help Robert, his words being "to do something useful" although Susie did say she would be monitoring the contribution much to Robert's amusement and David's annoyance. Talking with Susie and David over dinner he asked whether they would like to use his house whilst he was in the USA knowing that they found their flat to be noisy, and without a garden. They were thrilled to accept. After a simple meal with David having no alcohol Susie sent him off to bed and asked Robert to stay.

"Bob, I need to talk to you."

Robert thinking it was about David immediately started to say that he thought David was improving albeit slower than everybody expected.

Susie shook her head. "No, it's not about David. It's about Leanne. She poured her heart out to me the other night."

Robert sat down quietly.

"She's in a terrible state. She thinks you're the most wonderful person on earth. She is just so miserable that you have shown very little interest. I know that you have been out a few times, but she feels that you are keeping her at arm's length." Robert started to say something, but Susie said, "No let me finish," but Robert pressed on.

"I am interested, Susie, but hell I'm not exactly Clark Gable what with a scar on my face and a gammy leg. And there's just so many things happening in my life."

Susie smiled at what Robert said. "Dearest Bob. I am very fond of you. If you and Leanne became a match, I would be very pleased but if you are not interested then put her out of her misery. I'm not aware of anyone else in your life."

Robert interrupted. "Before the surrender there was someone, but she had a bad time in a camp in Sumatra and is now more or less permanently in hospital in England."

"I'm really sorry, Bob. I had no idea. I would never have raised it now if I had known. I just don't want two people I love to be hurt."

Robert stood up. "Look what I promise, Susie, is that I will write to her when I am in San Francisco and explain things and if she is still interested then when I get back, we will take it from there. What worries me Susie is that I am quite a bit older."

"You clearly don't know women, Bob. You could be the hunch back of Notre Dame and forty-five but that would make no difference if she were interested. She may be twenty-three coming up to twenty-four, but she behaves as a thirty-year-old."

Robert for a moment and was quiet and then said, "And here's me thinking you wanted to talk to me about David. I am glad he will do that little job for me until I get back."

Susie came across and gave him a kiss on the cheek. "Don't worry if he can't I will get involved. You just be careful in San Francisco. I hear the women are dangerous."

"God, that's what my landlady in London said about the women out here.

Chapter 27

The plane touched down at Kellang airport nearly two hours late. The Pan Am plane from Manila to Bangkok had been delayed and it had meant that Robert missed his connection to Singapore. First Class travel had its creature comforts but palled after 36 hours of flying from San Francisco with extended landings in Hawaii and Manila. After months away Robert couldn't wait to be in his own home.

He knew that Susie and David had moved into his house and had been enjoying the space it offered and its lovely gardens. With David no longer earning an income, he knew they couldn't afford to move from their cramped flat in Cathay House. David had never really recovered from his imprisonment in a camp in Sumatra with most of his fellow internees dying of malaria and other jungle fevers. Robert was sure that David would have benefitted from the fresh air, and Susie, well she would just enjoy having a garden. And more importantly she could keep her eye on Chunggy who was liable to do something silly.

Coming through customs Robert took no notice of the people at the entrance, greeting passengers. He didn't expect to be met as he hadn't detailed his travel arrangements to anyone. He said goodbye briefly to a local businessman whom he knew slightly and pointing out his luggage to a porter he set off to clear the entrance when he heard Leanne shout his name.

He turned around and smiled across to her as she came up shyly and almost impetuously kissed him on his new cheek. "God, it looks wonderful," was all she said as she kissed him again. "Come on, Bin Lau, has your car outside." Robert said very little, just taking in the bundle of feminine allure that had come to meet him. Nothing surprised him anymore. Leanne turned round and linked her arm into Robert's, chattering all the time, as they followed the porter outside to where Bin Lau, grinning broadly, was waiting in a VIP car space. Thinking about it afterwards Robert wasn't sure he actually said anything until they got into the car.

It was on the way to the city that finally Robert got a word in with Leanne constantly chattering about what she and her mum and David had been doing in the past four months; much of which Robert already knew about as he had exchanged airmails with David and Susie on half a dozen occasions. He had also written a long letter to Leanne explaining much about what he wanted to do with his life and saying that he hoped she would have dinner with him when he got back and he had received an airmail, almost by return, to say she couldn't wait.

"How the hell did you know that I would be on that plane?"

Leanne giggled. "Rebecca gets the lists of passengers who're flying in as many have to make transfer arrangements by train to KL, or ship to Kuching, Palembang or Batavia. We knew that it would be in the next few days so I told her I would never talk to her again if she didn't regularly check the lists and she gave me a call this morning to say you were on a transfer flight from Bangkok. I changed my shift as I thought it would be nice for someone to meet you."

"I didn't send Bin Lau a note as I wasn't exactly sure when I would arrive", Robert said.

"So I discovered this afternoon when I went over to your place with mummy. I told Bin Lau what Rebecca had told me, so he kindly said he would collect me and bring me over. He even found out the plane was late."

Robert was enjoying the ride. The person next to him smelt delicious and Bin Lau was driving him through his favourite city. As they were talking, he could see familiar sights, places he had thought about every day when lying in hospital, and afterwards recuperating in a small hotel on the coast twenty or so miles north of San Francisco. One of the doctors had recommended it and Robert found it to be a wonderful tonic giving him time to relax and release himself from all the stresses of the last five years. Taking short walks along the beach with the sea pounding away at his feet he found new invigoration and time to make plans.

Robert turned to Leanne. "So, what about dinner."

"What now"

Robert grinned back." I think we best make it tomorrow night as I'm liable to fall face first in the soup and ruin any prospects for the future."

Leanne snuggled closer to Robert as they both enjoyed the warm evening air. "I can wait one more day."

Bin Lau drew the car outside the bungalow on Beach Road where Leanne lived with Rebecca. "You working tomorrow night?" Robert asked, and Leanne shook her head. "Then I'll pick you up around 8 o'clock. I presume you eat anything."

At that Leanne giggled, "Not frogs legs. Or chicken's feet."

Robert got out the car and helped Leanne out. "I can see why David said you were expensive to feed." Leanne leaned forward and kissed him lightly on his lips and turning ran up into the house.

Robert got back into the front of the car. "Right Bin Lau. I presume I still live on Tanglin Road?" Seeing Bin Lau grin Robert sat back in the passenger seat. "Take me home, Bin Lau and while you're driving tell me all the real news.

Tanglin Road hadn't changed; it just seemed cleaner and more settled. Robert wondered whether "settled" was the right word. It just seemed more established. It was just wonderful to be home.

At the house the new gates he had ordered before he left for America, were closed but when Bin Lau tooted the horn someone appeared immediately and unlocked them. Even in the dark Robert could see it was Sunni. Sunni had started life as a cabin boy on his uncle's steamer ploughing the seas around the Malay States, Sumatra, Borneo and Java; somehow when the Japanese had sunk the *Lancashire Lass* in January 1942, in the Musi River, Sunni had escaped capture and made his way back across the Malacca Straits to his home. Not bad for a fifteen-year-old boy.

As far as Robert could find out no other crew had survived and when Robert had seen Sunni at his aunt's home in the kampong north of Malacca in late 1945, he had been told that the Japanese had shot anyone who came out of the ship as it was sinking. It was the first mate who had covered Sunni as they lowered themselves into the river only for the Japanese to shoot the first mate as Sunni drifted away.

As the car drove under the frangipanni trees and up to the house Robert shouted a welcome to Sunni and watched him run behind the car to catch up. At the veranda steps Bin Lau got out quickly and raced round before Robert could get out and opened the car door for him. "Welcome home boss. "The door to the house opened and

Chunggy came out looking very smart in a new outfit. "Mr Drapa, you home at last. We all miss you. Many people want to see you." Robert could only grin at Chunggy and shake his hand. Chunggy still mixed his words and dropped his "r's" when he got excited.

Robert turned to Sunni who was standing at the end of the car helping Bin Lou to get cases out of the boot. "How's Aunt May?"

"She well, Mr Draper. She said to tell you she has many good vegetables for you." Robert just nodded and walked up the steps into the house.

It smelt fresh with flowers in the hall. "Mrs Masters, she stay many weeks, with Mr Masters, and then they move out last week but she comes every day and puts fresh flowers in the rooms," Chunggy said fussing in front of Robert.

Robert just wandered through the rooms touching things he had missed before turning and saying, "I don't suppose you have something for me to eat," almost knowing before the answer came, "I have chicken curry ready, Mr Drapa."

"I wish I knew where he got his chicken from. I would have bought shares in the business." Robert mused as he followed Chunggy through to the dining room where Chunggy had already laid out a place for him with Mrs Lin Yuen's best china which had survived the Japanese occupation, hidden away under Chunggy's

little house. Chunggy brought over a large stengah as Robert sat down.

"No work tonight Chunggy. I just want to enjoy being home."

Chapter 28

Robert sat with Leanne in the garden at *Salisbury Crags* laughing at the contents of the parcel laid out in front of him. Lady Copeland had somehow sent it via the RAF - a large cardboard box full of goodies. Robert had not a clue how she had managed to get them when everything was still in short supply, but she had. There were two pots of Robertson's strawberry jam, one jar of Robertson's marmalade, a stick of rock with Blackpool through the centre, and half a dozen other little memories that Robert had told Lady Copeland he missed when one night they were camped by the side of the road, on the way to Malacca.

Robert spent the next few moments telling Leanne about the journey from Segamat to Malacca and how they had rescued four girls; one of them being Lady Copeland's granddaughter, and another was her granddaughter's best friend, Sara. Robert went on to explain that the other two girls turned out to be sisters who had been orphaned because their parents, missionaries in south China, just disappeared in the fighting in that part of the world.

Lady Copeland had taken all the girls under her wing and Robert suspected that Lady Thomas was instrumental in arranging for them to stay at the High Commissioners Residence until Sara's parents arrived just before Christmas 1945. Sara, he knew, had eventually been spirited away by her parents although from the infrequent letters from Lady Copeland it was obvious that the two girls were joined at the hip. What Robert didn't know was what had happened to the two sisters, but he was pretty sure that Lady Copeland had taken care of everything.

How she had got the pots of jam was beyond Robert as they were a rarity in Singapore but the most wonderful present of all was a photograph of Lady Copeland with Lady Bertwyn, taken in the summer, at Windermere by the looks of it. Robert almost choked telling Leanne about the lovely old lady who had given him advice under, well near to, the Pili Nut tree in the grounds of the High Commissioners Residence. Leanne sat quietly smiling and laughing as Robert told her the story of the invitation for a meal in the first-class restaurant on the SS Narkunda and how his friend, Harry had devoured a full second plate of fish.

"Leanne, Lady Copeland must have used up half her coupons for months. I must send her a present."

Leanne smiled back, just happy to be part of the lovely moment. "Why don't you send the girls something? I'm sure she would love that just as much."

"Well, you can jolly well come and help me pick something appropriate." As he was saying it Robert was rifling around in the packaging and emerged with a separate letter to the one that had been with the presents. It was from Lady Bertwyn. Robert turned it over. Memories were flooding back of the happy times before December 1941 and the Japanese invasion.

Leanne saw the change in his face and took the initiative. "Right that letter is obviously going to take a while to read so let's have a drink while you read it. I'll get Chunggy to telephone Raffles and put back our dinner by half an hour. But I'm not giving up the dinner. Remember you promised to take me dancing and show off this new set of feet you have, and Raffles won't wait all night for the performance." She stood up to go and tell Chunggy. "Go on, Captain Scarface, read your letter." With that she touched his face and ran her hand very gently down where you could barely see the scar.

****

Raffles in 1947 was still living with its 1941 clothes on but it was the place where you should be seen, and this was important to both of them. The relationship had blossomed with Leanne very tolerant of Robert's single mindedness and sudden inspirations for business. Robert found that as time went on that he was more and more dependent on Leanne and loved her being part of his life.

At Raffles, Robert had arranged for them to have a table well away from the dancing as he always found it to be so irritating when people tried to get past tables to go to and from the dance floor. It was perhaps ten minutes after they arrived when Robert noticed

Major Comber sitting at the far side of the dining room with a female companion. Major Comber was looking across at him. Robert acknowledged the wave and eventually it was Major Comber who excused himself from the lady he was with and who crossed the busy dining room.

"I'm sorry to spoil your evening Mr Draper but I wonder if we could meet tomorrow morning. It is important that we keep up to date."

"I remind you Major of what I said when we last met. I am not in the service of MI6 or whoever. "Robert sighed anxious to get rid of the Major. "I have site meetings from nine tomorrow. I could be up at Nassim Road for eleven thirty".

Major Comber shook his head. "Why don't we meet somewhere else? It's best not to be too official."

Robert anxious to get rid of Comber said, "Then make it Beach Road. The far end: you will see a sign for Hussain builders. Meet me there before nine, let's say eightish. That gives us an hour to talk through the information we have." Robert started to enjoy bossing around the head of MI6 in Singapore. Major Comber merely nodded and as he walked away, he said he would be there. Leanne watched after him before she turned to Robert and said, "Not one for introductions or for the niceties of life."

Robert shook his head. "It's not like him. I understand he's quite a ladies' man. Obviously, something important has come up. He's not even waited to phone me at home and arrange a meeting. I suspect if you hadn't been with me, he would have spirited me away to some dark and dingy cell." He said the last sentence as Leanne suddenly started to get cross.

"Who does he think he is? I expect it's to do with that stupid gold of yours."

Robert shook his head and started to laugh. "No, I suspect it's more likely the High Commissioner has run out of his favourite tea and thinks I can get my hands on a regular supply."

"Don't you try and change the subject, Bob. You're in far too deep with these nasty people. I thought since you had been back that it was all behind you." Standing up she said, "I think I would like to dance, please."

Chapter 29

Bin Lau drove Robert down to Beach Road with both of them conscious of another car following them from the corner of Margaret Road. They had heard that both the Kuomintang and the MCP had cars on the streets and that the MCP was kidnapping prominent businessmen for ransom. They both decided with some relief that it was just them getting paranoid as the car following them stopped outside Raffles as they continued down Beach Road.

When Robert had a drink with Peter, a few nights before, Peter had said that he thought he had been followed in an unmarked car. He had telephoned Neil at police headquarters just in case it was the communists preparing to kidnap him which had only just happened the day before to a senior Hong Kong banker when he had travelled by car up to KL. The banker was still missing.

Peter was seeing less and less of Robert as the bank began to open up for business and Robert in any case was busy with his many new business interests. Nigel had been sent up to Penang to manage the bank's branch but was finding life difficult and Robert had at Peter's request made a visit shortly after his return from the USA to see if he could encourage local businesses to use the bank. Peter had hired two or three more Brits but more and more he depended on Chin Lee and other Chinese clerks; gone was the old colonial dependency on British managers.

As Bin Lau drove the car onto the building site, Robert looked across at the bungalow next door; there was no movement and he remembered that Leanne was working at the General from late morning so presumably a long lie in for her although Rebecca had office hours and had probably set off before the day got too hot.

Robert spent the next few minutes just wandering around the site, deep in thought. The security men the Hussain Brothers employed knew Robert well and left him to wander; Bin Lau sat in the car reading the morning paper. The security staff carried metal lathis and Robert well remembered their use by the Indian guards, on him, in the YMCA. About ten minutes later Major Comber turned up driving an old Singer car that had seen better days, wearing a grey linen suit that looked as if it too had seen better times. Robert was surprised to see that he did not have a bodyguard.

They shook hands and then Robert took him round to the back of the site out of the way of prying eyes or for that matter people with big ears. Robert asked one of the security men to provide some chai but Major Comber shook his head. "One mug then, Sarpinder." As they walked round to the back of the site Robert merely added, "He makes the best Chai and always with condensed milk. I usually manage to get a couple of tins from the American base for them when I'm over there."

Major Comber sat on the bricks piled ready for laying as Robert sat down on some planking. Without more ado the Major said, "We have been told that Kenneth Chen has been moved on as Chin Peng is making a real effort to remove him. I presume you know this?"

Robert shook his head. "This must very recent. When I last saw Kenneth, he did tell me that Chin Peng was targeting members of the party and he was having to be more careful but that was months ago before I went for my surgery."

Major Comber nodded as he got his cigarette case out and Robert shook his head when offered. "We found out yesterday afternoon. Our sources have told us that Kenneth Chen has relocated to China although exact location not known at this point. Don't suppose you know his likely location?"

Robert merely raised his eyebrows. "At a guess it's probably Shanghai as Nanking and Peking look as though they have gone to the communists or are about to fall. I suspect you are more up to date on these developments?"

Major Comber again just nodded. "Our information is more or less the same. Kenneth Chen was a useful contact. Our view is that Jai Mung may take over although his influence will be very limited because of his age and his lack of authority. His father would have been better, but he has poor health I understand. Do you know much about Jai Mung?"

Robert shook his head as he drank the sweet tea that Sarpinder had just brought round. This was what Comber was after, he mused.

"I have only met him the once when I was taken to see Kenneth Chen at a safe house which I think was near Tajong Ris. That must be eighteen months ago. I am surprised that he is Kenneth's successor." Robert was quiet for a moment and then said, "It doesn't say much for their desire to make Singapore a major centre for the future. My information is that some of the funding sources are drying up. Have you heard the same? "

Major Comber gave nothing away just making a ring of smoke from his cigarette. Robert took that to be a "yes".

Major Comber had clearly come about Kenneth, and anxious to see if Robert could help in developing a new strong contact. He shifted his position to look more at Robert and said, "Have you any more ideas about the missing gold."

Robert smiled back. "I've only been back a few weeks and most of my time has been spent with my business interests. Anyway, I thought with the Tan Choo Sin incident we had more or less solved the problem; it's obvious that Shee Yang Chen and Lai Tek had squirreled the gold away for a rainy day. When I think about it, it could only be Lai Tek not Chin Peng who got the gold that was going up to the Batu Caves and seeing the photographs in the garage nailed Lai Tek. Sorry but it was only a matter of time before Chin Peng put two and two together. Lai Tek was on borrowed time and from what I hear there was an investigation underway in the Malay Communist Party. Shee Yang Chen may have got away with it too but even that I doubt. Chin Peng when he found out the connection, would have gone hunting. As to there being more gold, well maybe there is but at this time I have hit a brick wall and I'm not in a rush anymore now that Lai Tek has been sorted. If there was more gold, then it had to be connected to Maurice Levy and not Ernest Beverley. Beverley was supposed to have escaped to Australia, so he was unlucky to be captured. I doubt he would have known of Maurice and the Tan Choo Sin connection. As Maurice was out of the frame almost immediately that leaves whoever was the go between with Tan Choo Sin. As I said Ernest was not supposed to be in Singapore but safe in Australia so that makes it improbable that he was privy to all the arrangements. The poor devil picked a ship that was sunk trying to escape the surrender and he was brought back to the Island. There were one or two of his colleagues interned in Sime Road who were lifted by the *Kempetai* in late October 1943 but I still doubt that they had any direct connection to the gold. Sadly, they all died in Outram Road gaol and if they did say something it doesn't seem to have helped the Nips much in their hunt for more gold. All Ernest knew in my opinion was that Maurice had organised a gold shipment system but as Maurice was already dead the Nips would get nowhere. They interrogated people like me in the hope that we had a piece of information that might help but it was wishful thinking. It's clear to me that Lai Tek had some information because he knew about Tan Choo Sin but not much more and what he gave to the Nips he gave piecemeal, and he conveniently made sure that Tan Choo Sin was removed without revealing that he was involved in delivering gold. It looks as though Lai Tek played a clever game in order to survive the war. We have to give him credit for that."

Major Comber sat there stoic as always. He had been listening attentively as Robert analysed the situation. Finally, he said as Robert finished. "Shee Yang Chen was a severe embarrassment to us having become high profile and advising the HC on business development on the Island. Since his disappearance his businesses have gone into receivership. As to the photographs you say were on the garage's office wall, they were lost when the garage burnt down.

Robert said, "I presume you know that Maurice Levy looked after Tan Choo Sin's banking affairs, even financing the setting up of the lorry business in '32 or '33. I think the photograph I saw was of Maurice cutting the ribbon in the lorry park at the back of the garage sometime in 1934."

Comber this time did nod.

Since Robert had got back in the late Autumn 1946, he had seen Major Comber on a number of occasions and the atmosphere between them had mellowed although Robert suspected that he would not be allowed too much slack. Certainly, the relationship was much more based on Robert supplying information and providing names of possible contacts. The fact that the Major had admitted that the Government's relationship with Shee Yang Chen was an embarrassment was tantamount to an apology as far as Robert was concerned.

The meeting was drawing to an end and Robert got up from the planks. It was almost as an afterthought he said, "There were other traitors as well you know, not just the obvious ones."

Major Comber guessed that Robert was referring to Mohan Singh and his colleagues who had started being helpful to the Japanese in 1942 but had quickly disappeared into POW camps as they fell out of favour with their new colonial power. There was much talk in Singapore of action being taken against these collaborators.

Comber chose not to respond to the point made by Robert and instead he brought the discussion back to the gold by saying, "I have been talking to some of the Force 136 survivors about whether they had come across any link to the missing gold. Presumably you know that they ended up having to bring in large amounts of gold and dollars after the Batu Caves massacre to fund the communist fighters and the Kuomintang." Comber offered no further information and afterwards Robert decided that the people Comber had talked to knew little or nothing about the Singapore gold.

Robert moved his position more into the shade as the heat was starting to build up. "No, in my view the source was broken from mid-1943 thanks to the zealousness of the Japanese in removing Tan Choo Sin. So, if there was more gold, Lai Tek had lost the only person likely to be able to name the source. For that reason, I am sure Lai Tek and Shee Yang Chen planned the whole thing – get rid of the MCP Central Committee and end up with a nice big bag of gold." "I think Lai Tek gave, the *Kempetai,* Tan Choo Sin as a person not to be trusted. They disposed of him not knowing that he was the courier for the gold. I also don't think Tan Choo Sin would have told them of the gold. Lai Tek did well to last out the war." Changing tack Robert asked, "I don't suppose you're going to tell me if Ronnie Millar left any records?"

Major Comber looked surprised at what Robert said. "How do you know about Ronnie?"

Robert could see he had touched a nerve. Ronnie had been the Government's contact with the unions and the MCP before the war, so he was an obvious link in getting any insurgency organised against the Japs."

Comber said nothing and left it to Robert to guess that if Ronnie had had such records, they were not for public consumption. Robert had already decided that Ronnie Millar when he was taken from the internment camp knew he was going to die in the YMCA so had given Captain Ishiguru false information. Robert smiled to himself as he mulled over the information. Robert said to himself, *"Lai Tek was probably the one who had betrayed Ronnie to provide another offering."*

As Robert was deep in his thoughts Major Comber finished his cigarette and walked up to him. He spoke, breaking into Robert's thoughts, "I want to know how you knew about the execution of Heenan?"

Robert had said at a previous meeting that Lieutenant Heenan had been executed down at the docks on 15 February 1942, but Comber had not followed up the conversation at the time. Robert finished his chai and threw the dregs over the ground at his side. "Heenan was executed by a group of Military Police. Some Chinese coolies saw them do it and then throw the body in the water. I have a Chinese servant who plays chess sometimes at the Chinese Mission and one of his chess friends told him that he had been told by a rickshaw runner who had been told by a ………."

Major Comber put his hand up, "I give in. It's probably a true account as we don't have any paperwork or official report of any execution. Whatever, he deserved to die for what he did."

"Will others who betrayed us get the same summary execution?

Major Comber became irritated. "You know it won't be the same. You also know that it wasn't anybody in the military who betrayed you. If you say it was Lai Tek then so be it. There may have been others, but they are not obvious. If any of them are ever caught then there will be a penalty to pay but that will be decided by the powers that be, not by you or I."

Robert moved out of the shade. "Look if I get news of what is happening with Kenneth Chen, I will let you know. From what I know Kenneth was destined for a more important role. As I said with him going, I suspect the Kuomintang are going to downgrade the work at this end. After all they now have their hands on the China Bank money and the other gold, if it exists, could be small beer. They just don't want the communists to get it." Robert watched Comber smile at this comment before he added, "Kenneth is held in high regard from what I can see so presumably there is a lucrative job for him in China. As for me finding out anything more, the truth is that all the sources have dried up thanks to the efficiency of the Japanese, and Lai Tek and Shee Yang Chen doing a runner. God help them when the communists get their hands on them. I think even Chin Peng will choose revenge over finding more gold. It just seems to me that the British Government is all in a dither about bags of the stuff lying hidden in some chamber pot. That makes me suspicious that you do have information about how much there was and how it was split up." Robert stopped talking for a moment and then added, "Chances are that there are a few boxes out there somewhere on this Island, but we shall never know." As Comber made no reply Robert finished by saying, "If you want a meeting with Jai Mung I can arrange."

Robert started to walk away with Comber following a few steps behind. "Unless you have anything else, Major, I suggest that we call it a day. There are workmen on the site and they'll be getting curious. I'll lay you odds our meeting will have been noticed and will be reported back to Jai Mung and more likely Chin Peng."

"I can arrange the meeting with Jai Mung," was all Major Comber said as Robert watched him get into his car and drive off. Turning back, he walked through the building site and across to the neighbouring bungalow and climbing up the veranda steps he knocked on the back door which was opened by a young Chinese girl. She recognised Robert and said, "Missee still in bed."

Robert just said, "Tell her I called, Peggy" and he walked round to the front knowing that Bin Lau would have brought the car around from the building site. "Give me five minutes, Bin Lau. I just need to speak to Ali about some of the work here and then we can go and have breakfast; somewhere quiet where I can work out what Major Comber was really after and then we need to go up to Flower Road."

Chapter 30

Robert sat in the officers' mess at Kellang Airbase watching an enormous US Air Force plane come into land. He had been invited to lunch by Chuck's successor, a large, easy going Texan who seemed to take everything in his stride. Lunch on the Air Base seemed to be a million miles away from life in the Orient. The airbase was a little bit of the USA. What Robert already knew was that the Texan was keen on making Singapore his final assignment before he went back into the law practice he had left four years before in some place Robert had never heard of in the mid-west.

He and Major Bentz were sat on easy chairs in a lounge that made Raffles look threadbare, enjoying the view with somewhere in the distance the blue of the sea just discernible. In the air-conditioned lounge, it was difficult to believe that outside the temperature was near enough 100 degrees Fahrenheit with the poor men working on the planes having to deal also with a high humidity factor.

Robert took another drink from his beer as they watched the great plane taxi to a halt about a hundred yards away. "Milk and fresh food for the kids," was all Bentz drawled as they watched the hive of activity now surrounding the plane. Almost as an afterthought "Four planes a day from Darwin." Robert nodded; he knew all this already. More than two years after the Japs had surrendered and the Island was still heavily dependent on the Americans for fresh food and milk being delivered from Australia. The staple rice diet of the local population had greatly improved with the Thais now supplying some of their surplus, but other commodities were still in short measure. Chunggy's vegetable patch at the end of Lin Yuen's garden and surplus food from his step aunt's plot were still essential although there did seem to be more food on the stalls in the markets.

They had had a meal of giant steaks together with large bottles of beer followed by fresh fruit that the Major said had been flown in from Manila. Robert just shook his head at the whole set up. He thought back to 1940 and the life he had led then. True it had been privileged in comparison to the local Chinese and Indian population but even then, he couldn't remember being offered a twelve-inch steak with all the trimmings. As he always did when he had the pleasure of an invitation to the base he asked after the Major's family who were stuck nearly 4000 miles away and who had not seen the Major for more than a year.

"I'm hoping you can help me, Bob. I've got permission for my family to come out for the last few months of my posting and I was wondering about somewhere nice where we could stay. There's only limited accommodation on the base and they've never stayed in service accommodation. Talking to my wife on the phone the other day she said she would like to stay in the city if that's possible. I told her that Singapore is not like Vermont where she originates from but she says she would like to try, so what about it. Any ideas?

Robert sat for a moment digesting the news and shaking his head when a steward came up to ask if the gentlemen would like more drinks. "I presume she has never lived in the tropics, Casey?"

He watched the Major shake his head before he answered, "We went to Tijuana in Mexico once for two days."

Robert grinned at the reply and shook his head, "I think she will find it very different than Tijuana. We also have a security problem. The Indians have quietened down but the communists are causing a problem and by all accounts they are only just getting started. A friend of mine, Mike Sanders is up in KL, as the senior police officer, and was ambushed and badly wounded the other day."

The Major nodded his head. "Yeah, I saw the report in the papers. We have upped security around the camp but hell there are only occasional incidents. I go into the centre every day and it seems okay. Our intelligence boys say that it is mostly over the causeway where's there's problems."

Robert didn't answer the point and instead asked, "When does she come, Casey?"

"She is on her way to San Francisco to stay with friends for about a week and then she will fly out here. Maybe two weeks and she should be here. I've arranged for the boys to go to the International School on Hill Street."

"If you're determined to live off base then I have a large house on Flower Road that should be safe. It's in Siglap not far from here. It was an old plantation house on a coconut estate. There's no air conditioning though; I know what you Yanks are like. I have an Australian army officer and his family occupying one part and a navy chap and his family occupying another part but there is still a lounge and three bedrooms with bathroom and so on. There's a joint kitchen arrangement with Chinese catering staff and there's a couple of Malay gardeners to maintain the grounds. It's probably best that you stay in this type of accommodation as it scares off the commies and the police are close by if there ever was trouble. It's about thirty minutes from Kellang, maybe ten minutes from the beach. I think the army chap is likely to move in the next couple of months as his term here is nearly finished. You can have the accommodation for as long as you like. It's all been done up recently courtesy of help from yourself." Robert grinned as he said the last sentence before then continuing, "An RAF family was staying there until last week but they're off back to England. If you're free tomorrow morning I can take you over and you can decide. If you don't like it then there's a smaller place in Tanglin but I don't think it's as good."

Major Bentz raised his cup. "Well, I reckon I had better look at it. I can make myself free after my meeting with the General, let's say ten." This time it was Robert who raised his glass in acknowledgement.

"I look forward to meeting your family, Casey. Now have you heard from Chuck? I had a letter about two weeks ago and he said he was on the move to New York from Phoenix, Arizona. That sounds a bit of a shake up."

****

Major Bentz came out of the kitchen and walked down the short corridor into the main hallway where Robert was standing talking to a Malay gardener. "How does the kitchen work, Bob?"

Robert finished what he was saying to the gardener and then he turned to face the Major. "There are staff employed by each of the three households. They share the kitchen facilities. If you like the set up I can introduce you to Mai Lau who has been looking after the RAF family. If you have particular types of cooking then if your wife can show her the first time how you want it prepared then she will take over. I think if you speak to Captain Sherwood's wife upstairs, she will tell you how she and the Australians arrange the purchase of food. In your case it should be easy because you have the shop on the base. It will have more choice than you can get in the shops in the city."

Major Bentz nodded and then went for a second look around the accommodation. About ten minutes later he joined Robert on the lawn in front of the house where he was again talking to the Malay gardener. Robert clapped the Malay on the shoulder and said thank you to him and turned to Major Bentz who had stepped into the shade under the large porch that ran the length of the frontage. "Well Casey what do you think?"

"It's certainly very different from what Julia is used to but she says she wants the real thing."

At that Robert laughed. "You didn't tell me you wanted to stay in a kampong with no electricity, no running water and cooking outside. I'm sure I can arrange that for you."

The Major laughed embarrassed at the suggestion. "No, no. I think she would die of fright if I told her that she was going to be in a kampong with no facilities. I don't think the boys will mind these arrangements. I think it's managing servants and not doing everything yourself. She's liable to be in the kitchen organising hot dogs and the like."

"I think living on the camp sounds safer, Casey. I have a colonel in the Sherwood Regiment who has enquired and will be interested in this accommodation. So maybe we just say that you have made enquiries, and a service bungalow is the best for the year you have left out here. "

"What about the bungalow in Tanglin?"

"It's smaller, Casey and less room if you want to entertain. Here you have the general lounge as well as your own lounge. And there's the veranda and gardens. The bungalow has only a small garden. You would still have the problem of Julia having to manage at least two servants, one of them in the kitchen."

"Don't you have anything with a pool?"

Robert shook his head. "Like gold dust, Casey. The few that are around were emptied during the occupation and used as sewage dumps or as vegetable plots. Even the High Commissioner hasn't got one although I think he has plans.

The Major just shook his head. "Take me home, Bob. I'll telephone Julia and tell her the situation."

"I tell you what. I can keep the property open for forty-eight hours as the Colonel is up in KL at some army conference about the troubles with the communists. If you want the property, you must tell me by Thursday as I expect him to be onto me as soon as he gets back from KL. I understand his wife is on her way from England and wants to be off the camp just like Julia suggested. In her case though she has done a stint in India so is used to the set up."

Bin Lau drove into the airbase as they finished discussing the very few options on the Island and Casey said he would be in contact. Robert watched a Dakota plane coming into land as Bin Lau turned the car round and they drove back into the city. In the time

Robert had been with Casey, perhaps two hours, he had seen at least a dozen American planes come and go from Kellang Air Base.

"Take me down to the *Mata Hari*, Bin Lau. I need to speak to Tong Chee Tan ", was all Robert said as he watched some large ships at anchor about a mile or so offshore. They seemed to be waiting to go into Keppel Harbour. To Robert there was definitely more shipping which was good.

Chapter 31

Robert, by all accounts had been forgiven for exposing Lai Tek without warning and ending his use as a double agent. Indeed, the High Commissioner had never raised the matter when he invited him to be a member of the security advisory group he had formed. The exposure of Shee Yang Chen might well have saved the Island Government from embarrassment had it later come out that he had stolen Allied gold intended for use in fighting the Japanese and Robert took this to be a major factor in why he was being invited to meetings concerning the security of the Island and Malay States. He now sat with the leading business and security leaders of the community. Henry as the Superintendent of Railways also attended. There were perhaps a dozen attendees at such meetings and when he looked round at those present Robert realised, he had come a long way in seven years.

The meetings always included Chinese, Malay and Indian leaders of their communities and Robert saw this as a recognition by the British Government that things had to change. The new High Commissioner, Sir Franklin Gimson, had taken up office and wasted no time in putting in place changes in the way the Island and the Malay States were governed and how he communicated with each of the separate communities.

At the time still trying to keep a low profile on his return from the USA Robert had been greatly surprised when the invitation had come through from the new First Secretary for him to attend the meetings. Henry and Peter when he had drinks with them a few nights later were much amused that he had received the invitation and he had added, "who knows they'll be asking me to join the Singapore Club next", only to be told that both of them had been invited to become members. It was Peter who had said, "Of course, we did tell them that you were not quite the type we should have but I suspect they haven't listened. I think there's probably an invitation on the way." Robert had shook his head in disbelief at this development.

The High Commissioner now had monthly meetings with the security group to discuss the unfolding problems of communist attacks in the various Provinces on the mainland and the situation on the Island, with particular concern about how the communists had changed their tactics and were now targeting police stations and public institutions. Robert for his part had suggested that this tactic was entirely predictable as Chin Peng would want to demonstrate that the Government was not in control.

Robert, as he sat in his third meeting of the group, looked around as the High Commissioner said, "Superintendent Sanders is still recovering from his wounding and will be absent for a good few months so the Police Commissioner has asked Neil Forsyth to take over for the next six months." It was the first Robert knew that Neil was back from Scotland; he had made a second visit at short notice for family reasons. He must have literally landed in Singapore and then been shipped off. He hadn't seen his name on any of the shipping lists that were printed in the Straits Times so presumably he had managed to scrounge a lift on a military plane from England.

The Commissioner continued what he was saying. "His wife will be arriving in the next few days and will be staying down here for the foreseeable future." More news. Neil had said in his last letter to Robert, a few weeks back that he had met someone special, but he hadn't said that it was that serious. He jotted down a note to contact her as the High Commissioner brought the Police Commissioner into the discussion and invited him to give more detail of the situation in the Malay States. From the corner of his eye Robert saw Major Comber enter the room and slide into a vacant chair at the other end of the table. He saw Comber nod at a few people before nodding at Robert.

Life on the Island was taking a shape that was very different from the early days of Robert's time in Singapore. True there were large numbers of troops still stationed on the Island, but it was now to control the enemy within rather than to fight the enemy of the Rising Sun. From what Robert observed the enemy was still originating from the north only this time they were Chinese. The Kuomintang was more and more losing ground and certainly the

China Bank, the unofficial bank of the Party, was no longer visible. Jai Lee Kwan and his son, Jai Mung, may well be in business and collecting donations from rich supporters but it was no longer done through the auspices of a bank. Jai Mung was now the figurehead of the local Kuomintang, but from Robert's observations few Chinese businessmen were greatly influenced by the young man who was quite elusive and afraid of the communist threat. Peter had managed to obtain the release of the China Bank gold that had been taken with other gold reserves to Australia, just before the Japanese could get to it in 1942. Robert knew that it had taken a great deal of argument with the Australian Government, with the British Government also involved, and both Peter and Robert were surprised when suddenly the Australian Government agreed to the funds being sent back to Singapore. Where it had gone after its release to Jai Lee Kwan was anybody's guess but a cynical Peter suggested that it was probably back in the British Government's hands as payment for arms supplied to the Chinese Nationalist Government.

In the two years since the Japanese surrender the old colonials still living in Singapore had sought to return to the old ways only to be told by the British Government, and by an increasingly vocal local population, that things had to change. The Indian population still regularly demonstrated about independence issues in India but with much less animosity to the British population. The newspapers sadly were still filled with articles and pictures of mass riots in India. But to the average person living on the Island, it was not the Indian population that was the concern but the mixed attitudes of the large Chinese population and the less and less vocal voice of the small Malay population. The High Commissioner recognised this, as presumably did his masters, the British Government, and he was making it clear that the Government was open to discussion on the way forward; Robert although having no real interest in politics strongly supported the idea of an elected assembly.

The Lin Yuen Trust which he now managed was as he quickly discovered a large fund of property and money intended to benefit the poorer communities although it was not entirely clear how or where Mrs Lin Yuen had obtained the funds. She seemed to have spent the last years of her life collecting donations from many sources, nearly all Chinese, from what Robert had been able to find out, which made it all the more interesting that she had chosen him to take on the management of the trust when she died. He had only known the lady for a short period but had grown very fond of her and it seemed that the love had been reciprocated.

Increasingly he found himself dragged into discussions about how the fund should be used in the poorer communities bringing him into conflict with landlords and occasionally the trade unions. Of one thing Robert was absolutely convinced and that was that the continued mistreatment of the coolie population was untenable and in Robert's view to continue the old regime brought with it the real possibility of pushing the poor working class into the hands of the communists if they were not already tied in with them. His arguments at the security meetings he had attended so far were for the Singapore Government to come up with legislation that would improve the lot of more than half the population of the Island.

Having drifted momentarily from the purpose of the meeting he was brought back with a bump when he heard the High Commissioner say, "Now Major Comber do you wish to add anything to what the Police Commissioner has just outlined. " Robert expected the Major to say something about the fact that the Kuomintang were in trouble but it seemed the Major had other things on his mind. The High Commissioner saw Comber shake his head seemingly to indicate to say he could add nothing new, and then turning back to the rest of the attendees he took a question from one of the Chinese businessmen at the meeting.

The Chinese businessman who Robert knew to be heavily into shipping, asked, "Why is it necessary to change the present arrangements with regard to the Government of this Island? Is it not better that we limit control to those who know how to govern the people?

The High Commissioner pursed his lips before replying, putting his hand up to stifle the protests that had come from Zhang Lee John, one of the other Chinese in the room, who was sitting by Robert. "Mr Tan, we are not here today to debate how we might develop the governance of this Island. I have invited you to be a member of this advisory body that assists me in deciding how we should direct our security forces in protecting the people of this Island and the Malay Peninsula. You and I have had private discussions about the idea of a possible Assembly, and I can understand why you are asking the question, but the answer is obvious. As I have said to you before we are no longer living in a world as it was governed in the 1930's. We are living in 1947 and the people on the Island want a greater say in how they are governed. I suspect I will be the last High Commissioner to have absolute power on behalf of the British Government. We are here today to discuss the present security situation not the governance of the Island. Now other questions, gentlemen, if you please."

The meeting went on for about another thirty minutes before the High Commissioner brought the meeting to a close and Robert and his fellow attendees retired to a dining room where they had drinks and lunch. As soon as there was an opportunity Major Comber headed for Robert and drew him to one side. "Well, have you had any contact with Kenneth Chen?"

Robert shook his head slightly at the Major. "I have spoken to Jai Mung, and he doesn't know Kenneth's whereabouts, but I've had a message to say Kenneth is safe. My guess is that he's in Shanghai as it seems to be the best place where his talents for raising cash could be most appropriately applied although I understand the communists are now attacking the city." Robert raised his eyebrows as he made the comment and as Major Comber said nothing he continued, "Surely Jai Mung has told you this?" As always Comber gave nothing away. Robert again addressed the Major who was watching Robert's face all the time, "I spoke to Peter Connaught, and he says that Shanghai is the obvious place. Nanking is too risky with the communists effectively in control of the city, and Canton is in turmoil."

Again, Comber said nothing, merely drinking a little of the beer from the glass he held.

"Anyway, what's so important about Kenneth Chen? He is the least of your problems. Surely the schism in the Malaya Communist Party is more worrying. If Chin Peng gets full control of the MCP, then we are in for a tough fight. My information is that Chin Peng has been removing certain commissars who don't support him and he has all but got what he seeks. Surely you have an inside source that will confirm that information? "

Major Comber spluttered on his drink and stepped back. Forgetting that they had been talking quietly he said in a loud voice, "What makes you think we have an inside source?"

It was Robert's turn to talk out loudly. "I think I have hit a raw nerve. Whatever. Can I suggest you tell your source to be very careful? Chin Peng in charge will be a very different kettle of fish;

he may start to draw conclusions from what has happened in the Malay Communist Party over the past eight or nine years.

Robert was saved from further argument by the announcement that lunch was served. Sitting between the leader of the Indian community in Singapore and Zhang Kwan Lee he could feel Major's Comber eyes watching him.

"You seem to have given Major Comber something to worry about, "Zhang Lee John said half way through the meal as they watched Major Comber getting up and excusing himself, offering apologies to the High Commissioner and saying that something urgent had come up.

"I only told him the obvious, Mr Zhang. The Japanese were taken for a ride, and I suspect the British Government have been as well. Chin Peng has had enough and from now on is going to raise the stakes. What is happening in China is strengthening his hand, so we have to be more ruthless."

Zhang Lee John nodded and said, "My interests in China will shortly be lost and my son is there at this time trying to rescue what he can. I am not hopeful. That is why I feel we must support the idea of an elected body on the Island. If it is given teeth, it may deflect those hot heads who believe that a communist state here would give them a better life. It will not be so, Mr Draper, as we both know. The people would exchange a colonial rule for an authoritarian regime." The conversation around the table had died away as other people heard Zhang Lee John's statement and it was the High Commissioner who said, "Mr Zhang, well said. I think you are right. We must get the people interested in the governance of the Island although it will not be easy as there are so many interests, all wanting different outcomes."

The High Commissioner smiled at Robert. "As for you Mr Draper, you seem to upset Major Comber every time you meet. He tells me that your contacts seem to surpass any he seems to be able to make. In these difficult times I can only ask that you work with him. I invited you on this advisory body as I value your knowledge of the communities and I am convinced that you are part of the future." With a wry smile the High Commissioner added, "Major Comber has an almost impossible task in getting information about the communist activities and I suspect you are telling him things that are highly sensitive and not in the public domain."

The High Commissioner turned away to talk to the person sitting on his right and Zhang Lee John spoke to Robert. "Perhaps we could have dinner, Mr Draper. I think we may have mutual interests."

Chapter 32

Robert and Leanne were with family and friends in the garden having drinks before tiffan. Robert was standing beside Henry who was in deep conversation with Ethel Connaught, who always looked unhappy and not comfortable with life in Singapore. Robert watched Sunni bringing a tray of drinks over to the Masters' who were sitting under the shade of the mango tree talking to Peter and Zhang Lee John, who was now a regular visitor to Robert's home. Somewhere over to his right Robert could hear Brian and his girlfriend Miranda, a very recent addition to the gathering, laughing and talking with Rebecca. Mona and Mrs Zhang were missing, probably in the house exchanging ideas on silk material, so Robert guessed as they seemed to always be talking about such things when Robert ever saw them together. The gathering was almost complete; all they waited for was for the Davison's to turn up. The Davisons' had finally got their pharmacy up and running on Orchard Road and it seemed to be going well. Their delay in arriving for the lunch was because they had been seeing off their two girls on a Cunard ship back to England where they were to complete their education and go onto college.

As they stood there all enjoying the day before it became too hot Robert heard Mrs Di Lavio, the new housekeeper he had taken on, ushering the Davison's through into the garden. The Davison's were welcomed by everyone with a great deal of noise and laughter and in some cases there was a yell of surprise as Robert had not told his guests of his invitation to the Davisons to join them for lunch. Chunggy looking quite disorientated appeared and asked them what they would like to drink and then disappeared back into the house. He had accepted Robert's decision to have a housekeeper with little argument as Robert had been at pains to say that Chunggy would still have his little cottage at the bottom of the garden and would still be able to go on Tuesday evenings to the Chinese Mission to play chess and meet friends; Robert even said that he would ask Bin Lau to take him in the car and bring him home.

As they enjoyed drinks most of them had moved under the shade of the mango tree that was the boundary with the newly renovated house next door; the undergrowth now completely cleared with a path laid out between the houses. The excitement over the arrival of the Davison's had died down and Leanne nudged Robert who smiled back at her.

"Eh, friends, I wonder if I can just have your attention for a moment. Leanne and I have an announcement. I am pleased to tell you that Leanne and I have decided that we are going to be married."

There was a roar of congratulations and laughter and somewhere in the background Robert heard someone say, "We've known for months." For the next ten minutes or so everyone was talking and congratulating Robert and Leanne who was showing off the ring she had put on as Robert made the announcement.

"We told mummy and daddy yesterday but asked them to keep it a secret until today. Rebecca has known for ages but sworn to secrecy," Leanne said to Mary Davison and Mona who had come over to inspect the ring. "It's one from Mrs Lin Yuen's collection and I thought it would be so nice for Robert to see it on my finger."

As they were all talking Robert saw Mrs Di Lavio signal that the buffet was laid out and he raised his voice above the noise, "Tiffan is served folks so let's go and eat."

Robert sat between Henry Preston and David Masters with Peter and Mike Davison opposite. Other than Peter all those sitting nearest to Robert had been in Sime Road internment camp. There was a bond between them that would remain throughout their lives. Zhang Lee John had been dragged off by his wife to sit at the far end to talk to Mona about some ideas the wife's had about a small charity they wanted to set up; Brian sat with his girlfriend next to Leanne and Rebecca telling them about the state of KL where he had been working until recently. As always Susie took in hand Ethel who increasingly found life in Singapore difficult.

Around Robert there was an air of confidence. Things at last were beginning to happen. The High Commissioner had got things moving and the economy was starting to pick up. True there were shortages and regular outbreaks of rebellion by one community or another but there just seemed to be a feeling that the worst was behind them.

"So, what are the arrangements" asked Peter referring to Robert and Leanne's announcement. A Peter who had only just returned from Batavia as he still called it and who over lunch would tell them of the chaos in Java with mass killings and large parts of Batavia on fire.

Robert grinned across at him. "I have no idea, Peter. Leanne said the other night that she wanted to make an honest man of me. All I said was that if we are getting married, I wanted us to move into the Reeves' old house, next door, as it's bigger if we end up having a family and that Susie and David should move into here. All agreed over drinks last evening. That right, isn't it, David!"

David finished eating a mouthful of chicken curry, trying to nod at the same time. "Robert has said that for some reason he wants us to have this house and Susie is over the moon with the idea. It's part of the deal. The flat in Cathay House is too small and I can't get out as much as I want so his generous offer is a wonderful surprise. The marriage isn't. Even if Robert didn't know it the girls have been planning it for months." Nudging Robert, David said, "You never had a chance old boy. All I can say is that she will make you a wonderful wife. Best thing that could have happened to you and anyway why should you escape."

There was much laughter at this and then the conversation changed to whether anyone had seen friends from the camp or from the "old" days and lunch proved to be a long enjoyable time as each of them gave information about friends and acquaintances who had been resurrected since the last time they had sat down as a group. At one point Robert saw Chunggy disappear across the garden to his little cottage behind the hedging, presumably for his afternoon nap.

Mike Davison now a solid part of the group had information on camp members who he had heard from since his return from England. "John Cole is now vicar for a church near Salisbury. When I saw him last year he was just settling into his new parish, and he seemed pleased with his patch. His latest letter says that his girls have settled well into school and Fiona is enjoying her new friends." Robert as he listened thought of his long discussions with the Rev. Cole in the camp, usually in the early evening, when they sat outside the hut waiting for the general alarm to be sounded which was the signal to say that everyone should attend for *tenko*.

Peter was able to also contribute on camp members who had returned to England. "Dr Robertson wrote to me the other day." Peter looked across at Henry. "You get a letter from him, Henry?"

"Mmm. He said he was now living on an island called Colonsay with his sister. He was trying to get used to the weather after thirty years out here and hoping that where he lives will be a million miles away from any more wars." Peter continued. "Dr Robertson asked me to give his kind regards to members of the Tanglin LDU and had asked if Robert was still getting into trouble." There was much laughter from those sitting at that end of the table with Robert saying that he never got into trouble until he met the Tanglin crowd.

"Wait till he hears that Bob's getting married, "Henry said, and again there was much laughter. The ladies sitting at the other end of the table looked up at the noise and it was Mona who said, "Less noise down there, we can't get on with planning the wedding."

Robert looked across at Peter and just shook his head. "I might need a loan, Peter."

After lunch the men sat on the veranda for a while with Brian and Zhang Lee John joining them. The conversation was about the state of affairs with talk in the newspapers that there had been a bad rice harvest in Thailand so there may be short supplies in the months to come. Brian said that when he had been working on the rail tracks in Johor there had been particular problems with rabid dogs but generally everyone was more positive about how the Island and things over the water were becoming more settled if only those terrible communists would go away.

The ladies drifted over from where they had been congregating under the mango tree to join in and the conversation changed in tone and became more light-hearted with laughter at the news that Martin had gone to live on a plot of land up near the causeway with his mule, in fact mules as it seemed two more had somehow come into his possession.

"Mrs Lin Yuen had a plot of land up there. Jungle really and when I mentioned it to Martin, he was all for clearing it so he's gone up with a couple of Chinese labourers and his mules. I'm going up tomorrow to see what he's doing. It's all swamp, snakes and nasties from what I can see but when I told him that, he just said it was exactly what he was looking for." Robert just shook his head at poor Mona who was looking very upset. "Sorry, Mona but I think you have bred a jungle lover." Brian made some comment about his younger brother had always been a bit queer and there was laughter at the comment with Henry just shaking his head.

"How's your step aunt settling in, in Siglap?" Susie asked Robert changing the subject seeing a very dejected look on Mona's face.

"She and her crowd seem to have settled in well. Aunt May has a small pension from the South Asia Shipping Company, and they have rented a plot of land and are growing vegetables which May says she intends selling at the market. They insist on being as independent as possible. Sunni still lives with them but stays over here when he's needed. I'm just glad they are away from the kampong they lived in as the communists were coming in almost daily and demanding food. Very scary for them."

Some of the women drifted off into the house as Peter said, "I'm not up to date on the security situation. Can you give me a quick rundown?"

A Meeting Under A Banyan Tree

Robert looked at Zhang Lee John who was sat next to him and across at Henry before outlining in a quiet voice the latest security situation and how the HC was proposing to handle it. "It has been agreed that we should discuss with the trades unions and other parties how we might set up an Assembly and what sort of powers it might have. As you can imagine some of the die hards will resist it, surprisingly it seems to be some of the Chinese businessmen who are most against it at our meetings with the HC. In some respects, I think they are very traditional and say that the coolies should know their place."

Zhang Lee John came in arguing that the quicker there was an Assembly with real teeth the quicker they could stop the spread of dissent on the Island. "It's going to be tough for a lot of people to accept the change", Peter said. "I can think of quite a number of people who will say that it's a step too far or at least too soon. Some at the Club have said they will leave and go back home if there are big changes. I'm only here a couple more years and then I retire, and chances are Ethel will have us back in Wimbledon the week after." Peter looked over towards Henry. "From the times I've talked it through with Henry, he has said that they plan to stay and it sounds like David and Susie will be staying." As he was saying this there was a gentle snoring from David whose face was covered by the large hat Susie had put over his face.

Henry shrugged a little before he said, "Other than back to India there's nowhere else for us to go. I would be like a fish out of water back in Blighty and Mona would hate it. She's never lived there; she's never even visited England. My family, what there was of them were never happy I married Mona. What's sad is that India with all its troubles doesn't look a good prospect if things go wrong here. Monas family in Assam have moved to Shimla but there's only a few of them so we wouldn't know anybody whereas here" Henry stopped what he was saying and then looked across at Mike, "You and Mary may have the right idea by starting a new challenge and if it doesn't work out then moving onto New Zealand."

Brian who was sat a little apart just said in a very determined voice, "This is my home and I have no intention of leaving. I fought for it. And I'm damn sure Martin will not leave."

The conversation continued for a few moments more with this sombre note with everyone suggesting possible outcomes and all aware that the next few years was a crossroads for Singapore. Finally, it was Robert who said, "Well I for one don't see why we can't make a success of it. Lee John and I have agreed to go into business together and that plus Lin Yuen's trust and my bit of property should keep me busy for years."

Henry said, "You're right, Bob, we must get on with it but it's not going to be easy especially with the communists gaining the upper hand in China. If they win the fight and it looks that way, then they may well spread their tentacles throughout the region. It only wants Thailand to go, or Burma and we will be very isolated. I saw the HC the other day and he suggested we may have to put the peninsula on a war footing in the near future or it will be too late. He's asked me to work with the military on ensuring that the rail line is not cut." Taking a breath he added with a cynical smile, "We might have need of your gold, Bob, to buy us a spot in paradise", bringing much laughter. The last comment coming as he furtled in the top pocket of his shirt for the cigarette case that Mona now insisted he use and not the proverbial battered packet of cigarettes.

Robert could see Leanne heading towards the group and he changed the subject. "You know presumably that Neil Forsyth is back from Scotland but has been shipped off to cover for Mike Sanders. By all accounts he could be there for months. I invited his wife for lunch today, but she had already accepted an invite from the HC's residence. "

As Leanne came over and stood behind Robert, putting her hands on his shoulders, it was Lee John who said, "I must be going, Bob. My wife and I have a function to attend this evening and we will need to rest for a little while after this most sumptuous meal. "There was a general murmuring by others that they too had things to do. The group started standing up as Leanne whispered something in Robert's ear. "I've just been reminded by the *mem* that we are proposing to have a bit of a do at Raffles to confirm that I have agreed to marry Leanne Masters and of course you are all invited." Leanne gently nudged him at what he said and there was much laughter. Sunni had come into the garden to see if anyone wanted more drinks and seeing the party starting to break up, he picked up a tray and started collecting glasses. Someone had nudged David who was now awake, and Leanne went round and helped him up.

Chapter 33

Robert was well aware that the Union & China Bank was having a tough time trying to establish a new commercial niche for itself after the War. By 1949 the bank could no longer count on it being a leading commercial bank in China with the country in turmoil and the communists making big gains. In fact, apart from a slice of territory near the Indo- China border and the stronghold of Hainan Island, with which the Chinese population of Singapore had strong links, it could no longer be said that the Kuomintang were the Government of China. The bank having started trading in the early 1900's in China was now likely to see its origin wiped out.

Most of Asia was preparing for the communists to take over and already Chinese business interests had moved out of China seeking new pastures but not it seemed seeking the help of the Union & China Bank. More and more it was with the international banks, in particular the American banks. In all the turmoil and demand for change, Singapore could no longer count on being one of the great centres of the Far East.

The French were hanging onto Indochina but it was obvious that there would be strong resistance to it remaining a French colonial outpost. In Thailand the Chinese communists seemed to recognise that a different approach would be needed as the Chinese influence was much less but in the Malay States and Singapore the large

Chinese community saw that a fight with the weakened British power could be successful.

It was in this atmosphere of turmoil and change that Peter as the Regional Director had the unenviable task of trying to pick up the pieces after the War and develop a successful commercial bank. Banks on the peninsula were particularly vulnerable with the communists undertaking audacious attacks on employees and customers with a number killed in rural banks and in KL. In these circumstances Peter spent more and more of his time setting up security systems to protect employees with some success, but the commercial opportunity was much less successful.

Large numbers of British troops had been demobbed after the war back to Britain having spent a good part of their youth fighting in the far outlying parts of the Empire. But in a rapidly deteriorating situation the penniless Labour Government had little option but to send fresh numbers of troops back to the peninsula and to Singapore to cope with the chaos, making it at times reminiscent of the terrible dark days of early 1942. To Robert with his experience of the last days of chaos before the Island surrendered in February 1942 it seemed to him that the National Service soldiers, now barracked in Singapore, were not much better trained or committed to the task than those who had been camped on the Island eight years before.

The Union & China bank's problems were compounded by the turmoil in the Indian sub-continent where independence had come at a terrible price with millions of displaced people and probably hundreds of thousands slaughtered in the religious war that followed. The bank had sought to develop commercial links in the largest cities in India in the early 1920's and these links had survived throughout the great economic downturn of the next twenty years, and the war years, only for the branches in Calcutta, Bombay and Delhi to find that independence brought with it a volatility that made banking almost impossible. On Peter's advice the bank's branch in Batavia had not even attempted to reopen because the political situation in the Dutch East Indies was so difficult.

Sir John Hatton as Chairman of the bank and as a past banker in Singapore had made a number of trips to Singapore since the Japanese had surrendered seeking to give Peter support and on each occasion he had made a very great effort to see friends who he had known when he had been Regional Director in the late 1930's and to see new friends such as Robert. That said, the numbers of friends had diminished to a handful, nearly all those who remained having been in Sime Road internment camp with Robert.

On the first occasion that Sir John had visited Singapore in mid-1946 he along with Peter had asked Robert and Henry to take them up to the Sime Road internment camp and show them around the site. It had been a moving experience for both Robert and Henry to see the huts, already falling down and strewn over the ground, and to see what was left of the women's camp where the concrete main buildings were starting to crumble. Many Chinese squatters had moved into what had been the north end of the camp presumably taking advantage of the cultivated fields and growing some food of their own. Robert talking to Henry later agreed that it was as though they had never been there.

As they walked around Robert had shown them the central buildings where he had spent many hours organising the routines of nearly 4,000 internees. The large mango tree near the entrance to the camp was full of fruit with little Chinese boys throwing sticks up and trying to knock the fruit down. The old barrier was still standing but the single wire that had signified the boundary on the Sime Road was gone.

"Here at the back is the building where General Saito had his office and where the guard house was situated. The prison box is also there where internees who were being punished were placed," Robert told Sir John and Peter as they walked down the side of the administration building. "I believe that the office that Saito used was General Percival's old office when this camp was Army HQ." Sir John and Peter didn't say much, just taking in the size of the camp; only occasionally they would ask a question such as how many were housed in a hut, who built them, where the hospital was located and so on. Walking round to the Japanese area they discovered that somebody had been before them and destroyed the punishment box.

They walked up to where the fields of vegetables had been grown and stood for a few minutes at the spot the internees called "the valley". It was Henry who explained that on Sunday evening, in the last twelve months of incarceration, the Japanese had allowed the camp to play classical music for an hour in the little dell that ran alongside the camp. "The men and women's camp were allowed to attend but not to mix. The women sat over there. "Henry waved at a small mound. Robert added that as the music machine was not very loud and the numbers attending needed to be restricted it had been agreed to let as many as possible of the married men who had wives and children in the women's camp go, so they could at least see their family.

It was when they later drove round to Changi Prison that the atmosphere changed. Both remembered without even discussing it the oppressive atmosphere the prison had generated; the constant fear of the *Kempetai* turning up and of them being beaten by the guards for some minor misdemeanour. Sir John and Peter said little as they walked with Robert and Henry around the outside of the prison, which now housed Japanese war criminals, realising that this was where civilians, in the early days, and later Allied troops, had endured terrible days of torture, starvation and never knowing if they would ever be free.

Robert had given evidence at the War Crimes Tribunals some weeks before and his nerves were still raw from the experience but in a way, walking around the walls was cathartic. Some of the demons seemed to come off his shoulders. On Robert's part he was able to breathe without gasping and feeling his heart thumping, knowing that the men who had ruled with fear were no longer able to create terror, some sentenced to be executed and others sentenced to long prison sentences. Henry just murmured that he had been bloody lucky.

It was as they walked back to the car that they heard the prison bell toll and they saw that the gates of the prison were being opened. They stood with a small crowd of onlookers in the midday heat as the Military Police brought out a dozen stocky Japanese soldiers in chains urging them towards a waiting army lorry. There was absolute silence from the crowd watching the *Kempetai* soldiers, only a child asking who the prisoners were. Robert and Henry stood looking, both feeling revulsion, at these men who they learned later were being transported to Japan for trial for crimes against American servicemen.

Not much was said on the journey back into the city and it was only as they dropped Sir John off at the Goodwood Hotel that any real conversation did take place. "Thank you for taking me, Henry, and you Robert. It was important for me to understand just what happened. I know it must have been difficult for you both, but I think it was necessary that now I understand just what you suffered. I promise you I will not forget." Robert still in physical pain from the three and a half years of imprisonment merely made a bit of a face and shook Sir John's hand and it was left to Henry to say, "John, I agree. We should not hide away from it. We lost a lot of friends, and we should try and remember them as often as possible. Certainly, my boys want to see the camp and I now feel comfortable to take them up." Peter said nothing and it was only later that he said that he should never have gone with the gold on the *Tenedos* and should have stayed with his friends. Robert told him in no uncertain terms that he did his duty, and it would have served no purpose to have another mouth to feed and in any case the *Kempetai* would have had him in their sights. He said nothing more, he didn't need to.

Sir John's visit in early 1949 was again to deal with the bank's problems with Robert no longer involved but knowing that the bank was having a torrid time. Robert had seen Sir John on a couple of recent occasions at social events, but Sir John had asked Robert to have lunch with him before he set off for another of the bank's outposts and Robert had suggested that they eat in the newly created private dining room he had had installed upstairs in the *Mata Hari*, which was a recent acquisition. Sir John was happy to accept the invitation and with Robert's agreement he brought Peter and Colin Warriston along with him.

The four of them stood on the veranda, overlooking Collyer's Quay, having drinks and watching the little boats going back and forth and watching the steady throng of traffic in the distance, over towards the Municipal Building. The noise from the thousands of people alongside the quay rose up to them in a cacophony of sound, the many languages vying with each other. Robert's mind momentarily went back to his first morning at the bank in Fullerton Square and coming out with Mr Yin to get more suits for work. *"Whatever happened to Mr Yin,"* murmured Robert to himself. But he knew. Mr Yin like thousands of others had been forced to swim out to sea on the 17th February 1942 and left to drown.

As they stood watching life in Singapore and feeling the heat of the day, Tong Chee Tan, the *Mata Hari* manager arrived with a note for Robert. "Someone has just handed this in for you, Mr Draper. He did not give his name. Only he said that it was urgent."

Robert took the folded piece of paper and excused himself for a moment. Handing his glass to Tong Chee Tan he opened the sheet and read the few words on it. He made a bit of a face and folding it he put it in his pocket. "Thank you, Chee Tan. Could you send someone over to the Cunard ship, the *Franconia,* and leave a message for Mr Summers that I will see him at 4 pm downstairs. If I am delayed, please look after him.

Turning back to the three guests Robert merely said that it looked as though he had a long day in front of him.

Over lunch the conversation was generally about the state of the old country with Sir John saying that the Americans were stepping up and providing some aid but nothing like enough with the recovery of Germany far higher on their list of priorities. Colin Warriston told a tale of his family business which his older brother had managed, now going to the wall after three generations. Sometime later Peter said that he had been over to Kuching to see if he could encourage business over there but had found things were stagnant, at least that's the word Robert heard him use.

During the lunch of fresh seafood and salad Sir John explained about some new British monetary regulations coming into place and how he thought it would make life even more difficult, before asking Robert about the commercial deal Robert was involved in with Zhang Lee John. "I see from the plans that it is a threefold exercise with the bank being involved in front ending the capital development in stages one and two. What I really want to know, Bob, is how you see the long-term development of the city."

Robert had been expecting the grilling. He had had detailed discussions with Peter and Colin on two occasions and taken both of them on a site visit. Zhang Lee John had been involved in these meetings, but he was away in KL so could not be present at the lunch. Robert went through the current situation and how he and Lee John saw the potential in incrementally developing the site up towards Bugis Street at the east end of the central commercial area. "We think that too big a development at this stage would create too much of a financial risk for all parties and that a three-stage development over four to five years would encourage new businesses to build on ones that have already taken advantage of the earlier stages. The Economic Division of the Singapore Government also see it as a more realistic step. I should add that we are now in discussion with an American company who want to locate at some point to this region and I have asked Peter to be involved in our next round of discussions with them. The plan of course allows for some flexibility, particularly a slowing down if the political situation becomes more difficult but we are optimistic that this development and others that will follow will encourage the promotion of new commercial activity. We understand that Symonds are planning something on a larger scale with support from Barclays over towards North Bridge but in our opinion that development is too risky. The social housing issue in that area makes it a potential problem."

Sir John was nodding. "I like the ideas you have put forward although my concern was your lack of commercial experience. As far as I can see your experience is in domestic capital projects, other than the evaluation process when you worked with us."

"Don't disagree, Sir John. I wouldn't be trying to persuade you to be involved in the project if it wasn't for Zhang Lee John's experience. He worked with the bank on a project in '37 in Shanghai to great effect and what we propose is not so different. I think the three-stage effect we believe offers security to all parties in that we will not need finance too far ahead and we should start to see returns as the second stage gets to a critical point. We already have a number of businesses keen in relocating to the development and our aim will be to keep them warm. We considered the option of getting two banks involved; still could, but we thought because of my association with the Union & China that we should give you first crack at the development."

Sir John sat quietly nodding at all of what Robert had just outlined, as the waiters' cleared plates from the table and reset it for the next course. Finally, he said, "Peter and I have been persuaded with the business plan for the development, but I think in reality it is because you are involved. Inexperience or not we think you will keep at it until it is a success and frankly the bank needs more ideas like yours and Zhang Lee John's." Sir John lent over towards Robert and offered out his right hand and as Robert shook it, he said, "We're on board. Now to more pressing matters. I understand you are to be married shortly and as I shan't be around as I have urgent matters to deal with in Hong Kong I need to know what can I give you as a wedding present."

When the bankers had gone Robert went down to the small office that Tong Chee Tan had at the back of the building and borrowed it for a few moments to put a call through to Zhang Lee John in KL. "All systems are go, Lee John. We can go ahead with the negotiations for the last piece of property. I leave that in your hands. I will try and ring you this evening with a fuller account.

Grahame Kerr

****

Frank Summers turned up a few minutes early wearing a Cunard uniform and Robert learned that he was the Assistant Engineer on the *SS Franconia* that had brought in a large contingent of British servicemen the day before.

As they shook hands Frank Summers said, "We are sailing at seven, so I have to be back for no later than six o'clock. The old girl needs to be warmed up before she will be able to set off for Hong Kong."

Robert took Frank over to a corner away from the few people in the bar and after he had asked if Frank would like a drink he said, "I know you weren't in Sime Road or Changi so where were you interned? All your note said was that you had been interned and knew something about the gold, and could we meet urgently."

Frank nodded and took a drink from the beer that had just been brought over by one of the waiters. "I was in River Valley Road initially with Laz who told me to contact you when I saw him a few weeks ago. I hurt my leg, tore it open and I was looked after by Knowsley our first aid guy. We became good friends. Anyway, I was okay for months and then I went down with fever. You know what it's like, good one day, out of your mind the next. The Nips wanted just fit men at River Valley as they were needed for repairing the ships and the like so they shoved me up to Adam Road."

Robert interrupted Frank. "How is Laz? He's hopeless at keeping in touch and the last I heard he was back in London having a bit of a break and that the City of London had offered him his old job back."

Frank laughed. "I suspect he'll always be the same. I saw him a few weeks ago for a few beers. He had some divorcee in tow. This one he'll have a job chasing off, although when I saw them, he seemed quite keen on her."

Robert smiled at the description of Laz. It did seem like him; he was always keen until the girl started getting serious. Whoever tied him down was going to have to use thick rope.

"Anyway, when I was moved up to Adam Road Knowlsey turned up there. Being Eurasian he seemed to be able to move around; the Nips seemed to be comfortable about letting him look after us. But this time he seemed very worried. Laz when I saw him said that he was sure he was a pharmacist; had a clinic on the Island and helped the children a lot. The Nips used him to treat injuries and the like at the camp and at River Valley. At the time he was the only medic we had, so the Nips needed him to sort out injuries, and to look after us when we went down with the fever. Was I glad to see him. I had been down with fever and was coming round that day and feeling a bit better. I remember he sat beside me and he told me he thought the Nips were after him and he gave me a bit of paper and told me to hide it. He said he would get it back if everything turned out okay. I asked him what the note was about but he said he hadn't read it; he had only just got it from someone who knew where there was a load of gold the Nips wanted. The Nips turned up an hour or so later and started searching for him. They knew who they were looking for. There was only maybe fifty of us in the camp and they started laying into us. Then they found Knowsley who had been hiding in a latrine and started on him. I wasn't in much of a state so apart from them throwing me out of my cot they left me alone, but they beat up some of the lads bad, real bad. If it hadn't been for Lieutenant Yamasta turning up, I reckon they would have finished some of us off. Yamasta said that we were vital for the repair of the ships and for collecting goods to go back to Japan, and he started yelling and remonstrating with the *Kempeta*i and telling them they should take the first aider if that is who they were after and get out. Believe it or not they did. They dragged Knowlsey out and left us. Yamasta, he could speak good English, then started shouting at us saying that if we were involved in drug smuggling or whatever then we got what we deserved but he needed men to repair ships and engines and we were on our last chance. A few days later they shipped some of the lads back to River Valley but a quack they now had at Adam Road said that me and a few others were not up to it, so they put us on fatigues clearing bomb damage and taking booty up to one of the warehouses up near Bugis Street ready for sending on to Japan. We were on that that for more than a year and then towards the end we were digging trenches in case the Allies invaded."

"Do you know when all this happened?"

"I think I was shipped off to Adam Road sometime in late '42."

"Any idea what happened to Knowlsey?"

Frank Summers finished his drink and Robert signalled for two more beers.

"After I was at Adam Road for a while there was a great explosion, in fact more than that, down at the docks and a couple of nights later some of the warehouses down by the canal went up in flames."

Robert nodded. "That would have been in the October '43."

"The Nips were going demented accusing us of being involved because we had to take stuff up that way every day. They rounded us up and made us do tenko for a whole day in the sun while the *Kempetai* searched our huts. There found nothing other than some extra food we had filched from somewhere. It turned out it was our lads blowing up the ships in the docks and the Nips were then all over the place searching for commandos."

Robert was nodding at this information. He knew it all already.

"Laz says that the River Valley lads got it in the neck until Yamasta pointed out that the ships had been sunk by limpet mines of the type used by the Allies so that it must have been commandos doing a raid. Ended up with Laz's mob having to try and repair the damage although he says they never got very far as they didn't have enough equipment to do a proper job."

Robert was sitting patiently and Frank watching his face said, "I know. I know. I'll get to the gold in a minute."

There was a small pause as Frank looked around and then he continued. "When I was with the fever; you know how it is your one minute lucid and another minute you're raving away. Anyway, Knowlsey was sat with me cleaning me up. I had come round a bit, and I could see he was very worried. All I remember is that he gave me the bit of paper and said that it was about where there was a load of gold the Nips were after. He said he thought the *Kempetai* were looking for him. I hadn't a clue what he was talking about, but he went on that he needed to see a Chinaman. I think he called him Tan Chinsin or something like that and he was going to make a break for it that night. He did say something about a Jewish friend was also in trouble. He said he wanted the piece of paper back if he survived. Then the commotion started and Knowlsey went and hid in the latrine. I don't really remember much after that."

"Do you think he said Tan Choo Sin?"

Frank smiled back. "I think that was it. Sorry I'm not good with Chinese names."

Robert said nothing thinking through the timescale of events. *"John Kwai Knowles could not have known that Tan Choo Sin had already been arrested,"* Robert mused. Then he said, "Do you still have the piece of paper?"

Frank shook his head, "It fell to pieces in the end. I did copy some of the signs though." He handed Robert what was a yellowed piece of paper with perhaps a dozen Chinese words on it." It seemed to be a code or direction about something from the quick look Robert made. He turned his attention back to Frank.

Frank continued. "Anyway, you know the rest. The *Kempetai* came that night and after battering the hell out of half a dozen lads they dragged Knowlsey away."

"So, you don't know what happened to Knowlsey?"

Frank shook his head. "Not a clue, Mr Draper, but when the *Kempetai* came to Adam Road just after the explosions they wanted to know what everybody had done in civvy life and one of our lads who spoke the lingo said they were after men who knew where a load of gold was hidden."

"Did they have an officer with them? A Captain Ishiguru?

Frank finished his beer and shook his head when Robert offered him another. "Got to keep a clear head if I'm on duty." As an afterthought he said, "There was an officer yelling at his men, but I didn't get his name." Frank got up, "Sorry but I've got to go."

Robert got up from where he had been sitting and proffered his hand. "You have been a great help, Frank. Give my kind regards to Laz when you next see him. Tell him I miss our drinking sessions. They were always different."

As they walked to the entrance with Frank laughing and telling Robert that a night out with Laz was an experience, Robert suddenly asked, "what I forgot to ask is how you ended up on the Island when we surrendered?"

"Oh, I was Assistant Engineer on the Empress of Asia and as she came in sight of the Island we were bombed by the Nips, about twenty miles from here. Hell, I was one of the lucky ones. Some of my lads were stuck in the engine room and went down with the ship. So did loads of soldiers. If it hadn't been for a ship called the *Lancashire Lass* I would have been a goner. It nipped in with the Nips still bombing us and took off hundreds. Even when she was hit, she wouldn't give in and got us to a destroyer who brought us into here. Last I saw of her she was listing to port but still working her way back to here."

Robert smiled at Frank Summers. "You've given me information that is more important than anything about the gold. The *Lancashire Lass* was my uncle's ship. The ship after some repairs went off and rescued some more people over in Sumatra and was sunk by the Nips. My uncle was the Captain and the bar in here is named after him."

Frank Summers shook Robert's hand again and smiled back at Robert before he set off for Clarke's Quay a few hundred yards away.

Robert walked back into the *Mata Hari* momentarily confused by the turn of events.

Chapter 34

Robert walked into Mike's pharmacy; he couldn't wait any longer to speak to Mike about *Knowsley*. The wedding was only a few days away and then he would be away on honeymoon for a month. Not knowing more about *Knowsley* and his connection to the gold was too much to bear. Mike as a pharmacist must know more about him. When he went into the shop Mike was dealing with a young woman with a little child and he just acknowledged Robert before continuing to deal with the customer.

Robert looked at some toiletries on the shelves and picked out some soap that he rather liked. Did you talk to your new wife about the soap you liked, or did it just happen? He smiled at the question and the fact that he didn't know the answer. He guessed that there would be many such things to be decided –Bin Lau had said that he thought it was a bit like going into a dark room. You had to walk with your new life partner around the room to find the window in order to draw the curtains and let the light in.

He was deep in thought about the wedding and the new life about to happen when Mike tapped him on the shoulder. "What can I do for you, Mr Draper? Have you got everything you need for the great day? I hope not and you spend a fortune as it may go some way towards paying for the outfit Mary has bought." He was smiling as he said it.

Robert shrugged his shoulders and smiled back. "I was just thinking about whether I will be consulted in future about such things as the type of soap I like."

"My dear chap I would worry much more about how long you can survive before you are told that you should not have apricot jam for breakfast as it is fattening or the colour of your tie does not go with your suit. Soap seems a small matter."

Mike not one for humour normally was clearly enjoying seeing Robert having the jitters. "You usually get the thumbs up after about ten years and then you know you are okay. What it means is that they have completed their training programme and her wishes have become yours."

"Isn't that a bit cynical," Robert looking across to where Mary was serving an elderly European woman whom Robert recognised. Both of them said nothing more as Robert handed over the toiletries he had chosen, and Robert walked with him over to the counter handing over some money. Mary finished dealing with the customer who smiled at Robert and wished him well as she left the shop. Mary turned to Robert and briefly saying "good morning" she looked over the purchases that Robert had selected.

"This soap can be very harsh on your skin. I'm sure Leanne would choose softer soap, Robert."

Robert saw Mike smirk. "Oh, it's just for Chunggy. He likes that particular soap and I promised him I would get some when I came to your shop this morning," Robert said. Mike continued smirking and Mary clearly didn't believe him. "By the way who was that lady? I know her from somewhere."

Mike answered. "Mrs Jeffries. Husband is the Chief Engineer at the power station." Robert nodded. At last, he remembered her.

"Why don't you two go off and have a coffee." Mary turned to Mike. "It's clear Robert came to talk to you but don't be all morning. I want to be away to see Mona and Susie around noon. I'm having lunch with them."

Mike took off his white coat without any argument and the two men walked out into the beating heat immediately feeling their clothes stick to them. Mike said, "Come on, let's try Mrs Wang's, she makes a decent cup, and the cakes are good." Mike was still smirking as he walked down a little side street and turned into the coffee shop with Robert following but in deep thought about the wedding and trying to decide whether he had made any decisions or merely agreed to what Leanne had wanted. He just wasn't sure; he hadn't thought about it before.

It was a few minutes later that Robert said, "Did you ever hear John Kwai Knowles being called "Knowlsey"? "

Mike shook his head. "Not in my presence."

Robert told Mike the story Frank Summers had told him.

"Well, it's got to be John. He was a pharmacist. He was Eurasian. But who the hell is the Jew that he was seeing and anyway why was the *Kempetai* interested unless they were trailing John or the Jew. Sorry I can't help on that part but I think it must be John and presumably when they caught John they also got a hold of Rachel, poor sod. She wasn't ever in Changi that I remember so they must have let her stay at their home because she was married to a Eurasian."

Robert shook his head. "Rachel was in the YMCA with me in '42 this is '43."

Mike said nothing, just looked puzzled.

"Why do you think he was working as a first aider?"

Mike sat thinking about it for a moment. "Well, the pharmacy wouldn't be open as the Nips were collecting all the drugs from the pharmacies and hospitals so John would be unemployed. If Rachel was not around he would want to do something. God knows what she had done to upset the Nips. We may never know. John was a great one for helping people and I can see him being involved. It maybe that being a first aider also helped him if he was the contact with Tan Choo Sin."

Robert was thinking through what Mike had said when Mike added, "John and Rachel were great friends of the Bishop. I don't think he'll be much help to you though as he's away at this time; I seem to remember something in the newspaper. He has a secretary who was with him before the surrender so she may know more. She was in the women's camp. Her name's Celia Normanton."

Robert nodded. "That is helpful, Mike. Come on you had better get back. I'm very grateful. I'll see you on Saturday.

Mike stood up and as they set off to leave the café he said, "Don't worry, Bob. You're marrying a gorgeous woman and she will make you a great wife." Laughing he added, "Just go with the flow."

****

Bin Lau drove Robert down to Saint Andrews Cathedral. "I can't make head or tail of the words on that piece of paper, boss. Can I show it to my auntie? She's good with clues and the like. She lives over Mount Faber way so maybe we can go there later." Robert nodded at what Bin Lau had said just noticing as they parked that there were a number of cars he recognised.

Inside the Cathedral he could hear voices he definitely recognised.

"Hullo, darling." Leanne appeared from nowhere. "I didn't know you would be here."

Robert was totally at sea. "What's happening? I thought we had a rehearsal last week?" He kissed Leanne and then looked around. He could see Susie and Rebecca some distance away as well as two other young women. Somewhere he could hear other women's voices.

"Darling, you look completely lost. Mummy was having a coffee morning to discuss final arrangements and we decided to come down and look around again. Two of my school chums have arrived so it was an opportunity for them to see the Cathedral before Saturday. They're staying at the Goodwood, so they know where the reception is to be. Oh, and there's a surprise for you. You better come and see." Leanne linked her arm in Roberts and led him down towards the altar.

There standing talking to Susie was Kay. She turned as they approached and gave him the most wonderful smile. She rushed up and gave him a kiss. Robert was speechless and it was Susie who said, "Well that's one for the record books. A speechless Bob Draper."

"What are you doing here, "was all Robert could say with now seemingly half a dozen women round him.

"I'm on my way to live in Dunedin and I arranged to stop off here for a few days and when I turned up at Mrs Lin Yuen's old house, I was met by Susie who told me the news. It's wonderful."

Robert still wasn't taking it all in, he was completely off tangent. All he could say was, "I came to see the Bishop's secretary."

Kay was telling everybody that the last time she had seen Robert was when she was loaded onto the back of an army lorry to go off to the docks, from Sime Road, and Robert had stood with a crowd of other well-wishers shouting their best wishes.

Leanne had a hold of Robert's arm and tried to swivel him around to introduce him to her friends, but Robert was not to be put off. "But why didn't you write. I would have sent you an invite."

It was Leanne who answered. "Darling that's all arranged. Kay doesn't leave until Sunday night so she and her husband will be at the wedding."

That was the last straw. Robert shook off the arm. "Hang on a minute. I am totally unsure as to what is happening. Did you say they're married?

"Yes. You'll meet him tonight. He has gone off to the General to see some old friends."

Kay was however by this time answering questions from Susie and telling her about the Cathedral being used as a hospital and how Robert and his Unit had camped, exhausted, outside for nearly two days until the Japs had turned up so Robert gave up and turned back to be introduced to Leanne's friends. Robert was getting nowhere in the chaos. It was a few minutes later that Susie rescued him. "Come on, Bob. You need peace and quiet." Robert followed her like a lamb watching Leanne and her friends talking to Kay and laughing at something, no doubt about him he decided."

"I need to see the Bishop's secretary." Robert had stopped at the entrance to the Cathedral offices having been led there by Susie.

"The secretary's through there." Susie pointed down a corridor.

"I've not even said goodbye to anyone."

"In the excitement I don't suppose anyone will notice, Bob. Now don't forget dinner is early to suit David. I've invited Kay and her husband Stephen, so you'll get a chance to catch up on the news. Now disappear and I will take this noisy crowd off for lunch with Mona and Mary.

Robert went to find the secretary's office only to realise when he saw her that he knew her slightly. She had been in the camp although he had only seen her perhaps two or three times in the time he was at Sime Road. He knew nothing about her other than she worked for the Bishop.

Robert apologised for bothering her and explained that he thought, or at least hoped, that she knew or had known Rachel and John Kwai Knowles.

Celia Normanton came round from her desk and said she was pleased to see Robert and was he the Robert Draper that was getting married on Saturday. Robert nodded at this and repeated the question.

"Of course, I knew them. They were great friends of the Bishop. He is not here; he is in Calcutta at an ecumenical conference and will be back next week. You know the Dean is conducting your service."

Robert nodded again. He decided in a flash that there must be an easier way to live. Perhaps Martin did have the best deal just living with his mules and clearing a patch of jungle. As he was thinking about Martin, Celia Normanton had continued to speak and realising he had missed what she had been saying, he said, "Oh I'm sorry. I missed what you said."

"The Bishop always said that there must be a lot more gold left over and somewhere on the Island. We often talk about you and say that if you keep turning up stones it will be found." In a bit of a fluster, she repeated herself, "The Bishop is convinced you will find it."

"Miss Normanton, would John Kwai Knowles have been involved in keeping the gold?"

Miss Normanton raised an eyebrow and shook her head. "I don't think so. The Bishop presumed that when poor John was tortured it was because he knew someone who was involved and he must have mentioned the Bishop and that is why the Japanese then again arrested the Bishop. John if he did know anything must have been very brave not to say where it was. Such a terrible death and Rachel as well. Did you know Rachel, Mr Draper? Such a lovely person."

Robert for seemingly the hundredth time nodded. "I was in a cell with her for about two weeks. She was a very brave woman." "Do you know the name Tan Choo Sin?"

Miss Normanton shook her head and went back towards her seat by the desk. Then she stopped. "Wasn't there a lorry firm before the war with Tan Choo Sin on the side of the vehicles. I think they used to deliver to us."

Robert couldn't remember seeing lorries with Tan Choo Sin on their sides; life would have been so easy if he had remembered them. He said nothing in response to what she said. Instead, he said, "Did you know Ernest Beverley?"

"Of course, Mr Draper. He was an elder and a warden of the Cathedral. He was great friend of the Bishop and was also quite friendly with Mr Knowles. I think he gave some money to a charity that Mr Knowles ran for sickly children.

Robert thanked Miss Normanton and started to leave. He was actually through into the corridor when he turned back and asked. "Does the Bishop have connections to other religious groups, say the Jewish community?"

Miss Normanton smiled at Robert as though he was demented. "Of course, he has. He often has meetings with the other religious leaders that live on the Island. Some are very good friends."

"Would he have had contacts during the war?"

I can't say Mr Draper as I was in the women's camp but it must have been possible as many of the Jewish men were interned from November 1943. A few of the Jewish traders on Serangoon Road I think were left to their own devices, but most were interned. You must know that as you organised the fatigues in the men's camp."

Robert smiled and thanked her and left looking for Bin Lau who he found smoking under a tree near to where many wounded people had lain on 16th February 1942. "Come on Bin Lau, let's get out of this mad house. Let's find a tea house or better still somewhere where I can have a beer and then we can visit your auntie."

Bin Lau finished off his cigarette and laughed at Robert. "Boss you look exhausted. The ladies have left and headed for Raffles so best we don't go there. I know a good place on Robinson Road."

Chapter 35

Robert arrived late for dinner with Susie and David and guests. It wasn't as though he had to travel across to Cathay House as Susie had arranged the dinner party in Robert's home as the flat in Cathay House was much too small for more than a dozen guests. A very apologetic Robert arrived late to his house and then asked to be excused for ten minutes whilst he had a quick shower and dressed in his best tucker. As always Chunggy had anticipated his needs, and everything was laid out ready for him. As he was getting dressed a very excited Leanne came in and ignoring Robert's pleas that he was trying to get dressed she came over and kissed him.

It was perhaps Chunggy's entry carrying polished shoes that stopped Leanne from being even more amorous. Poor Chunggy was most apologetic, and it was Robert who said, "Don't you dare leave Chunggy. I need a chaperone." Kissing Leanne again he swirled her round and pushed her towards the door. "Out before my reputation is completely ruined. I will be down in two minutes."

Leanne left but only after saying that it was not only his reputation that was ruined, as she had also lost a lot more. Robert was heard to say "bloody hell" as he completed getting dressed.

Downstairs two minutes later Robert was apologetic to all and sundry although he learned quickly that most hadn't noticed he was thirty minutes late as they had been enjoying the contents of his drink's cabinet. Looking for Leanne, he found her with her two school chums laughing at some joke which came to an end when Robert came up beside Leanne.

"Anyway, why are you late? Mummy is not pleased with you," Leanne said intertwining her arm with Robert's who had been handed a large stengah by Sunni who was for once smiling and not looking stern. Robert had asked Chunggy why Sunni always looked stern at the social occasions and had been told that Chunggy had told him that he must look serious for such occasions. The next time Robert had seen Sunni, he had told him to smile and ignore some of Chunggy's daft ideas.

"I had to go up to Mount Faber to see Bin Lau's auntie and then go to the Jewish cemetery on Thomson Road. It took ages as the traffic was awful and then getting back was just as bad. Anyway, I'm here."

"Well don't think that's going to get you off the hook with Mummy." Robert watched Susie come in with David from Mrs Lin Yuen's old bedroom. Susie glanced across at him and he signalled across to her that he was sorry. She just shook her head and then turned and started talking to Kay and Stephen who Robert hadn't seen as they had been on the veranda enjoying their drink with Peter and Ethel.

At dinner Susie had thoughtfully placed Robert next to Kay and he spent a good bit of time catching up on the news. It seems that Kay and Stephen had had a whirlwind romance culminating in a special licence as Stephen had landed a consultant's post in Dunedin and the hospital needed him urgently. "It all happened in about six weeks. Engaged, married, resigned, a family get together for both of us and then off. Not quite the leisurely trip on the *Narkunda* that you and I had, Bob. God, do you remember the awful food."

"I'm thinking that only three of us have survived."

"I met Jenny's mum about six months ago. She was lovely. She knew about Harry and said that she was sure they would have made a great couple."

Leanne who was sat on Robert's other side could hear some of the conversation and asked who Jenny was; she knew that Harry had been Robert's house mate.

Kay answered "There was three of us, all nurses. Laura and Jenny did their training in London, and I did mine in Birmingham and we teamed up on the ship coming out to here. We met the three reprobates on the ship and Harry and Jenny instantly clicked."

Robert added, "The last time I saw Jenny she was working with Laura in one of the emergency wards outside the General. They were looking after people injured by the bombing. Laura in fact was on her last shift before she left to go and work in a military hospital, they were setting up in Port Moresby. She was going with her fiancé, a South African medic. All I know is the ship never made it."

"So, who was the third reprobate?"

"Oh god. Surely you've heard of Laz. A woman's nightmare."

At that Robert, with the noise in the room growing quite loud with laughter, added to the noise by roaring with laughter as he remembered his friend. "Never mind a woman's nightmare. He was our nightmare. A night out with him and anything could happen. There was this place up in Siglap, Rosies. Jenny threatened Harry that if we went again, she was calling off the engagement. You couldn't take him to the tennis club as we never knew what he would do."

It was at a later period in the evening that Kay saw Robert standing on the veranda momentarily alone. Leanne was deep in conversation in the dining room with Rebecca and her two school chums presumably about last-minute detail as the three were to be her bridesmaids. Other guests were enjoying the cool air in the garden and sitting under the mango tree with Sunni being very attentive.

Kay came over. "A lot has happened since those eight weeks on the *Narkunda*."

"I'm glad you've met someone Kay. I've only had a few minutes talking to Stephen and he seems a good match for you. For god's sake, let's not lose touch."

Kay smiled and shook her head. "You're right. Too much has happened and we mustn't forget it. If I have children, I will want to bring them one day to the Island to show them what happened."

They both talked for a few moments about friends alive and dead who they had both known and then Kay said, "I saw Joyce a few months ago. I'm sorry Bob but she didn't know who I was. The Connors have placed her in a special hospital in Warwickshire and they have bought a cottage nearby. Mrs Connor sees her most weeks, but she doesn't even know her mother. Professor Connor keeps himself busy doing his research. It's all very sad."

Robert nodded at what Kay had just told him. "The Connors sent me a card last Christmas and said that Joyce had taken a turn for the worse. Poor girl. It's my fault. I made her catch the ship out on the 12th. She had no chance."

Kay shook her head. "No, you're wrong Bob. It was the fault of those idiots up on Nassim Road who wouldn't make a decision about getting civilians out until it was too late. Anyway, nothing could have come of it between you both as she would have wanted to come back to Blighty and you would have stayed here. Mind you how anyone wants to live there is beyond me; last winter was beyond all reason. Even the boilers in the hospital didn't work for days and we ran out of coal for the house. It was freezing."

"How warm is it in Dunedin," Robert asked smiling at a good friend.

"I don't know. Anyway, I've got my own hot water bottle," Kay replied looking across at Stephen who was in deep conversation with the Cummings.

Leanne came up behind them. "So, have you two caught up on all the news? "

Kay turned and gave Leanne a hug. "Just look after this daft sod. He's so single minded he forgets what planet he is on sometimes. Is he still trying to find the gold?"

At that Leanne groaned. She took Robert's arm and looked up at him. "Kay, he even had to leave the Island because half the thugs in the Far East were closing in."

Robert smiled down at a very happy face. "My darling is exaggerating, Kay. It was mainly the British Government, the Kuomintang and the Malay Communist Party. All perfectly nice people as you can imagine."

Chapter 36

The night before the wedding Robert had been invited out to dinner with Henry, Peter, Mike, and Brian who Robert had asked to be his best man. Bin Lau picked the Preston's up first and collected Robert on the way to Raffles Place where Henry had organised a dinner at a Chinese restaurant. Peter had arranged to be taken down in the bank's car and he collected Mike on the way.

Robert just sat back with Brian doing most of the talking and Henry enjoying the cool air wafting through the open top.

At the restaurant it was no less than the owner who came out to meet them and Henry who was very much in charge. Robert wanted to know what Bin Lau would be doing but all he got was a smile and "I'll be around boss to take you home."

In the restaurant they had a private room upstairs with a balcony overlooking everything in the long square. Robert was handed a large stengah without even being asked what he wanted, and the others had beers, so Robert presumed it had been arranged. When Peter and Mike finally arrived, there were more drinks before at last they were told the food was ready and they went into the private dining room.

As always, the first thing they did was to toast absent friends and all those who did not make it to the end of the war. They now knew that their great friends the Thorsby's, and their sons David and Jay who had grown up with Brian and Martin, had died when the ship they were escaping on had gone down off Banda Island on the 14th of February 1942. There had been a possibility that David Thorsby had survived as some of the rescued passengers thought they had seen him but there was no further sighting or information.

Inevitably during the evening Robert was asked for the latest information he had on his search for the gold. Robert explained what had happened over the past few days.

"So, what does the piece of paper say, "asked Brian enjoying the experience of being in the inner club.

"That's the problem really, Brian. Because Frank Summers copied what he could remember it is not very accurate. Bin Lau's auntie agreed it was some sort of directions as well as a sign we should look for but that there seem to be words missing."

"What about the Jewish connection? "Mike asked.

"In think the person John Kwai Knowles was meeting was under surveillance. I think the Jewish chap knew he was under surveillance and passed the note onto Knowles as to where the gold was hidden, probably in desperation. Knowles was just a courier, the link between the source and Tan Choo Sin; at least that's what it seems. Frank Summers says that from what he can remember Knowles said that he and the Jewish man were seen together; they were probably meeting about the gold not knowing that Tan Choo Sin had already been betrayed. I think the Jewish man, his name is David Abadi by the way, knew he was under surveillance, and he had to try and keep access to the gold open, so he had no choice but to tell John Kwai Knowles, but they were then seen together." Robert was looking very smug as he said it.

Henry watching Robert's smug look said, "Alright young man, what else do you know?"

"Bin Lau took me this afternoon to see Ben Nazario. You may remember him, Henry, and you, Mike. He was the hut leader for the Jewish internees in hut 46. He helped me get messages to the gardener at the Waterloo Street synagogue who Maurice Levy had arranged would hide money for me. Anyway, Ben Nazario was pleased to see me, even knew about the wedding. He said that the *Kempetai* arrested one of his community in 1943, for black market selling. He said they also made a surprise search of the community up on Serangoon Road a few weeks later and there was a shootout. They killed a man called David Abadi." There was a pause as everyone took in what Robert has just told them. "Apparently David Abadi was a Jew and a friend of Maurice Levy. He wasn't one of Ben Nazario's community but had asked for somewhere to hide when the Japs started to look for him."

"Ah Ha, we have the connection," Henry said.

Robert nodded at Henry and then smiled around at his friends. "I think we now know who the keeper of the gold was, and that John Kwai Knowles would contact him and tell him the communists needed gold and Abadi would arrange a shipment. Abadi would tell John Kwai Knowles where Tan Choo Sin could then collect the gold. I can only think Abadi agreed to a larger than normal shipment because it was becoming more difficult to make trips off the Island or because they were much more difficult to get to because they were based in the jungle. I also don't think that Lai Tek knew who authorised the gold only that Tan Choo Sin was involved."

"Lai Tek seems to have killed off the link to the gold when he betrayed Tan Choo Sin. The link to John Kwai Knowles and David Abadi was lost," Peter said quietly.

Robert shook his head at what Peter said. "I think Lai Tek betrayed Tan Choo Sin because he wanted his hands on the gold, and it suited him to kill off any link. If he had not betrayed Tan Choo Sin, Lai Tek would have been under pressure to continue helping in the search for the gold whereas the betrayal meant that the *Kempetai* had killed off the link to where it came from. Lai Tek could tell them other names knowing that he was safe with his gold.

"Hang on. If the large shipment meant that a lorry had to collect it from the source, then Tan Choo Sin or his driver would have had to go to the source; Tan Choo Sin would surely have told them under torture where his driver had collected it ." Brian had been sitting quietly enjoying being included in the conversation.

"It doesn't look that way, Brian. Tan Choo Sin under interrogation by the Nips must have given John Kwai Knowles's name but I can only presume not the source. All I know is that John Kwai Knowles was arrested sometime after Tan Choo Sin disappeared and that David Abadi was probably already under surveillance because the *Kempetai* just didn't trust him. My guess is that they met to arrange a shipment not knowing that Tan Choo Sin had been lifted and had given John Kwai Knowles' name under torture. The *Kempetai* started looking for Knowles only to see him meeting David Abadi who they were already suspicious about. Somehow, they both escape; Knowles to hide at Adam Road camp and David Abadi up Serangoon Road "

Peter asked another question," Why do you think the *Kempetai* were already interested in David Abadi?

"David Abadi was a Lecturer in Asiatic Languages at the Raffles College. It was closed down during the war and was the HQ for the Japanese Army. The *Kempetai* kept a close watch on all the staff as they didn't trust anyone who was a member of the middle classes. Abadi from what I now know was quite important in the Jewish community worshipping at Waterloo Road and a good friend of Maurice Levy. The small Jewish community up on Serangoon Road suffered because they hid him; a good many of them ended up in Sime Road."

Peter replied, "David Abadi may well have been the keeper of the gold but why did he give the note to John Kwai Knowles in a Chinese code?"

"I think that Frank Summers misunderstood what he was told. I think David Abadi gave John Kwai Knowles a note of where the gold was hidden as a fall back in case the *Kempetai* took more interest in him in order to ensure that the gold could still be accessed. Remember he didn't know about Tan Choo Sin being arrested or that they were looking for John Kwai Knowles. The note was not in plain script but John Kwai Knowles would have known how to interpret the note. Remember Frank Summers did not copy all the note just bits he could remember, and it was in Chinese script. Abadi giving Knowles the note was just some form of insurance."

Henry who had been smoking a cigarette and absorbing all the information asked, "What do we know about Abadi. Why did Maurice Levy trust him with such a big job?"

"It seems that Abadi was brought up in Shanghai and his first language was more or less Chinese. As he was Jewish, he was not interned. He was a family friend of the Levy's; he was married but his wife died some years ago and he never remarried." Robert said all this watching the faces of his friends, finishing with "so Ben

Nazario told me". "In my opinion the *Kempetai* had John Kwai Knowles watched after Tan Choo Sin gave them his name under torture and were fortunate to see him meet with David Abadi. I think neither could have known when they met that John was being watched and Abadi gave the note to Knowles because he thought he might be on borrowed time because he knew he was under scrutiny; they knew nothing about Tan Choo Sin having been betrayed. Hundreds were being arrested and tortured because of the godown incidents and the *Kempetai* would have looked for people with influence in the community. Abadi would have fitted the bill. Maurice never spoke to me about Abadi but Ben Nazario said that Abadi was quite important and often helped Government officers as he had lots of contacts."

"So why was Knowles not just arrested when Tan Choo Sin gave out his name?" Brian asked.

"The answer is, I don't know. It maybe they thought that he could lead them to the location of the gold which if Tan Choo Sin did know of, he had not betrayed before his death. It could be that when Tan Choo Sin was told to pick up the gold from a location, he did not realise that it was where other gold was hidden. The *Kempetai* nearly pulled it off, with Knowles and Abadi just escaping and both dying only a few days later; well weeks in Abadi's case."

Robert after a pause whilst he took a drink then continued. "Knowles could not say where the gold was as he had not translated the note and I don't think the *Kempetai* could have known about the note, only that Knowles was a link. If Knowles did confess that Abadi knew the location of the gold that did not help the *Kempetai* because when they do corner Abadi there is a shoot-out and Abadi dies. All links to the location are dead or seem to be.

Brian looking very pleased with himself couldn't wait with his next question and was asking it as Robert finished what he had been saying. "Well, have you worked out where the gold is?

"Brian I am hoping that it is your jacket pocket. I gave it you not thirty minutes ago."

"No not the bloody wedding ring. Do you know where the gold is?"

It was Brian's father who intervened. "Brian, it's obvious. We first have to decipher the clues that David Abadi left in John Kwai Knowles' care."

"Well, all I can say is that my best friend is the best winder up I've ever come across. He's sat there with a face like a Cheshire cat. I thought he had worked it out."

"Well now we know all this, where does it take us?" Mike said shaking his head at all the interruptions and questions.

"It takes us nowhere, Mike. It will just have to wait. I am going to be away for a month on my honeymoon." Robert turned to Brian sat on his left, "Now have you got your speech ready. "

"You can bet on it. I have a few tales to tell."

Robert looked at Henry. "I'm beginning to think I asked the wrong son." Turning back to Brian, Robert added, "Just remember there will be ladies present as well as the HC and also remember I have to live here afterwards."

The evening continued in this vein with much laughter from Robert and his friends but with Robert never admitting that Bin Lau's auntie had worked out a good deal of what was on the piece of paper that Frank Summers had given him.

It was on the way home with Brian sitting in the front talking to Bin Lau and Robert sat in the back with Henry that he was again asked about the gold.

Henry smoking his last cigarette of the day said, "Are you sure that Abadi is the link to the gold?"

Robert smiled across at Henry and for some reason keeping his voice low, "It could only have been him. Ben Nazario was quite clear. He said that he had a few conversations with David Abadi, whilst he was in hiding, who told him his days were numbered. Ben Nazario said that he knew that Abadi was friendly with Maurice

Levy and that they both worshipped at the Jewish synagogue on Waterloo Street. Apparently, the Jews on Serangoon Road have their own synagogue but only a few of the local Jews who were shopkeepers used it. We know Maurice couldn't leave the Island because his wife was dying and was in the General. That's why he did voluntary work at the hospital; so he could be near her. I saw Maurice in the evening of the 15th at the synagogue. He was having a meeting about the surrender and what might happen to the Jewish community. He didn't say anything about Abadi, but he did say that he just hoped all his plans would work. Abadi told Ben Nazario that he couldn't be taken alive. I assume that Maurice knew he also had only a short time to live after the surrender as the Japs would have had information from their inner source about who had been involved with the gold shipments."

"You're determined that somebody in the Colonial Office was an informant."

"More than ever. I even think Comber has an idea who it was or is, but I suspect it will never be revealed. It would be too embarrassing for the Government. I also now think that Ernest Beverley helped to arrange the connections but did not know where the gold was. As far as I can see he was killed by Sato just about the time that David Abadi died so any possible link was again broken."

"Has Bin Lau's aunt had a good go at the piece of paper?"

"Mmm. She agrees that it looks like an inscription you put over a doorway but some of its missing. There are also directions about going to a location but not where to start from."

Henry finished his cigarette as Bin Lau drove them into the driveway of the Preston's house. As Henry started to get out, Robert said, "I meant to ask. When you got married did Mona change the soap you used?

Henry raised his eyebrows, "I haven't a clue what you're on about. I have enough to worry about at the station without worrying about what soap Mona buys. If I don't like something I say so."

Brian had got out and come around to stand by his father. "God, she is changing your soap already."

"Now don't you wind him up. It's bad enough when he does it to you." Turning back to Robert, Henry said, "Bob, go and get a good night's sleep. Tomorrow is a big day." With that he turned and walked up the steps to the house with Brian just saying, "I would get Chunggy to get a secret supply."

Chapter 37

Robert sat on the veranda having his last breakfast in Mrs Lin Yuen's house. Chunggy was fussing round making sure he had coffee and his favourite caraway cakes; Robert was reading the newspaper and pretending he wasn't really interested. Robert could see the little old Chinese man in the Reeves' garden sweeping the leaves and tidying up before it became too hot. There was chatter on the patio below and he could hear Sunni and Mrs Di Lavio talking so he presumed that Sunni had come in for an hour or so before going back up to Siglap to bring May and her two daughters down to the cathedral. Susie had said that she and David would be moving in later the following week and Robert knew that she had had discussions with Sunni about certain changes she wanted in the back garden to make life easier for David.

"You going to come down with me in the car?" Robert said to Chunggy who shook his head.

"I come down on bus."

"If you're not at the church on time, then I'm not getting married."

"Mr Draper, I will be there. I catch eleven o'clock bus. It get me there, plenty of time. I don't like fuss. I watch wedding then go home." Chunggy had refused to come to the reception after the wedding ceremony despite Robert saying that both he and Leanne would like him there.

Robert got up and wandered back into his bedroom for the last time. He had a shower and then just pottered around until Brian arrived just before eleven; Bin Lau having gone to collect him. "All ready, Bob." was all Brian said on arrival.

Robert nodded as he finished dressing and said, "I thought when I left the bank, I would get rid of penguin suits and here I am on the most important day of my life wearing one again." Finishing what he was doing he said, "Come on I need a drink?" They walked into the downstairs lounge to find that Chunggy had laid out a bottle of whisky and two glasses. "The sod knew I would need a drink," Robert said as he poured two measures into the glasses. "Here's to us, Brian. May we survive and be happy in this turbulent world."

They clinked glasses and drank back the neat whisky as Bin Lau pipped the car horn to tell them to get a move on.

****

Robert stood in the shade of a large mango tree looking at the hundred or so people at the reception. Leanne and Robert had stood under the tree and welcomed all the guests as they arrived. The formalities had finished, and Robert had already signalled to one of the waiters that he need a drink. He had asked Leanne if she wanted one and she had murmured something as she talked to one of her school friends and Robert presumed it meant "yes". Her school chum reminded him of Fiona for a moment with her loud excitable voice. Whatever had happened to Fiona? He knew she had escaped from Bangkok on 5 December 1941 with a few dozen women from the British and US embassies with the help of a Thai Foreign Office Minister who knew that the Japanese was ready to spring an attack. They had made their way to Rangoon on a small freighter only to have to escape again, this time to India. By all accounts the journey on the freighter, to Rangoon, had been terrible with the ship being strafed and bombed. He had never heard of her since nor for that matter did he know what had happened to Fran, a girl friend, except that she had made it to England. Robert was brought back with a jolt; someone was speaking to him.

It was Martin with the little Chinese girl who now lived with him up at the Woodlands where Robert was getting Martin to clear the ground. Robert already knew that Mona did not approve of the girl. "Why can't he marry a good girl? We know nothing about her." Martin would just say that they weren't married so what did it matter. Brian would say nothing nor did Henry.

"Bob, great wedding. Helen and I want to congratulate you and Leanne and to say we hope you will be very happy." Helen said nothing as Martin, standing to attention, said this as though he was addressing an officer in the army.

Robert looked at them both. They were both so young it made Robert suddenly feel very old. He had done so much in the past eight years. Robert thanked them for coming and for their best wishes and then added, "I know you're not comfortable with this crowd, Martin. And you, Helen. You know you can stay as long as you want but I understand if you want to disappear. I'll come and see you when I get back from my honeymoon and we can discuss what you need up there." Helen smiled at Robert and thanked him and they went off hand in hand. Robert saw Mona watching them as they left and he just shook his head.

The High Commissioner and his wife had attended the ceremony at the Cathedral and then made their apologies to Robert and Leanne as a Parliamentary delegation were due in later in the afternoon and the HC would be on duty.

David had done his stuff in taking Leanne down the aisle and afterwards Susie had taken him off to rooms in the Goodwood Hotel that Robert had hired for guests who needed a rest or to change.

The meal later in the afternoon went well with Brian enjoying himself telling stories of Robert leading the LDU and of his bravery in saving a child in a burning building on Thomson Road with Japanese fighters strafing the road and of the time in KL when he had millions in gold and nothing to spend it on. He had done his homework and found a story to tell about Leanne as a child refusing to go for a shower only for her ayah to find a snake in the shower room.

May and her two daughters, in traditional Malay dress, stayed for the meal but in the early evening they excused themselves promising to have the happy couple round for a traditional Malay meal on their return. Bin Lau who had brought his mother and brother with him to the reception took them home also after the meal, returning later in the evening to take Robert and Leanne to catch the late flight to Hong Kong on their journey to honeymoon in America.

Chapter 38

Twenty Five Years Later

Molly came into the kitchen only half awake. It was already hot and her mother, at least she presumed it was her mother, had opened the French windows out onto the veranda which was sheltered from the rays of the sun by a large canopy.

"Where's Maria, mummy?

Leanne looked across at her daughter. "Good morning, darling. You look as though you have been dragged through a hedge."

Molly groaned. "Good morning, mummy. We went to The Sky Bar and danced till god knows what time. Geof brought me home." Leanne said nothing, just continued getting things for breakfast and putting them on trays.

"Do something useful and take the trays out. And for god's sake tie up your gown. You know your father hates seeing you half undressed."

"Where is daddy? He's not in his office; the doors are open." Molly picked up one of the trays and went out onto the veranda and it was only when she returned that her mum answered, "He's gone down to Robinson Road for some early morning auction. I dread to think what next he will bring back."

Molly giggled in a throaty sort of way as she took the second of the trays. As she went through the open doorway she again asked, "Where is Maria?"

Leanne lifted the coffee pot to carry out. "Oh, she's gone up to Malacca for a few days, to see her friend Rosa. Your father asked Bin Lau to give her a lift as he also wanted to visit some relatives up there. She's back on Monday night by train as Bin Lau plans to stay a bit longer.

They both sat in the shade under the canopy enjoying the smells from the garden combined with the rich smell of the coffee. As they sat momentarily enjoying their own thoughts, they saw a vision emerge from around the mango tree walking up the path that led from the house next door.

"God she's never going to work like that", Molly said quietly watching her older sister walking towards them in a white silk suit with black high heels and all the trimmings. Molly shouted across at Lucy. "Have you got an appointment with the queen?"

Lucy looked at her sister but did not reply as she walked the last few feet up to her mother and kissed her on the cheek. "Good morning, Mumsie." She took off her hat and placing it on the table she sat down in one of the spare chairs. "Daddy is taking me to some reception up at the old Bidadari Cemetery. The Government have finished the social building project and daddy has an invite to the cutting the tape ceremony because the trust has contributed money for a community centre and a small shopping mall."

Molly seemed to lose interest in this information and turned to the laid-out breakfast table and started eating. It was Leanne who said, "Well you'll get more of these functions now you're working at the trust." Mischievously she added, "Your father used to drag me along, but he prefers younger models these days."

Lucy smiled back at her mother. "You know that's not true. He even took nana to that do up at the Woodlands last year. He has given me notes on what I can say and who I should get a hold of. It's like being in the army."

"You're not going to follow them are you, "Molly said trying to eat some cereal at the same time.

"She better had," a voice from behind her suddenly said making Molly choke and Lucy grin at her sister's discomfort. Robert had come through the kitchen onto the veranda as the ladies were talking; he had obviously been listening. "And I do wish you would dress a little more for breakfast. There's more flesh on display than at an abattoir."

Molly just groaned as Leanne said, "Bob, really there's no need."

"And I do take your mother out to do's. I'm taking her to the Chinese Restaurateurs Annual Gala tonight. Never let it be said I don't splash out."

Leanne looked across at Robert who had sat down and grabbed the coffee pot. "Before you say anything there are no caraway cakes this morning because you agreed that Maria could go off early with Bin Lau. She didn't have time to make any. And furthermore, I thought we got free tickets for the Gala every year."

"Ah yes but you get a new dress for the do."

Leanne looked across at Lucy and shook her head in despair.

Lucy said, "You told me to be here for nine dressed to the teeth and you're not even ready. What time are we leaving?"

"I'm ready. When I've finished my coffee we're off. Now remember I want you to chat up that young assistant of the Environment Minister, what's his name Lee Yang Shu. I think he will have the information I want about that new eco reserve on Pulau Ubin Island."

Lucy said nothing with her mother looking shocked. "My god Robert it's come to something when you have your daughter pimping for you."

Robert finished his coffee and stood up. "Needs must, old bean." He kissed Leanne on the cheek she had turned to him. "Right Luc let's go and enjoy ourselves. Oh, nobody touches that vase I've left in the hall."

Leanne and Molly watched them disappear through the kitchen doorway out to the waiting car.

"Daddy is up to something. You can tell by the way he's behaving."

"Darling you may be the baby of the family, but you already know the signs. As long as we don't have a menagerie in the garden I don't care. Now can you clear up as I want to go and see your nana? I thought she and I might do a little shopping. After all I've just been told I have to have a new outfit for tonight."

Molly smiled back at her mother.

Chapter 39

Sunni drove the car up the main highway towards the causeway as Robert and his eldest daughter sat quietly in the back, enjoying the relative cool before the heat built up. It was Robert who broke the peace.

"How are you finding your new responsibilities?"

"I told you only the night before last daddy that it will take time to get the marketing of the Trust up to scratch. I will need at least three months. I've only been doing the job for a couple of weeks so I'm still finding out things. I spent yesterday with Mrs Wong going through all the files looking for bits of information about the foundation of the Trust and about Mrs Lin Yuen."

"No need, little one. I can tell you everything."

Lucy ignored her father's attempt to soften the discussion. "I prefer the real thing daddy; not just what you remember or think you do."

"I have a pretty good memory."

"When it suits you. What about your wedding anniversary." As she said it, she could see Sunni smiling in the rear-view mirror.

"Nonsense. That was just a clerical error in my diary. I wrote it down in the wrong month."

"It must have cost you a fortune, that's all I will say. And what is that vase in the hall? It looks awful."

"It could be Ming."

Lucy just shook her head. Everybody said she was like her father; God help her if she ended up like him.

"I came across newspaper cuttings from 1946 with you on the front page. It was all about you looking for gold and getting into hot water with the Chinese Nationalists and the Malay Communist Party. What was all that about?"

"Oh, that's old hat. Everything's all sorted out."

"Was the gold ever found?" Lucy asked.

"Ah here we are. Not been up here for ages. God, doesn't it look different," Robert said getting out of the car as Sunni opened the door on the other side to let Lucy out. There were flashes from cameras as photographers milled around with half a dozen journalists all asking questions which Robert ignored as a young Government assistant escorted him and Lucy towards where the official party was already collecting.

A Meeting Under A Banyan Tree

After various introductions Robert disappeared off with the main party but not before he had pointed Lucy in the direction of the young assistant from the Environment Department. "Don't forget. Get as much info as you can," Robert whispered in a rush.

Lucy put on her best smile and started chatting to some of the many guests and working her way towards the young assistant who when she got closer seemed about her age. She was soon talking to him, and the rest of the morning went in a blur with Robert even at one point cutting a ribbon and saying a few words, at the entrance to a community centre which was to house a surgery and nursery as well as social facilities. Lucy looked at a father who was very calm as he said a few words and cut a ribbon; she had seen him cut the ribbon at other ceremonies and as always, he was short and to the point.

She was chatting to Lee Yang Shu and agreeing to meet for a drink when Sunni came up to her. "Mr Draper, he is ready to leave, Miss." Lucy nodded and saying goodbye to Lee Yang Shu she followed Sunni out to where Robert was already in the car talking to someone in the back. Sunni opened the door of the front seat for her to get in and turning round Lucy smiled at her uncle, Alex Masters.

Alex had been back in Singapore for a few years after fifteen years working in London, and Hong Kong, and was heavily into financial developments and Lucy had no doubt he was involved somewhere in the financing of the Bidadari site.

"Hello little one", her uncle said as he leaned forward and kissed her on the cheek. "You enjoy yourself."

"Mmm. I was sent on a mission. All very secretive. But yes, I did enjoy myself."

Her father sitting in the back raised an eyebrow and said, "Bloody hot. I told the Straits journalist that he should contact you Lucy about any information on the Trust. I just said that we wanted to work with the Government on social issues and would continue to do so in the future. You going to come and have some lunch with us at the Club?"

Lucy shook her head. "No, after we've dropped you off, I'll get Sunni to take me home to change and then I want to do more work in the archives."

"Don't need to do too much, you know. A lot of the old records will not help to get the true flavour of the Trust."

"We shall see Daddy. Anyway, I am rather enjoying the trip down memory lane."

All Robert said was that he hadn't realised that Mrs Wong kept everything.

A Meeting Under A Banyan Tree

****

Later that afternoon Robert turned up at the Trust offices he had purchased for them near Coleman Bridge and wandered through saying hello to staff, some of whom had been with him for years. Asking where his daughter was, he was directed to the Board Room one floor up.

Opening the door to the room he stopped amazed at the sight. Mrs Wong was on her knees, with her back to him, rifling through thousands of bits of correspondence and paper cuttings. There seemed to be some semblance of order as little mountains had emerged on two sides with a river of paper in between.

Robert could hear Lucy, under the Board table at the far end, sifting through papers as she talked to Mrs Wong.

"Mai Wong, did my father really look like that; he looked like a pirate. I had no idea his scar was so vivid. Why mummy married him is beyond me. He would have been better placed in a chain gang." Robert in that moment could only think that Lucy was looking at a photograph of himself in 1946.

Mrs Wong giggled, something Robert hadn't heard her do for years.

"Still, I suppose my mum had to take him on for the sake of the country."

Mrs Wong did not reply, she had shifted her position and seen Robert's feet. Slowly she looked up at Robert. Robert held out his hand and Mrs Wong took it, and Robert helped her up. Lucy was continuing to talk at the far end saying things she remembered about her father. Finally, Robert spoke.

"Lucy, I have no idea what you think you're doing but I expect a bit more discretion."

"Daddy, I knew you would turn up," was the instant response as a brunette peeked her face over the end of the Board table. "Actually, I knew you were there. I could see you in the doorway from the mirror."

Robert looked down to the far end where a full-length mirror was fastened to the wall and sure enough, he could see himself standing in the doorway with Mrs Wong looking like a scared rabbit.

As Lucy climbed out from under the table Robert turned to Mrs Wong. "I thought as a grandmother of two you would set an example to my daughter, not participate in her crazy ideas."

Mrs Wong looking miserable said that Miss Draper only wanted to know everything, and Robert stepped aside and let the rabbit escape.

"Daddy you are mean. Mai Wong thinks the world of you. It's Mr Draper did this and Mr Draper did that. It's quite sickening really."

"What the hell do you expect to find in all this?" Robert asked waving his arms at the mounds of paper on the floor, in piles at the side of the wall on his left, on the table itself and by the sound of it under the table.

"I hadn't realised how famous you are."

"Infamous you mean", Robert growled as Lucy continued talking.

"I've just been reading about you being a witness at the War Crimes Tribunals and somewhere about here there's an article about you serving on some committee trying to stop the communists from taking over. You never told me any of this."

Robert waved his hands again at the mounds of paper. "What has this got to do with Mrs Lin Yuen and her Trust?"

A young woman with her hands grubby with printers' ink and with her dress looking as though it had seen better days came up to her father and kissed him on the cheek. "It has everything to do with Susanna Lin Yuen and her picking you as her successor. You've made the Trust into what it is; Lin Yuen merely got the Trust started but you have made it an important part of the life of lots of people on the Island. I'm very proud of you. That's the story we must get out for next year's 40th anniversary celebrations."

Robert had started to mellow under the calming voice of his daughter. *"Damn her she's old beyond her years. She's her mother all over."* he murmured to himself as Lucy went off to the far end of the room. Robert followed her in a trance, almost bumping into her beside the chair he sat in at board meetings.

"Look at this daddy. It's a picture of you and Uncle Neil at his leaving party ten years ago. Isn't that the prime minister that Mummy's talking to? It's a lovely picture. Oh, I also found this. "Lucy went under the table and emerged with a black and white photograph.

Robert instantly recognised where it had been taken. "That's in our garden. No rather your Nana's garden. There's the old garden cottage that Chunggy lived in. That's Laz and Harry and Jenny. I think that's Laura and my god that's your Aunt Kay in the background. Who the hell is that she's talking to. And there's Mrs Lin Yuen." By this time Robert had sat down in his chair not noticing that it had papers on it. "Why are all these things here, Lucy? They're not really to do with the Trust."

"According to Mai Wong you ordered Chunggy to have a clear out at home and he decided they should be kept and passed them on to her. I'm halfway through them and we should finish tomorrow.

Now I think you should go and find Mai Wong and say you're sorry as you scared her to death."

Robert just nodded totally lost in memories of 1940.

Chapter 40

It was a week later. Leanne was sitting in the lounge sewing and talking to Maria who was sitting at a small table that had a Singer sewing machine on it. From what Lucy could make out as she walked in, they were making a party dress for a little girl. Both ladies were engrossed in their handiwork and didn't notice Lucy at first.

"I guessed you would be here doing something like this. I presume dad has gone off with Uncle Brian and Bin Lau, drinking."

Lucy went over and kissed both her mother and Maria. There were the usual questions about "how's your day been" and Maria said "just give me a minute to finish this hem and then I'll get us some drinks."

Maria was technically the housekeeper, but she had become an integral part of the family after twenty-six years living under the same roof as the Drapers. Unless Leanne was entertaining her friends or Robert was having an evening in, which was rare, Maria would invariably join Leanne in the lounge or they would end up in the kitchen, hatching ideas and enjoying the quiet of an evening. Leanne's mother, Susie, only yards away in Mrs Lin Yuen's old home, occasionally joined them but more often than not she had her own circle of friends. Sunday was the day when most of the family came together for tiffan and a catch up on the news.

Maria finished the hem and got up from the small table and said, "Right what would you like to drink?"

"I think I want something strong, Maria. Can I have a small G&T, plenty of ice."

Maria nodded at the young woman whom she had known since she was born. "You sound like you have had a bad day?"

Lucy just shook her head. "Not really, Maria. More one of those days when you don't seem to be getting anywhere."

Maria looked across at Leanne. "A glass of wine?"

Leanne shook her head. "I think I fancy a cup of tea. Are you having one?"

Maria nodded and disappeared off into the kitchen to make the drinks as Leanne put down her sewing. "Your father being difficult?"

"Mmm. He's evasive when I ask him for a full list of the donators to the Trust. He says that a good deal of the money is derived from investments made years ago. As far as I can see there are millions sloshing around."

"Well, he always was very good at making money. He and Zhang Lee John made some very good business developments in the 1950's."

"Mmm. Do you know why we bank with an Arab bank based in Qatar? Why not with a bank in Singapore?" Before her mother could answer Lucy continued. "We have accounts with a couple of local banks, but they have pennies in them. Daddy says he wants me to take over at some point, but he expects me to just take up the reins from today without questioning the past."

Leanne looked across at her daughter. "I know your father is always up to something. He loves to be involved in some deal or other, but I doubt it's shady or dishonest. As to banking with an Arab bank I can't help you. He told me years ago that he thought it was better for the Trust to spread its resources just in case we had a bad time on the Island. Knowing your father, he continued banking with them because they give the best interest."

As Maria came in with the drinks Lucy just said, "Mmm" and accepted the G&T.

"Have you asked your father these things?"

Lucy nodded and shook her hair loose for a few seconds before answering. "As I said Mumsie, he just doesn't answer my questions. He just says that he pooled all the Trust money together, around 1950, when he met someone who said that he would get a much better return for the Trust if it was invested in certain stocks. He did that and it did so well that he has remained with the Arab bank. It's not even a proper bank, it's a family bank run by a man called Mahmood Shebari."

"Oh, I know him. He's had dinner here a couple of times. Very quiet chap, quite traditional. Not recently mind you, it was quite a few years ago. What I do remember, darling, was that your father had to make some very quick business decisions in 1950 when the Korean War started going badly and we were in danger of losing it.

Maria who up to then had been sitting quietly taking no part in the conversation said, "Bin Lau used to go over to Dubai and Qatar in the early years. I remember that because he went one time when Zee Ping was due to have her baby. She was not pleased that her husband had to be away at that time."

Leanne nodded at Maria. "I had forgotten that. I do remember that everything was in a turmoil because we still had the emergency here and yet we had to send a lot of our troops to Korea. We all had instructions about what to do if civil war broke out here in support of the Chinese involvement. Quite scary especially as I had you, Lucy, only months before. Your father even talked about sending us and Nana and Granddad back to England until things quietened down. He was worried there would be a repeat of 1942. "

The conversation drifted onto other matters and after Lucy had finished her drink, she excused herself and walked back through the garden to where she lived in the upstairs of Nana's house.

"She sounds worried, Li, "Maria said at one point later in the evening.

"Mmm. I'll have to speak to her father. "

"You could speak to Bin Lau?"

"Fat lot of good that'll do. All he will say is talk to Robert. Anyway, has Bob said anything to you about this shop he's thinking of opening in Fullerton Square. Something about discerning things for the well-off tourist."

Maria shook her head as she laid out the party dress on the settee next to Leanne. "There I think that should fit Sandra. He's said nothing to me. Sunni must hear things but never says a word. They're like the mafia. I sat with Bin Lau in the car up to Malacca and all he talked about was his kids and how Zee Ping is too soft with them."

"Come on let's clear up and call it a night. I've got a big day tomorrow."

Chapter 41

It was some weeks later. Robert had been working on plans for a new development at Kranji near the causeway that joined Singapore to the Malayan peninsula. He had rarely been into the Trust offices, other than to sign some papers, and on one occasion to say a few parting words to one of the staff who was leaving to go with her husband to live in Penang.

He arrived unannounced one morning and found Lucy working upstairs in the hallway outside the Board Room, working her way through proofs for the publication that she had drafted for the Trust to celebrate its 40th anniversary. "Good morning, darling. Hard at it I see." He stopped what he was saying as he looked at the pile of paper set out on the floor. It was hot in the hallway as Lucy had switched off the fans presumably to prevent the pages being blown around. He watched her as she knelt on the floor going through the publication line by line before saying, "Wouldn't you be better working at a desk?"

Lucy hadn't acknowledged her father up to that point. It was only as Robert bent down to look at a photograph she said, "Don't touch a thing. It's all in order. I'm correcting grammar now. Anyway, I like to spread out and I can't use the Board Room desk. It's covered in papers." As an afterthought Lucy added, "I need to move the photographs around and check that what I say about you is accurate. Mind you I don't want it to be too bland, a bit of controversy will make people take more interest."

Robert who had started to go through to the Board Room stopped in his tracks. "You wouldn't dare. Anyway, what do you know that I wouldn't like to be made public."

"You'll have to read it, Daddy. You also need to spend some time in the office catching up on other things. Mrs Si Chen has been trying to get you for days about a new roof for the nursery up at Tajong Ris."

"Alright, alright. I will arrange to come in for the rest of the week, from tomorrow."

"I will finish the proofs by tonight so I can let you have what I've done, and you need to read it thoroughly."

"Yes. Yes. I will do it."

"Anyway, why did you come in?

"I can't remember. You've quite made me forget." Almost with exasperation Robert said, "Oh I know; I need the latest accounts. Mr Thuranggunu always leaves it on the Board table for me at the beginning of each month."

"Oh, I have them. You did say you wanted me to take up the reins at some point, so I took the liberty of studying the figures. I think we are in very good shape. In fact, we could probably buy the Island if it was up for sale."

"You exaggerate my darling. We must remember that much of the money is earmarked. There are many calls on the cash."

"I think I was more interested in the reserves and investments we hold, not current spend."

As she said it Lucy had raised an eyebrow at her father's excuse. "You and I need a really good chat, Dad. And this time without you being evasive. I love working here and I know I can make my mark in developing the interests of the Trust, but I want the truth about how we came to be so rich. The other thing, from what I can see, is that the Arab bank investments are in a separate set of accounts and only the dividends seem to appear in the final accounts; the investments seem to be recorded in some associated company."

Robert was standing in the Board Room doorway as they were speaking. He turned and looked at Lucy. "You may only be 24 but you could run this Trust with your little finger. I can see that. Well do you want to know everything?" Seeing Lucy nod he said, "Go and ask someone downstairs to make a good pot of coffee for us and then come through. Tell them downstairs we do not want to be disturbed."

****

"Mrs Lin Yuen left me with a Trust that had property in Seletar, Woodlands, Changi and Siglap. She had investments mostly in American shares that obviously escalated over the war years. In addition, she had cash reserves in the Hong Kong Bank. None of it was recorded other than in a little book she had in her bedroom drawer. From what she told me, and later Chen Zhu Lee, her solicitor, the money was donations from wealthy Chinese families as well as a significant amount of money that her father had accrued from his business. From what I've found out over the years her father was a bit of a pirate come market trader who made money from a range of shady deals. Anyway, the money was all there hidden for when I got out of the Internment Camp. It was exactly the right time, property prices were at rock bottom so I purchased property dirt cheap, sold it on a few years later and invested in stocks and shares."

Lucy took this all in, drinking her coffee and enjoying watching her father dig a hole for himself. "That accounts for about half the money, daddy, "she said sweetly. "Now tell me about the money that seems to have come into the Trust in the late 1940's. And don't tell me that we got it by rattling collection tins around Fullerton Square."

Robert sat more upright in the Chairman's chair. "We found some more of Mrs Lin Yuen's money after I came back from my honeymoon with your mother. We had a wonderful trip up the West Coast of the United States."

"I know where you went on honeymoon with Mumsie. Don't try and distract me. I want to know where you found this money and why did you suddenly change your banking arrangements?"

"God, you have done your homework. I presume you know about the search for gold during the war, by the Japanese?"

Lucy just kept watching her father's face and at one point she said, "Mmm" as her father went through the long story.

Lucy handed a scrap piece of paper she had in her pocket. "What is this? Who is Frank Summers?"

"Summers gave it to me only three days before your mum and I were getting married. He had been in an internment camp down on Adam Road. He talked to someone the *Kempetai* were looking for and he did his best to remember what he had been told before the *Kempetai* got the poor devil. How did you get the note?"

Lucy straitened her skirt and looked across at her father. "It was in an old photograph album Chunggy passed onto Mai Wong."

Robert said nothing about what Lucy had just said, he merely shook his head and made a bit of a face, before continuing with his story. "Frank Summers didn't speak Chinese or write it. So, some of what he remembered was inaccurate. But we did think it might help if we could understand some of the scribble. Bin Lau had an aunt up on Mount Faber who was good with cryptic notes so we went up to see her. She said she thought it was partly an inscription, maybe something you see over an arch and then she thought there were directions from the arch to another location. She also said it might be the sort of inscription that you put in places like churches. We talked about it when we left her as the gold was looked after by a Jewish chap called David Abadi; we tried to think what he might have meant in the note. I remembered that the entrance to the Jewish cemetery up on Thomson Road had an arch so maybe that was where the gold was hidden. We went up there but no luck- there was no inscription only a small notice saying the cemetery was no longer in use. Anyway, I left it that Bin Lau would have a look around and see if he could find an arch and we would look for it seriously after I got back from the States."

"Dad, will you get to the point."

"Yes, yes. I just think it is important that you know the whole story. Even your mother doesn't know all of it."

Lucy said nothing. She uncrossed her legs and stretched out and reset herself in her chair.

"When I got back from the USA, I had things to do with the development that Zhang Lee John and I were involved in up at Bugis

Street and also some things with the Trust so I couldn't put my mind to trying to work out how to trace the inscription. Anyway, a few weeks later Chunggy said he was going up to Lin Yuen's grave and as I hadn't been up for age's I said that Bin Lau would take us up. You won't know I don't think" Robert said hesitantly, "that Lin Yuen and her family had a small vault up at the top end of the old Bidadari Cemetery. You know the one the Government has just built the large social housing complex on, where we have just donated a community centre and shopping mall."

At that Lucy sat up and started to look more closely at her father.

"The old cemetery had two entrances – the one on the main road was where the Europeans arrived and walked up to the graves but at the top end was a second entrance were Eurasian and Chinese usually entered the cemetery as it was closer to the plots given to them. Anyway, there was a funeral in progress when we arrived and we couldn't park at the main entrance so Bin Lau took the car up to the other entrance which in any case was quite close to where Lin Yuen's family vault was located. Chunggy had used the entrance before, but I had never been through it. Bin Lau dropped us off and I walked through the entrance under an archway with an inscription. Just above your head as you walked through. Something about the afterlife and ancestors."

Lucy was now giving her father full attention. Robert had stopped momentarily to drink the last of his coffee. "Well go on don't leave me in suspense."

"Well of course I didn't have the piece of paper so I couldn't do anything. I ran back to Bin Lau and told him about the inscription, and he parked the car up and came through the entrance with me. But he couldn't remember enough for us to go anywhere. So, in the end we went over to the mausoleum for Lin Yuen and her father and mother. Chunggy was cleaning up around it and we spent half an hour sitting on the bench beside the plot trying to remember what the piece of paper said and then helping Chunggy to clear some of the weeds around the entrance to the chamber which was locked up. I used to pay a little Chinese man to keep the plot clean, but I learnt from Chunggy as we tidied the plot up that the old man had died, and I would need to get another gardener. By the time we left and got home it was growing dark. From memory your mother and I were out at some function that night so it was a quick change and shower and I had to forget about it for another day."

"God, you are long winded. No wonder Mummy goes to sleep when you tell her some news. You can be so infuriating. Did you find the gold or not?"

"No. Well not gold that could be linked to what I boxed for the banks. When Bin Lau took me up the next day, we went to the side entrance. We parked the car and then followed the directions after we entered the cemetery, just as Bin Lau's aunt had interpreted the piece of paper. Nothing, all we got, at best, was the base of a tree or a monsoon ditch. Bin Lau went to find the Head Gardener to ask if the layout had been changed and I collapsed on a bench. It was sweltering and I remember I was filthy and sticky. When Bin Lau got back, he had brought some water and we sat drinking and working out if the directions were wrong. Remember Summers said he had copied the Chinese down as best as he could remember it. It was Bin Lau who said that if we could make head or tail of it then the Japs would also have been able to if they had got the information. The directions were right in that they led you to a ditch and a tree. The Japs would have had everything within fifty yards of the ditch, or the tree, dug up if they had followed the directions. We went back to the entrance, and we tried different ways of interpreting the directions. There had to be something missing. Finally, I suggested that we should do the opposite of what the directions said and go left when it said go right and so on and see what happened. We did that and we ended up at a big vault next to Lin Yuen's. It was badly tended, and Bin Lau disappeared off to find the Head Gardener again, who came back with Bin Lau. He was new to the job but said that it was the family vault of a wealthy Chinese merchant family; he understood they had died out in the 1920's with a small legacy to maintain the plot but the money had run out years ago. The Head Garden knew nothing about the family. "At this point Lucy could see that her father was positively enjoying himself.

"So why should the vault interest you?"

"The vault was of the Shee Yang Chen family. That was the same name as the man who was in league with Lai Tek." Lucy nodded as she had already been told the story of her father exposing the conspiracy between Lai Tek and Shee Yang Chen. Robert continued, now well into remembering the detail. "Only the man involved with Lai Tek was not really Shee Yang Chen. We think he was called Phuoc Trong Si. He worked for Tan Choo Sin who I told you about earlier. He must have taken the name Shee Yang Chen when Lai Tek found out the gold was hidden in the vault. Maybe he and Lai Tek decided to change their names to avoid being traced by people from Indo China who were after them but it served their purpose later when they came into possession of the gold that was supposed to be given to the communists at the Batu Caves. At least I am pretty sure they got their hands on it. They must have found out where Tan Choo Sin had collected the gold, possibly from the driver of the lorry that was sent up to the Batu Caves. Phouc Trong Si saw it as a way of changing his name and buying out the Tan Choo Sin business after the *Kempetia* had removed Tan Choo Sin."

Before Robert could continue there was a timid knock on the door and it was Lucy who shouted, "Come in, please."

A young Eurasian girl looked nervously round the door.

"Come in, Jenny Mai," Lucy said.

"Please Miss Lucy, do you wish me to get some lunch for you and Mr Draper. Mrs Wong is worried that you will be hungry."

"No thank you, Jenny Mai. My father is taking me out for lunch." With that Lucy stood up and made her way round the table to where her handbag was lying on a spare chair. "Come on, Daddy. From what I can see there is much more to come so you can take me for a decent lunch and finish the epic tale whilst I have a large glass of Chardonnay."

They walked down to the front entrance of the Trust building and out into the busy street with Robert not protesting or seemingly even fully aware of how his daughter had taken charge. Somewhere at the back of his mind a little man was talking to his brain telling him that this is what it is going to be like from now on. Lucy waved down a taxi and in no time at all they were deposited at the Tanglin Club where in only a few moments a table was found for them in the restaurant.

Lucy had disappeared off to the rest room and Robert sat at their table not bothering with the menu knowing what he was going to have and waiting for the stengah he had ordered. He saw people in the distance he knew, and he waved back but didn't go over to speak to them, too deep in his thoughts on what was in his past.

Lucy returned from the rest room and taking the glass of wine the waiter had just deposited in front of her she raised it to her father. "Daddy, I'm looking forward to the next instalment. "

Robert inwardly groaned. *"Where had he gone wrong? Hadn't he paid for his daughters to be educated at the best schools and universities? One turns out to be a hard businesswoman and the other – god knows, he never really saw her sober; she spent her life partying and appearing in the social pages of the Straits Times."*

Both father and daughter sat for a few minutes quietly enjoying the atmosphere in the restaurant and looking out across the grounds. They ordered, predictably Robert a seafood starter followed by a small steak with Lucy preferring a salad tossed with lots of nuts. Other people they knew waved at them and on one occasion an old school chum of Lucy's came over and hugged her and they arranged to meet up.

Finally, as Robert's seafood starter arrived and their drinks had begun to course through them Lucy said, "Right Dad. Let's have part two."

Robert took a few more mouthfuls of lobster and king crab and then said, "Where did I finish?"

Lucy picked up her fork and helped herself to a piece of her father's lobster at the same time saying, "You know where you ended. Shee Yang Chen's vault."

"Ah yes. Well, the Head Gardener didn't have a key to the vault and it had a grill across the door with a bolt and padlock. The Head Gardener asked if we were relatives and when I said we weren't he said that only Chen Zhu Lee ever had a key but he had not been to the cemetery for years. Apparently, he knew him when he was just a grave digger."

Lucy just shook her head at her father's long-windedness.

"Remember Chen Zhu Lee was Lin Yuen's solicitor," Robert said between mouthfuls of lobster. "I met him during the war, and he was one of the poor sods who was killed by the Japanese immediately after the surrender. The Japs took large numbers of them out in the days following the surrender and drowned them at sea."

"Yes, I know about the Sook Ching Massacre. Everybody at school had lessons about it. "

"Bin Lau took me down to Smith Street to Chen Zhu Lee's old offices, but they were now a small textile factory. Anyway, Bin Lau went into the neighbouring shops and found out that one of his assistants had opened up a practice in a business centre off Robinson Road. So, we went over there, and we found her."

"Her." Lucy queried as she signalled to the waiter for a second glass of Chardonnay.

"Mmm. I remembered when I met Chen Zhu Lee that he had said to me that if anything happened to him that I was to contact Mrs Helen Yang and she would help." Robert had finished his starter and waited until the waiter had removed his plate before continuing. "She was very helpful. Told me immediately that Chen Zhu Lee had been the solicitor to many of the leading families. She remembered the story about a Shee Yang Chen doing a bunk in 1947 and the communists looking for him; she said she had assumed the same name was just a coincidence and was not connected to the Shee Yang Chen who had been a client of Chen Zhu Lee, who it seems was also the solicitor to Lin Yuen and to Tan Choo Sin. Remember Singapore was a small place then. Mrs Yang produced a box file with some papers about the Shee Yang Chen family; apparently, she had been able to retrieve them from the bombed-out offices in Smith Street. She also produced a set of keys she said she thought had something to do with the vaults up at Bidadari Cemetery and said she could see no reason why we couldn't use them as there were no descendants of Shee Yang Chen and I was the inheritor of Lin Yuen's estate.

The waiter arrived as Robert finished his sentence and for a few moments they sat as their meals were served and Robert ordered another stengah. In the distance Robert saw his wife arrive in the restaurant with friends; they had obviously been playing tennis. Robert said, "Your mother's here."

"I know. I've just signalled that we're in a business meeting."

"I think I should go across and just say hello."

"I think you should enjoy your steak, Daddy. We can say hello later."

"I took the keys off her, "Robert said assuming that Lucy would understand who he was talking about. "We went back up to the cemetery and opened Shee Yang Chen's vault. Lo and behold there were empty bank crates all over the flour. All broken into as though someone had been in a rush. There must have been six or seven boxes. I even remembered some of the numbering on them; I had stencilled the numbers onto those boxes. They were China Bank boxes."

The waiter took away the finished plates and Lucy just said that they wanted coffees to which the waiter nodded.

"You said you found gold."

"Ah but not bank money."

"God Daddy you are infuriating. What has all you told me to do with finding money for the Trust?"

"Oh, you are impatient."

"No wonder. It's beyond me how mother has not murdered you years ago."

"Now that is going too far. Your mother is besotted with me."

"Now that's going too far," said Leanne having walked up behind Robert. Robert jumped in his chair and started to get up. "Stay where you are, darling. The *Kempeta*i are nothing compared to Lucy when she gets her teeth into something. I can guess what this is all about and I will speak to Lucy later to check the details with what I know." Leanne had bent down and kissed her husband on the cheek before going round to kiss her daughter. Leanne looked across at her husband, "Good luck; see you later. Maybe." Robert heard Lucy giggle.

Robert watched Leanne walk back to her table and then said, "After I came out of the vault and Bin Lau had locked it up, we went down to Thomson Road where Major Comber was based at the time."

"You didn't go in Lin Yuen's vault?"

"No, no. The boxes were empty. It was important to put Major Comber in the picture."

Lucy groaned. "Who is Major Comber?"

"Come on. You remember Han Su Yin; your mother did voluntary work with her, over in Johor."

"At the hospital?"

"Yes, the very tall Chinese lady. She was a doctor and for a time she was married to Major Comber who was head of the security services out here. MI5 or was it six?"

"I remember her. Mumsie helped her at a little hospital. Children had malaria. She took me over there a few times to see the children."

"Major Comber was the bane of my life, for that matter so were the communists. Oh, and the Kuomintang." Lucy said nothing. She knew about the Kuomintang as Robert still had a friend, Kenneth Chen who had been someone important with the Kuomintang and who had sent Xmas presents to her and Molly when they were little; her father still corresponded with him in Formosa. "They all thought I knew where it was which I didn't. In fact, I always thought the British Government knew more than they were letting on. It meant they didn't have to pay their debts to one or more of the banks. Comber was up to his eyes in the troubles at the time but even he could not resist going up to Bidadari Cemetery to see the vault. He went straight back with us with an unmarked police car following us. Great hullabaloo with them banging on all the walls to see if there were any secret cavities; even wanted to see inside the coffins until I reminded them that we needed a search warrant or whatever from the coroner. Anyway, that seemed to end Comber's interest. Then I showed him the paper from Summers. He got quite excited and took it off me as well. Never saw that paper again"

Robert waited a few seconds and then grinned. "I had made a copy first."

Lucy had finished her coffee as had her father. She grinned across the table at her father. "You know I do love you, Daddy. You tell a great story. I remember the stories you used to tell me at bedtime. Mumsie always said you made them up but I'm beginning to think there's more to you than meets the eye."

Robert looked pleased with himself. "I aim to please."

"So, what about Lin Yuen's gold."

"As you can imagine there was quite a fuss and Comber let it out to the press. Journalists all over the place interviewing people including yours truly. Headlines for a day or two until the Chinese communists captured Shanghai and that was the end of the Nationalists at least on the mainland. They had Formosa, and Hainan Island for about a year. Bin Lau had family on Hainan so things were difficult for him." Robert looked around the restaurant that was now very thin on diners. "Should we move?" Lucy shook her head.

"About three or four weeks later it was the anniversary of Su Lin Yuen's birthday and Chunggy wasn't very well so I said I would take some flowers up to her grave. Bin Lau took me down with Sunni who was learning to drive the car. I think from memory we had to take your mother somewhere first to meet friends. Anyway, at the grave I put the flowers in the large vase beside the little door down into the vault. The new gardener had done a splendid job and spruced the plot up. I suddenly noticed that the padlock on the door was the same type as that on Shee Yang Chen's vault. So, I got out the keys I still had for Yang Chen's vault and one of them fitted; it was pitch dark inside so Bin Lau went back to the car and got a torch. He went down first – he said in case there was snakes but really, he just wanted to be first. Inside there were three coffins on plinths about three feet high. Bin Lau had brought Sunni back with him and the three of us banged on the walls. There was nothing behind the walls or on the floor; there was no hiding place. The coffins looked in good nick and when we looked at Lin Yuen's we could see that it had been moved at some point on its plinth or was not well fitted so we decided to move it a few inches and when I shone the torch down the hole all I could see was canvas bags. I tried dragging one out but it was too heavy so I got Sunni to lift it out. It was full of gold coins. There were dozens of bags. We lifted the coffin off the plinth and all we could see was canvas bags of gold. Lin Yuen when she died on New Year's Day 1942 must have requested that all her gold be stashed away with her."

"You crafty devil. That gold must have been from next door."

"No. There was no indication that it was anybody else's gold. She was a very wealthy woman."

"So why had she hidden all this gold before she died. You crafty devil." Lucy was thoroughly enjoying herself.

"No. No. She had collected gold over the years and hidden it in the vaults, probably for tax reasons. She did leave everything to me so the gold in the vault was mine or rather the Trust's as she left me specific instructions in her will about what was mine and everything else was for the Trust. Anyway, we put the gold back, replaced the coffin and tidied up and left the vault. "

"So how did Mahmood Shebari get involved?"

"Well, I couldn't exactly go down to the bank with a bag of gold and exchange it for dollars, could I. Half the Island would have been accusing me of something or other, and Comber would have had me in a cell. Even your Uncle Neil would have disowned me."

"I should think he still would."

"About eighteen months later I was trying to get finance with Zhang Lee John for a major development. The idea was ahead of its time and would work now but the Island wasn't ready at the time. I was at a convention in Bombay trying to get foreign investment and I met Mahmood Shebari. His family ran a small bank with the permission of the Emir, in Qatar. I told him that I had some gold to invest, and he said that this was entirely normal in the Middle East and he could help for a small fee and he knew an Arab dhow that traded with Singapore and would be happy to collect the gold. He would give us the value in American dollars. There was too much to take down to the ship in one go so we got Sunni to take down a few bags at a time; the dhow visited every six weeks and for the next three years or so Sunni took bags down. It was very simple really. In the end it worked so well that I invested the money through Mahmood in the New York stock exchange and the rest is history,"

"I should think that if this ever comes out, they will do you for theft, money laundering, plundering graves and god knows what else."

"Nonsense, young lady. I should simply deny any of it. Bin Lau and Sunni will not admit to anything. The Arab Bank will say that the money was given to them by Su Lin Yuen for the Trust."

"Wasn't Comber ever suspicious? Empty gold boxes, the Trust always in the money and you suddenly not interested in looking for the lost gold." Lucy looked sceptically at her father. "I can't believe he wasn't suspicious."

"I suppose he must have been, but he had bigger fish to fry what with the Korean War starting and then he got involved with Han Su Yin. The Malay Communist Party was also at the height of their atrocities and keeping him fully occupied. By 1950 he had quite a big team working for him. I remember we had a beer once and he asked why I thought the boxes had been empty. I had been expecting the question. I said in my opinion Tan Choo Sin's driver had collected the gold from Shee Yang Chen's vault by arrangement. He had Lai Tek with him and once he knew where it was he could collect it at his leisure. I am sure he then betrayed Tan Choo Sin to remove him from the scene and let his friend Phuoc Yang Si take over the business. David Abadi may have removed some of the gold when he knew his days were numbered or there could have been more than one place it was hidden. "Robert couldn't help smiling a little as he said it but Lucy didn't pick up on it. " Lai Tek then got Shee Yang Chen involved and they helped themselves to the remaining gold in the vault to buy businesses in Singapore and up north.

"Wait a minute, Daddy. How would Shee Yang Chen get into the vault? He didn't have a key."

"Easy. Once Lai Tek knew where the gold was stored, he could get at it any time. Shee Yang Chen would have been able to obtain tools to open the vault. Lai Tek betrayed Tan Choo Sin so he could not stop them from stealing the gold in that vault. John Kwai Knowles did not know the location and David Abadi did not know that Lai Tek knew where it was. He gave John Kwai Knowles the directions to where it was hidden not aware of Lai Tek's involvement. Fortunately, Lai Tek and Shee Yang Chen knew nothing about the gold in Lin Yuen's vault.

"Right, Daddy. Enough for today. I have had nearly five hours in your company which must be the longest on record. Take me home. No more work today."

In the taxi on the short journey home Robert turned to Lucy. "Get a few more months under your belt and understand the culture and I will make you the Operations Director. I think you will be a real asset being involved in the projects."

Lucy leaned across and said very quietly, "You are a dark horse. Nana once said that Grandpa called you a dark one and Uncle Alex has said the same now that I come to think of it."

"Just don't tell anybody the tale I told you. Even your mother doesn't know everything."

Lucy smiled at her father as they got out of the car and Robert paid the driver. As they climbed up the steps into the house Robert heard Lucy murmur, "I think Mumsie knows more than you realise."

From the bottom of the stairs as Robert disappeared into his study Lucy shouted, "Don't forget you need to read the manuscript thoroughly. I will give you the draft sometime tomorrow."

Chapter 42

It was some months later. Robert and Leanne were sitting on the veranda outside their bedroom enjoying the breakfast Sunni had carried upstairs from the kitchen. Robert was toying with the little caraway cakes with honey he always had whilst Leanne was savouring the mixed fruits that Marie had cut up for her. It was almost a ritual that they started their day having breakfast on the veranda and talking through their plans for the day before getting dressed and facing the world. The heat was already building up as they sat enjoying the quiet. They could hear Marie somewhere below talking to Sunni and they could see some movement at the far end of the garden as the gardener, a young Malay who was partially crippled following an accident, working on a new flower bed that Leanne had decided was necessary.

Leanne suddenly said, "Lucy seems to be taking an interest in the Chinese boy you introduced her to."

Robert deep in thoughts of his own perked up at the remark. He had been going through the itinerary for the long holiday that he and Leanne were due to take in only a few days to celebrate their 25th wedding anniversary. "I knew she had gone out with him. They went out to some rock concert or something." He finished by mumbling "Didn't know it was any more than that."

"Well, she has suggested we go out for a meal."

"He's not going to go on his knee and ask my permission for her hand or anything, is he," Robert grumpily said dreading the thought of a meal with two young people looking into each other's eyes.

"You are a grumpy so and so at times, Bob. Lucy just wants us to have a meal together before we set off for England. Molly will be there as well."

"What with that waste of space she knocks about with."

"By all accounts he's very good at his job with Barings."

"Bloody easy these days. Not like in my day."

Leanne sighed. "My we are in a grumpy mood today. What's the matter? The new Operations Director told you not to interfere."

"She doesn't know everything. I just offered her some advice, that's all. She bit my head off. Told me I was out of date."

Leanne laughed, well more of a throaty giggle as she finished her coffee. "From what she's told me she has masses of money to spend before some journalist or Government Inspector starts to delve into the Trust's financial history."

"Nonsense. There's nothing to hide."

Leanne got up to go back into their bedroom and then came behind Robert and put her arms on his shoulders. "Darling, I shall always love you. Even when they cart you off to Changi. Daddy said that I should not expect a quiet life with you, and he was right. I just hope that you have squirrelled away enough money to keep me in the luxury I am used to."

Robert groaned. "That's it. Think of yourself. Here's me worrying about how far Lucy will go and the consequences."

"Oh, don't worry about her. She is just like you. She will make the best of the money available. "Leanne moved off to the bedroom shouting as she went. "No different than you." It was a few seconds later she shouted, "I will tell Lucy to arrange a dinner for the weekend at Romero's. I like their Italian dishes."

Robert said nothing now deep in thought about a new project he had been telling Leanne about; the possibility of working with Alex and the Australian developers; this increasingly interested him. He already knew in his mind that Leanne would arrange the dinner for the family; her telling him was merely to announce her agreement to the meal, he never had any option. Anyway, Molly was the real worry even if Leanne kept telling him that she would end up getting married to a millionaire and having five kids.

He finished his coffee leaning against the veranda and watching Susie in the next garden talking to the young Malay gardener who was now over there. Finally, turning he walked back into the bedroom to shower and dress. Leanne was already dressed when he came out of the shower and he watched her collect her handbag and hat.

"I shouldn't be late tonight. The hospital is quite quiet at the moment so Mrs Simms and I should be able to finish around four." Leanne and other volunteers worked at the children's hospital that had been partly set up by the Lin Yuen Trust just over the causeway in Johor. She had worked as a nurse during the early years of the hospital being set up and then as Lucy and Molly had come along she had reduced her commitment and now she only did voluntary work for one or two days a week. Robert just nodded at what Leanne said. "I'll tell Sunni to go over and collect you then around four."

Leanne came across and kissed Robert just saying, "Leave her to get on with the job. You go off and do your work with Alex. The ideas for a development up at Changi sound right up your street. When we get back from holiday the paperwork should be ready so you can get your teeth into it."

Robert shouted after her, "Not Sunday evening I've got plans." As he finished dressing, he was already thinking of another idea. He murmured to himself, *"I will buy the old bank premises. It will be nice to tell Peter when I see him that I have bought them and converted it into an auction house and gallery."*

On the Saturday evening Sunni took Leanne and Robert down to Romero's, with Susie. Molly and Lucy were already down at the restaurant with their two young men in tow both looking decidedly nervous. Robert had had instructions from Leanne and come to that, Susie, that he was to be effusive and not to be grumpy and, yes, he was paying.

Romero's was packed but somehow Lucy had managed to get a superb table beside the window overlooking the sea and with the sunset in all its splendour. Robert recognised several people in the restaurant and briefly spoke to them as he worked his way through to the table. Susie told him as they followed the waiter that Alex had been unable to come because he had flown out to Australia to meet some business associates. Robert merely nodded; he knew all about Alex and the trip to Australia from meetings he had had during the week.

It seemed that Lucy was in charge, and it was she who arranged the seating making sure that her father was not isolated with the two young men. The manager seemed to know the preliminary arrangements and came over with waiters and drinks for everybody with a large stengah to keep grumpy happy, as Robert heard Lucy tell her Nana. It was as they were just relaxing that a lady, larger than life, descended on them.

"Robert, how nice to see you." The others at the table all looked up as Robert started to rise from his chair.

"Mrs Gionova. How nice to see you." Standing beside the table was a tall, attractive blonde perhaps in her late forties who spoke with a strong European accent. Robert bent down to his left. "Darling please meet Mrs Gionova. She and I are going into business together. I have agreed to buy the old Union and China bank premises and Mrs Gionova and her husband will be working with me to turn it into an auction house and art gallery. Mr Gionova has auction houses in Hong Kong and in Rome." As he was speaking Leanne had got to her feet and had shaken hands with Mrs Gionova taking in the news as though she knew all about it.

Molly whispered across to her sister as she watched the expression on her mother's face, "He's in for it now. She will do unspeakable things to him," giggling at the discomfort now on her father's face.

Mrs Gionova and Leanne spoke for a few moments with Robert adding little just watching the two women before Leanne said, "You must excuse us Mrs Gionova but I have guests to look after."

"Of course, of course. I am so pleased to have met you. Perhaps when you return from your holiday, we will be able to meet and get to know each other better. Robert has spoken many times about you."

Robert groaned inwardly at the last remark as Mrs Gionova turned and headed for a table at the far end of the room. Susie and the girls were looking at Leanne as she sat down at the table and Robert said nothing at first and looked round, before saying, "Well that's my secret out. I was hoping to tell everyone later this evening. It's a very exciting project and taking over the old bank premises is quite sentimental really."

It was Susie who said, "I doubt if you will live long enough to see it."

Leanne said nothing more and both she and Robert took part in the family get together laughing at the stories that circulated during the evening. To be fair Leanne said nothing when they got home and it was Molly who a few days later said, "This is going to cost you, dad."

"I know. I know. It always does but I have relented to an extra few days in Italy so that should settle everything."

Molly just shook her head.

Whatever Happened to

Bin Lau. He took over the management of Robert's property in Singapore and the Malay States. He married Zee Ping, a Chinese woman whose family were 3rd generation Singaporean and they had two children. Robert and Bin Lau became lifelong friends as well as business associates.

Brian Preston. He remained working for the railways in Singapore and the Malay States but never qualified as an engineer. What he didn't know about the railway network could be written on a postage stamp. He married young and had two children but things didn't work out and his first wife left him and taking the children she returned to England where she later remarried. Brian met a Eurasian lady when he was in his forties and they lived together until he died shortly after he retired from work in 1982. He and Bin Lau took up fishing in their later life and dragged a reluctant Robert along on some of their trips.

Martin Preston. He was never happier than when he was working in the jungle or on the land and after some years working on projects for Robert he landed a job as a Forest Ranger, on a nature reserve on the islands off Singapore. He and his wife, Helen, had four boys and kept countless animals including half a dozen mules.

Henry and Mona Preston. Henry remained the Station Master until 1956 when he had a massive heart attack and died. Mona remained in the family home on Tanglin Road until her death in 1971.

Mike and Mary Davison. They survived the difficult years after the war making their pharmacy a success and when their two daughters finished their education and married some years later with children, in England, they decided to return to Blighty to be nearer the grandchildren.

May Draper. Robert' uncle's wife lived for many years in Siglap selling her vegetables in the local markets. She died peacefully in her bed after a very short illness, in 1979.

Sunni Theragagaan. He remained happy working for Robert and his family transporting them around Singapore and the Malay States and just generally being useful. He never married.

Susie Masters. She lost David, her husband, in 1952. David never recovered from his ordeal in the Internment Camp on the Musi River in Sumatra and died of his many ailments. Susie lived in Mrs Lin Yuen's house for many years with Rebecca, her daughter, living there for some years, before she went off to live in Sydney with her second husband in 1968. Lucy on returning from university in the United States lived with her nana for a time until she found a flat that suited her. Susie's son Alex, finished his degree at LSE and worked for some years in London and Hong Kong before he returned to Singapore in 1966 to build a successful business, often working in collaboration with Robert.

Major Leon Comber. He was head of the British Security Service and in 1950 married the celebrated medic and authoress, Han Su Lin. His task in keeping one step ahead of the Malay Communist Party grew easier over the years as the British Forces learned ways of combating the insurrection. Robert, with his ability to communicate with many people on the Island and the Malay States, was always thought to be a probable source of information about communist activities. In 1958 Han Su Lin, always outspoken, published a book heavily criticising the progress of the British Government in combating poverty in the colony. Major Comber was forced to resign and take up a career in publishing in Hong Kong. He successfully developed this new career; he and Han Su Lin divorced.

Han Su Lin. With the support of philanthropists, including Robert, she set up a local hospital in Johor to help children with diseases, particularly malaria and leprosy. Leanne spent most of her married life working at the hospital in some capacity or other.

Lai Tek. The leader of the Malay Communist Party until he was exposed as a double agent of the British and Japanese, in early 1947. He had many names but it is thought he used the name "Truong Phuoc Dat" until the early 1930's when he changed his name to Lai Tek. He is thought to have arrived in Singapore in the late 1920's possibly a little later, from Saigon. His early career in Singapore is hazy but in the 1930's he emerged as a trade union leader arguing for the rights of textile workers and day work labourers (coollies). He is thought to have been recruited by the British Intelligence about this time. He joined the Malay Communist Party sometime during the mid-1930 and quickly rose to be General Secretary. In 1942, during the Japanese occupation, he arranged a meeting of the leaders of the MCP but failed to turn up. The Japanese army ambushed the meeting and most MCP members were killed except Chin Peng. Lai Tek's explanation for not turning up at the meeting in the Batu Caves was that his car had broken down. The question that must be asked, although it took the MCP some years to examine the issue, was how Lai Tek, a well-known trade union leader and communist, was able to drive around the Japanese occupied territories throughout the war. It was only after the war that it became obvious that Lai Tek was an agent of the Japanese betraying comrades, both communist and British. It emerged after the war that Lai Tek was also giving information to the British authorities before the Japanese invasion. What is less clear is whether he gave the British any information from late 1945 when the Allied forces reoccupied Singapore although this seems highly likely.

It probably does not matter whether he again worked for the British from September 1945 because by then Chin Peng and the reformed MCP had become highly suspicious, and Lai Tek eventually disappeared to Thailand and Indochina and he was assassinated in 1947 by supporters of the MCP.

There is no obvious reason why Lai Tek persuaded all the senior members of the MCP to meet at the Batu Caves; it would have been no easy feat to get to the caves from all over the Malay States. By this time John Davies, the leader of the Force 136 (the Allied Forces unit designated to continue the fight with the Japanese during the occupation), had done a deal with the MCP for their support in continuing the fight against the Japanese occupation force. What is known is that part of the deal was for the MCP fighters to receive payment for their continued fighting; as Malay currency was worthless the probability is that they were to be paid in gold coinage. It is highly likely that the MCP were meeting, believing that they were to collect gold to take to their fighters; gold which was being brought by Lai Tek who before the invasion we now know had connections with the British security services. We know from later information that Force 136 had to bring in shipments of gold from India because the source in Singapore and the Malay States had stopped being available.

Lai Tek continued to work with the Japanese throughout the war whether voluntarily or otherwise and we know that the *Kempetai* spent a great deal of energy seeking the gold. We know for instance that some of the arrests in October and November 1943 of European and Eurasian leaders in Singapore was not just about the attack on

Singapore harbour by Allied commandos or the attack by Chinese communists on the godowns beside Singapore River. The records clearly show that many of the men were tortured, some to death, in the quest to find the source of the gold. Lai Tek in all probability threw in names to deflect the Japanese from arresting him and in my opinion to remove people who might reveal where the gold was located. It is probable that he was merely buying time for himself.

Shee Yang Chen. It seems improbable that Lai Tek could have survived the war without help. In my book I have assumed that he brought a friend, Shee Yang Chen, with him from Indochina and he used him to front end his scam and to use the gold they came across as a potential back stop in case things went pear shaped with the MCP. In the 1940's many Chinese backed both the Kuomintang and the MCP waiting to see which one emerged as the predominant faction not only in China but also in South Asia. Shee Yang Chen disappeared in 1947 with Lai Tek and is never heard of again. The probability is that he would have been assassinated around about the same time as Lai Tek.

Chin Peng. The eventual leader of the MCP; a boy really when he became a central figure in the communist movement. He was born in 1924 so he was only 16 years of age when he became a leading figure in the MCP and in charge of one of the guerrilla companies fighting the Japanese. Indeed, he had been active before the Japanese invasion causing real problems for the colonial armed forces. He was a mere 22 years of age when he ousted Lai Tek and became the leader of the MCP. He was ruthless, being accredited with several killings in the period up to 1963 when he finally recognised that the MCP were not going to win the hearts and minds of the population. He then sought to go into politics but the new state of Malaysia despite reaching a peace agreement with the MCP always ensured that Chin Peng remained at arm's length. He is generally believed to have lived out his life in exile in Thailand. He never admitted to the killing of Lai Tek but he would certainly have approved of the act.

Joan Cramond. Like many of the women who were interned she never returned home to Britain preferring to remain close to where they had lost loved ones or as in the case of Joan Cramond because there was nothing back at home for her. Joan Cramond worked for many years for the prestigious department store, Robinsons, before becoming ill in her late 'fifties and having to retire. She continued until her death to live in her little flat in Cathay House on Orchard Road with friends such as Robert Draper supporting her financially.

Peter Connaught. He retired as Regional Director in late 1950 and Colin Warriston took over. The bank never recovered from the difficult trading times after the Second World War followed by the civil war in China and then the Korean War. In the end the foreign outposts were swallowed up by the Hong Kong Bank with the British branches becoming part of the then Martins banking set up.

Peter and his wife Ethel retired to England early in 1951 never to return to Singapore. He missed his lifelong friend, Henry, and was much distressed by Henry's death in 1956.

Sir John Hatton. He retired as the last Chairman of the Union & China Bank in 1954. He remained a non-executive director of various overseas businesses. In 1972 Robert visited him in a care home in Warwickshire. Sir John died a few months after the visit.

Eric Cassidy. He rose to be a Colonel, retiring in 1967. He and Robert exchanged Christmas cards for many years but gradually lost touch.

Neil Forsyth. He retired through ill health in 1963 just as Singapore became an independent state. After a short spell back in Scotland he and his family emigrated to New Zealand. He returned to Singapore as often as possible, staying with the Drapers.

Kay (Skipton). She and her husband, Steve, lived in Dunedin for the rest of their lives often having holidays in Singapore, and with the Drapers going over to New Zealand once during the 1960's.

Zhang Lee John. He suffered badly from the loss of his business interests in China when the communists took over, losing everything but through hard work and his business interests with Robert Draper he was able to recover successfully, only to be killed in a road accident just south of KL. Robert was always convinced that the communists had a hand in it as Zhang Lee John had been particularly outspoken about Mao Tse Tung's economic programme and how it was killing millions of Chinese. It did not serve the interests of the MCP to have someone speak so strongly against communist doctrine.

Frank Foley. He never returned to Singapore although he did have some contact with Robert over the years. He went into farming and settled in north Australia with a second wife.

Rachel Knowles. She died in the YMCA in October 1942 at the hands of Captain Ishiguru. Robert never found out what her connection was to the missing gold.

www.ingramcontent.com/pod-product-compliance
Lightning Source LLC
Chambersburg PA
CBHW070347170726
48291CB00001B/222